Praise for THE GRAV[...]
by Amanda Stevens

"The beginning of Stevens' Graveyard Queen Series left this reviewer breathless. The author smoothly establishes characters and forms the foundation of future storylines with an edgy and beautiful writing style. Her story is full of twists and turns, with delicious and surprising conclusions. Readers will want to force themselves to slow down and enjoy the book instead of speeding through to the end, and they'll anxiously await the next installment of this deceptively gritty series."

—*RT Book Reviews*, 4 ½ stars

"*The Restorer* is by turns creepy and disturbing, mixed with mystery and a bit of romance. Amelia is a strong character who has led a hard and—of necessity—secret life. She is not close to many people, and her feelings for Devlin disturb her greatly. Although at times unnerving, *The Restorer* is well written and intriguing, and an excellent beginning to a new series."

—Misti Pyles, *Fort Worth Examiner*

"I could rhapsodize for hours about how much I enjoyed *The Restorer*. Amanda Stevens has woven a web of intricate plot lines that elicit many emotions from her readers. This is a scary, provocative, chilling and totally mesmerizing book. I never wanted it to end and I'm going to be on pins and needles until the next book in The Graveyard Queen Series comes out."

—*Fresh Fiction*

Also by Amanda Stevens

THE DOLLMAKER
THE DEVIL'S FOOTPRINTS
THE WHISPERING ROOM

The Graveyard Queen Series

THE RESTORER
THE KINGDOM
THE PROPHET

THE PROPHET

AMANDA STEVENS

Recycling programs for this product may not exist in your area.

ISBN-13: 978-0-7783-1339-7

THE PROPHET

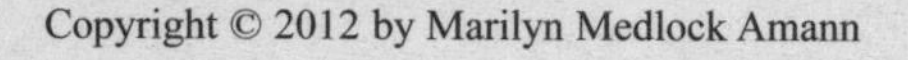

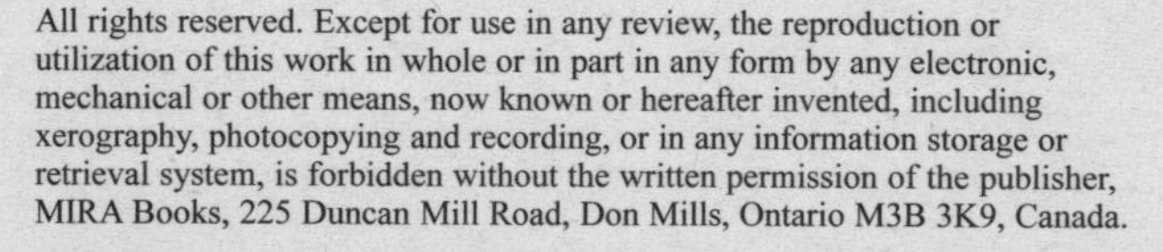

For questions and comments about the quality of this book please contact us at Customer_eCare@Harlequin.ca.

www.Harlequin.com

Printed in U.S.A.

THE PROPHET

One

Something had been following me for days. Whether it was human, ghost or an in-between—like me—I had no idea. I'd never caught more than a glimpse out of the corner of my eye. No more than a flicker of light or a fleeting shadow. But it was there even now, in my periphery. A darkness that kept pace. Turning when I turned. Slowing when I slowed.

I steadied my gait even as my heart raced, and I berated myself for having strayed too far from hallowed ground. I'd lingered too long at my favorite market, and now it was nearing on twilight, that dangerous time when the veil thinned, allowing those greedy, grasping entities to drift through into our world, seeking what they could never have again.

From the time I was nine, my father had taught me how to protect myself from the parasitic nature of ghosts, but I'd broken his every rule. I'd fallen in love with a haunted man, and now a door had been opened, allowing the Others to come through. Allowing evil to find me.

A car thundered down the street, and I tensed even as I welcomed such a normal sound. But the roar of the engine faded too quickly, and the ensuing quiet seemed ominous. The rush hour traffic had already waned, and the street was unusually devoid of pedestrians and runners. I had the sidewalk all to myself. It was as if everything had faded into the background, and the scope of my world narrowed to the thud of my footsteps and heartbeats.

I shifted the shopping bag to my other hand, allowing for a quick sweep to my left where the sun had set over the Ashley River. The mottled sky flamed like embers from a dying fire, the light casting a golden radiance over the spires and steeples that dotted the low skyline of the City of Churches.

It was good to be back in my beloved Charleston, but I'd been on edge ever since my return, the raw nerves a symptom of the emotional and physical trauma I'd suffered during a cemetery restoration in the foothills of the Blue Ridge Mountains. But there was another reason I couldn't eat or sleep, a deeper unease that made me pace restlessly until all hours.

I drew a quivering breath.

Devlin.

The haunted police detective I couldn't get out of my mind or my heart. The mere thought of him was like a dark caress, a forbidden kiss. Every time I closed my eyes, I could hear the whisper of his aristocratic drawl, that slow, seductive cadence. With very little effort, I could conjure the scorching demand of his perfect mouth on mine…the honeyed trail of his tongue…those graceful, questing hands….

Returning my focus to the street, I glanced over my shoulder. Whatever stalked me had fallen back or disappeared, and my fear eased as it always did when I neared hallowed ground.

Then, a bird called from somewhere in the high branches, the sound so startling I stopped in my tracks to listen. I'd heard that trill once before in the evening shadows of a courtyard in Paris. The serenade was like no other. Gentle and dreamy. Like floating in a warm, candlelit bath. I would have thought it a nightingale, but they were indigenous to Europe and by now would have made the three-thousand mile trek to Africa for the winter.

In the wake of the songbird, a fragrance floated down to me, something lush and exotic. Neither sound nor scent belonged to this city—perhaps even to this world—and a warning prickled my scalp.

I heard a whisper and turned, almost expecting to see Devlin emerge from the shadows the way he'd appeared to me from the mist on the night we met. I could still see him as he was then—an enigmatic stranger, one so darkly handsome and brooding he might have stepped straight from my adolescent fantasies.

But Devlin wasn't behind me. At this hour, he was probably still at police headquarters. I'd heard nothing more than the rustle of leaves, I told myself. The phantom whisper of my own longing.

And then, distantly, a child's laughter drifted over me, followed by a soft chant. Somehow I recognized the voice even though I had never heard it before, and an image of Devlin's dead daughter formed in my mind as clearly as if she stood before me.

Papa would have warned me to remember the rules. I recited them to myself as I turned slowly to scour the gathering twilight: *Never acknowledge the dead, never stray far from hallowed ground, never associate with the haunted and never,* ever *tempt fate.*

The ghost child's voice came to me again. *Come find me, Amelia!*

Why I didn't ignore her and continue on my way, I had no idea. I must have been enchanted. That was the only possible explanation.

The nightingale crooned to me as I left the sidewalk and followed a narrow alley to where an ornate gate opened into the walled garden of a private home. By entering, I ran the risk of being shot on sight for trespassing. Charlestonians loved their guns. But the danger didn't stop me, nor did Papa's rules because I'd fallen under that strange hypnotic spell.

Months ago, when I'd first seen Shani's ghost hovering at Devlin's side, she'd tried to make contact. That was why she'd followed me home that first night and left a tiny garnet ring in my garden. That ring had been a message just as surely as the heart she'd traced on my window. She wanted to tell me something....

This way. Hurry! Before she comes....

An icy foreboding clutched my spine. Danger was all around me. I could feel it closing in, but still I kept going, following the nightingale and that tantalizing scent through a maze of boxwood hedges and palmettos, through trails of evening primrose and midnight candy. The trickle of a fountain mingled with Shani's ethereal laughter and then the hair on my nape lifted as she started to chant:

"Little Dicky Dilver
Had a wife of silver.
He took a stick and broke her back,
And sold her to a miller.

The Miller wouldn't have her,
So he threw her in the river."

It was a ghastly rhyme, one that I hadn't heard in years, and the lines were made even more grotesque by the innocence of Shani's singsong.

Fighting that sinister lethargy, I turned to retrace my steps to the gate, but she'd materialized on the walkway behind me, a mere shimmer of light at first, and then slowly the outline of a child began to take shape as the garden grew colder. I was scared—terrified, actually—and I knew that I was treading on dangerous territory. I was not only acknowledging the dead, but also tempting fate.

None of that seemed to matter at the moment. I couldn't turn away. I couldn't tear my gaze from that delicate specter that now barred my exit.

She wore a blue dress with a matching ribbon in her hair and a sprig of jasmine tucked into the lace trim at her waist. A mane of wiry curls framed her tiny face, giving her a winsome loveliness that stole my breath. She was lit by the softest of auras, silvery and diaphanous, but her features were clear to me. The high cheekbones, the dark eyes, the café-au-lait complexion spoke to her Creole heritage, and I fancied I could see a bit of her mother in that gossamer visage. But not Devlin. The Goodwine influence was far too dominant.

Very deliberately, the ghost child plucked the stem of jasmine from the lace and held it out to me.

I knew better than to take it. The only way to deal with ghosts was to ignore them, pretend not to see them.

But it was too late for that. Almost of its own volition, my hand lifted and I reached for the flowers.

The ghost floated closer—too close—until I could

feel the death chill emanating from her tiny form. My fingers brushed the creamy blossoms she held out. The petals felt real to me, as warm and supple as my own skin. How that could be so, I had no idea. She had brought them with her from the other side. The blooms should have been withering.

For you.

She didn't speak but I heard her just the same. Her voice in my head was sweet and lyrical, like the faint tinkle of a crystal bell. I lifted the jasmine to my nose and let the heady perfume fill my senses.

Will you help me?

"Help you…how?" I heard myself ask her. My own voice sounded distant and hollow, like an echo.

She lifted a tiny finger to her lips.

"What's wrong?"

She seemed to fade as the air in the garden trembled and shifted. My heart was still racing, and I could see the rime of my breath mingling with a milky vapor that curled up out of the shadows. There was an odd copper taste in my mouth as if I had bitten my tongue. I felt no pain. I felt nothing at all except an icy fear that metastasized from my chest down into my limbs, paralyzing me.

The jasmine slipped through my numb fingers as the hair at my nape bristled. The night went deadly silent. Everything in the garden stilled except for that coil of mist. I watched, mesmerized, as it slithered toward me, twisting and writhing like a charmed cobra. The tension humming along my nerve endings was unbearable, as if the lightest touch could shatter me.

But when the contact came, it wasn't light at all. The blow was quick and brutal, propelling me backward with such force, I lost my balance. Tripping over a small garden statue, I went sprawling. The ceramic cherub shattered on the stone pavers, and a moment later, the sound of voices inside the house dimly registered. A part of me knew the residents must have heard the racket, but my attention was still riveted on the walkway. Another entity had formed in the garden, and she hovered over me, dead eyes blazing in the deepening twilight.

Mariama. The ghost child's mother. Devlin's deceased wife.

In one petrified moment, I took in the filmy swirl of her dress, the bare feet, the hedonistic spill of curls down her back. And that mocking smile. Terrifyingly seductive. Even in death, Mariama's mystique was pervasive, palpable. And so was her cunning.

Something Devlin had once told me about her flitted through my mind. According to her beliefs, a person's power wasn't diminished by death. A bad or sudden passing could result in an angry spirit wielding enough force to come back and interfere with the lives of the living, even enslave them in some cases. I had always wondered if that was her intent. To keep Devlin shackled to her with his grief and guilt. She sustained her existence on this side of the veil by devouring his warmth and energy, but the moment he let her go, the moment he started to forget, would she simply fade away?

I huddled there shivering, scolding myself for having followed Shani's voice and that strange songbird. I shouldn't have allowed myself to be lured into that garden. This was Mariama's doing. I understood that now. She was interfering in my life, warning me to stay away from Devlin.

I felt a sting and looked down to find my hand covered in ants. I shook them off as I scrambled to my feet. In that brief moment when my eyes left the ghosts, they'd vanished, leaving nothing but a lingering frost in their wake.

The back door opened, and a woman stepped out on the porch. "Who's there?" she demanded. She didn't sound frightened at all, merely annoyed.

I didn't know how to explain my presence in her garden so I grabbed my shopping bag and ducked behind a stand of azaleas even though I felt like a coward for doing so. I saw her shiver as she pulled a sweater around her body and gazed out into the shadows.

If I hadn't still been so shaken by the ghostly encounter, I might have made my presence known instead of skulking in the bushes like a thief. I could have made up some story, told the woman that I'd chased my cat through her gate, then offered to pay for the broken statue. I was on the verge of doing exactly that when I spotted the silhouette of a man behind her in the doorway.

"I thought I heard something," she said over her shoulder, and then he came out on the porch to join her.

My heart contracted as though from another powerful blow. I recognized the man, her companion. It was Devlin. *My* Devlin.

Now I knew why I had been enticed into this garden. I had been meant to see this.

Mariama appeared at Devlin's side, and I could feel her glacial eyes on me, taunting and mesmeric. Her hair tangled in the breeze, and the gauzy hem of her sundress wrapped snakelike around her legs. I could see right through her, and yet, she seemed at that moment as vital as any living thing.

Her hand lifted to Devlin's face, and she stroked his cheek, slowly, possessively, her gaze focused on mine. I didn't hear her in my head the way I'd heard Shani, but her message was clear just the same. She would never let him go.

My chest contracted painfully, as though an invisible hand had reached inside my chest and gripped my heart. I sucked in air, willing my heartbeats to slow even as my legs trembled and weakened. Something horrifying was happening to me in that garden. I was being drained, my warmth and energy usurped by an entity that had made me her enemy.

Papa had cautioned me so many times: *What the dead want more than anything is to be a part of our world again. They're like parasites drawn to our energy, feeding off our warmth. If they know you can see them, they'll cling to you like blight. You'll never be rid of them. And your life will never again be your own.*

The ghost laughed at me now as though she'd heard Papa's warning, too.

Shani materialized on the other side of her father and tapped his leg, willing his attention. He never looked down, never so much as flinched. He couldn't feel her. He hadn't a clue she was there. His focus was entirely on the brunette. He came up behind her and slipped his arms around her narrow waist. Her head dropped back to his shoulder, and the intimate murmur of their voices drifted across the garden to where I crouched in my hiding place.

He didn't kiss or caress her the way a lover might. Instead, he just stood there holding her as his ghosts floated around them.

I couldn't move or breathe. I couldn't look away even though it was quite possibly the worst moment of my life.

After a few moments, Devlin went back inside and his ghosts vanished. But the woman lingered, her gaze scanning the twilight as though she could sense my presence. I didn't dare move for fear of drawing her attention, but I was dying to get a better look at her. I could see little more than a shapely silhouette with a spill of dark, glossy hair over her shoulders. I knew she was attractive, though. She had an air about her, a certain vibe common to beautiful women.

She remained on the porch for several long minutes before following Devlin inside. I waited breathlessly to make sure neither of them came back out, then bolted from the garden and fled down the alley with barely a thought to my previous stalker.

I was so distraught by the sight of Devlin with another woman that I let down my guard and that wasn't at all like me. Living with ghosts necessitated vigilance, but as I hurried toward the street, my mind remained in that strange garden and the lapse cost me. The looming shadow appeared out of nowhere and the next thing I knew, I was grabbed roughly and shoved up against the stone wall, a forearm jammed to my throat.

The pressure on my windpipe precluded a gasp, much less a scream, but the attack was over in the space of a heartbeat. Even as I flailed for the mace I carried in my pocket, the assailant was already backing away. The arm dropped from my throat and I heard a sharp intake of breath. Then incredulously, "Amelia?"

Devlin.

I was so gobsmacked by his nearness, I couldn't utter a word. It had been months since I'd last seen him, but he'd visited my sleep nearly every night of our estrangement. Those dark, lush dreams allowed me to play out my every fantasy about him, but now I realized what a pale substitute the visions had been. Even with him standing there looking down at me so warily, I could think of little more than how much I still craved his touch. How much I'd missed his kisses.

"Are you all right?" he asked quickly.

Oh, that voice! That low, silky, old-world drawl that would always be my undoing.

I swallowed with some difficulty. "Yes, I think so."

"What on earth are you doing out here? And why didn't you say something? I might have hurt you." He sounded a bit rattled himself.

"You didn't give me a chance," I said defensively. "Do you always grab people without reason?"

"I had a reason. I was visiting a friend and we thought we heard someone in the garden."

"You mean a prowler?" How completely innocent I sounded.

There was a curious hesitation, then, "Yes, a prowler. I circled around to head him off." He glanced past me up the alley. "You didn't see anyone come out of here, did you?"

I shook my head as my heart continued to hammer.

"What about on the street? Did you notice anyone lurking about?"

"I didn't see anything."

His gaze was still on me, dark and probing. "Your turn, then. What are you doing here?"

"I…was just on my way home from the market." Lamely, I held up my shopping bag.

"You're a little off course, aren't you?"

"You mean the alley?" I moistened dry lips. "I heard something, too, so I decided to investigate."

His head came up and I sensed a sudden tension. "What did you hear?"

"It sounds crazy now," I said reluctantly.

He took my arm and a chill went through me, half alarm, half desire. "Tell me."

"I heard a songbird."

"A songbird?" Under other circumstances, his utter bewilderment might have been amusing.

"It sounded like a nightingale."

His grasp tightened almost imperceptibly and I could have sworn I saw a shadow sweep across his handsome features. Impossible, of course. Dusk was upon us and I could make out little more than the gleam of his eyes, but I had the distinct impression that my words had touched a nerve.

"There are no nightingales in this part of the world," he said. "You must have heard a mockingbird."

"I thought of that. But when I was in Paris, nightingales sang almost every evening in the courtyard of my hotel. Their trill is very distinct."

His tone sharpened. "I know what they sound like. I heard the damn things often enough in Africa."

Yet another detail I hadn't known about him. "When were you in Africa?"

"A lifetime ago," he muttered as he tilted his head to stare up into the trees.

Now I was the one utterly mystified. "Why does it matter what kind of bird it was?"

"Because if you heard a nightingale in Charleston—" He broke off, his head snapping around at the soft snick of a gate. Then he drew me to him quickly, dancing us both back into the shadows along the fence. I was too startled too protest. Not that I had any desire to. The adrenaline pulsing through my bloodstream was intoxicating, and my hand crept to the lapel of his jacket, clinging for a moment until a woman's voice invaded our paradise.

"John? Are you out here?"

When he didn't immediately answer, I slanted my head to stare up at him. Our faces were very close. So close I had only to tiptoe to touch my lips to his—

"I'm here," he called.

"Is everything okay?" she asked anxiously.

"Yes, fine. I'll be there in a minute."

"Hurry in." I heard the gate close behind her and a second later, the back door of the house slammed. But Devlin and I were far from alone. A breeze stirred, whispering through the leaves, and I felt the unnatural cold of his ghosts. I couldn't see them, but they were there somewhere, floating in the shadows, driving a wedge between us just as surely as the unknown woman's husky voice.

Devlin still held me, but now there was a distance between us. An uncomfortable chasm that made me retreat into myself. "I should be going."

"Let me drive you home," he said. "It's almost dark out."

"No, but thank you. It's only a few blocks and this is a safe neighborhood."

"Safe is a relative term."

How well I knew.

"I'll be fine." I was already walking away when he said my name, so softly I was tempted to ignore the entreaty for fear I'd only imagined it. I turned and said on a breath, "Yes?"

His dark eyes shimmered in the fading light. "It was a mockingbird you heard. It couldn't have been a nightingale."

My heart fell and I nodded. "If you say so."

Two

Devlin didn't call out to me again and I never glanced back. But the warmth of his touch lingered as did the frost of his ghosts. I'd spent many a sleepless night trying to convince myself that as long as I kept my distance, his ghosts wouldn't be a threat to me. After tonight I could no longer delude myself. I had done nothing to lure them back into my life. They had come despite my best efforts, and I hadn't a clue how to rid myself of them.

Shani had implored me to help her, and even now the memory of her voice in my head tore at my resolve. But I had to maintain a distance, my perspective. Whatever she needed, I couldn't give her. Whatever she wanted, I couldn't help her. I wasn't a medium. I didn't communicate with the dead—at least not intentionally—nor did I guide souls into the afterlife. Ghosts were dangerous to me. They were ravenous parasites. Hadn't Mariama just proven that?

If I were smart, I would ignore Devlin's ghosts just as I had ignored the hundreds of other manifestations I'd seen throughout the years. I would cling to the remnants of Papa's rules for dear life because, without them, I had little protection from any of the netherworld beings that crept through the veil at dusk.

Best just to put the whole disquieting episode out of my mind.

But…even if I somehow managed to disregard the ghosts, I knew the image of Devlin and that strange woman would torment me. I had no right to feel betrayed. I was the one who had broken things off with Devlin, and I'd done so without even a proper explanation. But how could I tell him that our passion had opened a passageway into a terrifying realm of specters that were colder and hungrier than any I'd ever encountered?

Drawing a shaky breath, I tried to soothe myself. I should be grateful that he'd found someone else. The sooner he moved on, the safer he would be. The safer we would both be. Hadn't I tried to do the same with Thane Asher?

But no amount of rationalization could ease the pain in my chest, nor did the sight of my home offer solace, though it was more than just a residence. It was a hallowed sanctuary, the one place in all of Charleston where I could sequester myself from the ghosts and hide from the rest of the world.

Rising from the remains of an orphanage chapel, the narrow house was built deep into the lot with upper and lower balconies and front and rear gardens in the Charleston tradition. I had the ground level to myself and that included access to the backyard and the original basement. A medical student named Macon Dawes rented the second floor. He was away at the moment, which gave Angus, the abused stray I'd brought home with me from the mountains, a chance to acclimate to his new surroundings before having to deal with a stranger.

Angus must have sensed my return because I heard him bark from the rear garden to welcome me home. I called out to him as the gate swung shut and I stood for a moment letting the scent of the tea olives settle over me. Later, we would sit out back together watching my white garden come to life as the moon rose over the treetops. It had become a nightly ritual, the only time that I actually welcomed the darkness. I had always admired the walled gardens of Charleston, but I enjoyed mine especially by moonlight when the moths stirred and the bats took flight. Sometimes I felt as if I could sit out there forever, dreaming my life away.

The old southern graveyards I restored held much the same fascination with their dripping moss, creeping ivy and, in the spring, the lavender gloom of their lilacs. Summer brought sweet roses; winter, luscious daphne. A perfume of death for every season. Each unique, each invoking a different emotion or a special memory but always reminding one of the past, of the fleeting nature of life.

I don't know how long I stood there with eyes closed, drowning in melancholia as I drank in the evening scents. Misery still held a firm grip, so perhaps that was why I didn't see him straightaway. Or even sense him.

When I finally spotted his silhouette, he was little more than a deeper shadow on the veranda, but somehow I knew who he was. *What* he was. I had the strangest urge to turn and dash back through the gate, but my muscles wouldn't obey and so I stood there suspended in fear.

In all my years of seeing ghosts, I'd never encountered one quite like Robert Fremont. He could emerge from the veil before dusk and after sunrise, and he could converse with me. Or at least…he communicated in a way that made me think he was speaking. He wasn't just in my head the way Shani had been. I could hear his voice. I could see his lips move. How he managed any of that, I had no idea. Nor did I understand how he could sit there so calmly on the steps of my sanctuary, a place no other ghost had ever penetrated.

That was the most frightening aspect of his manifestation. None of the rules seemed to apply to him, and so I was completely at his mercy with no way to protect myself from him.

The timing of his appearance couldn't be a coincidence. Nothing about this evening was happenstance. Not the nightingale, not my run-in with Devlin, not even Shani's disturbing nursery rhyme. Taken alone, each might seem incidental, but together they meant something specific. There was a word for such a string of events. Synchronicity.

And as I stood there staring through the deepening twilight at the murdered cop, I could feel myself being drawn into something dark and mystical. A supernatural puzzle for which there might be no earthly resolution.

Slowly, I walked through the garden, the crepuscular scent of the angel trumpets perfuming the air with an under note of dread. I came to a stop at the bottom of the steps to gaze up at him.

He looked much as he had the first time I'd seen him, his nondescript attire that of an undercover cop who needed to blend seamlessly into the criminal underbelly of Charleston. As always, his eyes were hidden by dark glasses, but I could feel the power of his dead gaze through those lenses. The sensation was chilling.

"Amelia Gray." The way he spoke my name was like the prick of an icy needle down my spine.

"Why are you here?" I asked.

"You know why. It's time."

The hair at the back of my neck lifted. "Time for what?"

"To make things right." His voice was deep and hollow like a well, and I shivered again as he watched me from behind those tinted lenses. I tried to avert my eyes, but he held me enthralled.

I'd forgotten how handsome he was, how perversely charismatic even as a ghost. Despite his dark skin—and the fact that he was dead—he'd always reminded me of Devlin. Both possessed that same smoldering charm, that same dangerous allure. They'd once been friends, and I had a feeling it was my association with Devlin that had allowed Robert Fremont into my world.

"We have a lot to talk about," he said.

"We do?"

"Yes. Maybe you should sit. You look a little unsteady on your feet."

Was it any wonder?

But I didn't want to sit. I wanted him gone, banished back to the realm of the dead, along with Shani and Mariama. I considered bolting past him into my house, into my sanctuary, but I wasn't altogether certain it would protect me from the likes of this ghost. For all I knew, he could follow me inside, and I didn't want to lose the peace of mind of a hallowed place, illusionary though it might now be.

My legs felt leaden as I climbed the steps, the burden of his unspoken demands already a heavy weight. He didn't rise, but then I could hardly expect him to. Why should a ghost be bound by earthly ceremony? Especially the spirit of a man whose life had ended in murder.

I sat down on the veranda, placing distance and the shopping bag between us. I felt nothing more than a faint chill emanating from his presence, and even that might have been my imagination.

"I told you once that I needed you as a conduit into the police department," he said.

"I remember."

"I need more than that now, I'm afraid."

I was afraid, too. Deathly so.

"I need you to be my eyes and ears in this world. The living world."

"Why?"

"Because you can go places I can't enter. Talk to the people who won't see me."

"No, I mean…to what end?"

"As cliché as it sounds, I need you to help find my killer."

I stared at his manifestation in silence. "How is it you can do all these things—converse with me, invade my sanctuary, appear to me as though you're still alive—and yet, you don't know who murdered you? Shouldn't you know? You told me once you had a gift. You said that's why you were called the Prophet."

"I never claimed to be omniscient," he said, and I thought he sounded annoyed, whether at my questioning of his ability or his current limitations, I had no idea. "I could never control the visions."

I could relate. I had no control over my gift, either.

"Haven't you read anything about my death?" he asked.

"Not much."

"That's disappointing. I would have thought after our last meeting you'd want to know more about me. You struck me as the curious sort. Or was I wrong about you?"

That aroused a spark. "I've been a little preoccupied since that night. I was almost murdered myself, remember? And I have a living to make, a business to run. But…" I paused to draw another breath. "I did look you up once. There wasn't much on the internet about you and I don't talk to Devlin. How else was I supposed to learn about you?"

He sighed. "I was hoping you'd be a little more resourceful."

I wasn't exactly thrilled with him, either. I really wanted him to just…vanish. "In that case, maybe you should look to someone else for help."

"There is no one else. I searched a long time to find you."

That gave me pause. "How *did* you find me?"

"That's not your concern."

"Not my concern!" My voice hardened. "Did it ever occur to you that I didn't look you up because I wanted nothing more to do with you?"

Careful, a little voice warned. I'd already been the recipient of one ghost's ire that night. It wasn't wise to provoke another.

He took a moment to answer. "You have a backbone, at least. That'll come in handy."

"Thanks. I guess."

"Maybe I was a little too quick to judge you. You have to know that I have a lot riding on this relationship."

We had a relationship? The notion of that made me shiver.

A neighbor walked by on the street. She gazed up at the house, then hurried on past. I saw her glance over her shoulder once. She must have thought me crazy, sitting out there in the dusk arguing with myself. I could hardly blame her. If not for Papa's ability to see ghosts, I might have wondered about my sanity a long time ago.

"What happened to you?" I asked with grudging curiosity. "I know you were killed in the line of duty—" I broke off. "Is it okay that I speak so bluntly about…?"

"I wouldn't have it any other way."

Good. I didn't want to have to walk on eggshells around him.

That drew me up short again. Even my internal dialogue was starting to freak me out. How had Robert Fremont managed to slip into my life so effortlessly? How had I allowed myself to accept him so readily?

He's a ghost. He's a ghost. He's a ghost.

I chanted the mantra to myself even as he continued to converse with me.

"I was shot in the back," he said. "I never saw my killer. My body was found the next day in Chedathy Cemetery. That's in Beaufort County."

My gaze had still been fixed on the street, but now I jerked around in shock. Mariama and Shani were buried in Chedathy Cemetery.

"You were a Charleston cop," I said. "What were you doing all the way down in Beaufort County?"

"I'm…not sure."

"What do you mean you're not sure?"

He said nothing.

I did not like the feeling of foreboding that knotted my stomach. "I'm still not exactly clear on what it is you expect me to do."

"I already told you what I need."

"I know, but—"

"*Just listen to me.* We have to act quickly. Do you understand? It has to be now."

His urgency took me aback. "Why now? It's been over two years since you were shot."

He glanced up at the sky. "The stars have finally aligned. The players have all taken their places."

Could he have sounded any more cryptic?

"Does that include me?"

"Yes."

I turned back to the garden, searching the shadows. "And if I refuse to be a part of this?" Whatever *this* was.

"Have you looked at yourself in the mirror lately?" he asked.

Now it was I who fell silent.

"Have you not noticed the dark circles under your eyes? The sunken cheeks? The weight loss? You're not eating or sleeping. Your energy is waning even as we speak."

I stared at him in horror. "You're *haunting* me?"

Three

My heart tripped at the implication of his words. I thought of my stalker, the elusive watcher who had been dogging me for days. Now I understood my lethargy and my insomnia. Fremont's very presence was draining me of my life force just as Mariama had siphoned my energy earlier. Or had that been Fremont even then?

"You have to help me," he said.

I gazed down at my trembling hands. "I'm beginning to realize that."

"As soon as we find him, as soon as justice is served, I'll leave you in peace."

"I have your word?" The word of a ghost. That was a new one.

"What reason would I have for lingering?" he asked.

I shuddered to think.

"You said find *him*. If you were shot in the back, how can you be so sure the killer was a man?"

"I'm not sure of anything," he admitted, and for the first time, I sensed some doubt. Maybe even a hint of fear. “I don’t even know why I was in the cemetery that night.”

“You have amnesia?” A surreal question if ever there was one.

“About the events surrounding that night? It would seem so.”

He gazed out at the street as I searched his profile. The detail I could see in the twilight was amazing. The strong line of his jaw and chin, the sharp shelf of his cheekbone, the outline of his lips. Even knowing what I knew, I still found it difficult to accept that he was dead.

“I suppose that makes sense,” I said, tearing my gaze away. “I’ve read that accident victims often can’t recall details leading up to the crash. This is similar. You suffered a severe trauma.”

“Yes, the trauma was severe,” he murmured.

“What’s the last thing you do remember? Before you died, I mean.”

He fell silent, and now I sensed some turmoil, some inner conflict. “I remember meeting someone.”

“At the cemetery?”

“I don’t know. All I remember is the scent of her perfume. The smell was still on my clothes when I died.”

“So the killer could have been a woman.”

“It’s possible. I have a vague recollection of an argument.”

“Do you know who she was?”

Another hesitation. “Her name eludes me.”

“What did she look like?”

In the split second before he answered, I could have sworn I saw a shudder go through him, but it seemed unlikely a ghost would be affected in so earthly a manner. Surely I was ascribing my own human emotions to him.

"I don't know. But her perfume..."

"Go on."

"The scent is still on my clothes," he said, almost in defeat. "I can smell it even now."

I thought of the exotic fragrance that had drifted to me earlier, riding the same ghostly breeze as the nightingale's song. If Fremont had been following me then, the scent might have come from him.

And then something else occurred to me. Had he seen Mariama and Shani's ghosts? Was that why he'd disappeared?

Could ghosts even see one another? Interact with one another?

Years and years of questions bubbled up inside me, but it was so strange to be able to ask them of a ghost. Stranger still that my fear had dissipated. Was I still under a spell?

Once again I found myself heading into dangerous territory, spurning Papa's warning and flirting with disaster. One door had already been breached because of my wanton disregard of the rules. Would my connection with a ghost open yet another?

"What's it like?" I heard myself ask him. "Behind the veil, I mean."

"It's called the Gray. The place in between the Dark and the Light."

The *place,* he'd said. Not the time. The distinction seemed significant.

"Does it still hurt? From where you were shot?"

"There's no pain," he said. "There's nothing really."

"But you feel something. You must. You're here because you want vengeance. That means you're still capable of human emotion."

"I'm here because I can't..." His ghostly voice trailed off.

"You can't what?"

"Rest," he said wearily. "Something is keeping me here."

"And you think if we expose your killer, you'll be released?"

"Yes."

I thought about that for a moment. His urgent need to find the killer corroborated what I'd always suspected. Not all ghosts were drawn through the veil by their rapacious hunger for human warmth or their insatiable desire to rejoin the living. Some were earthbound for reasons beyond their control. Apparently, Robert Fremont was one of them. I wondered if Shani was another. If Mariama's ghost kept Devlin chained to her by his guilt and grief, did those same emotions keep Shani bound to him?

"Can you see them?" I asked.

"Who?"

"The other ghosts. They're all around us. Surely you've noticed them."

"I keep my distance."

"Why?"

"They're insidious," he said with contempt. "Leeches preying on the living because they refuse to accept death. I'm not like that."

"But isn't that what you're doing to me?"

"Only for as long as I need your help. I have to sustain myself until I can find a way to move on," he said. "I don't want to be here any more than you want me here."

"So, what do we do first?"

He moved, stirring the air, and I felt a faint chill creep

up my spine. I had to remind myself yet again that, despite our strange arrangement, he was still a ghost and, therefore, dangerous to me.

"We follow the clues," he said. "No matter where they lead us. Understood?"

"I..."

"Understood?"

I almost jumped. "Yes. Understood."

He nodded and turned away. "Someone was in the cemetery after I was shot that night, someone besides the killer. We have to find that person or persons and get them to talk."

I gave him a skeptical look. "Did you see someone?"

"No," he said. "But I sensed a presence."

A *presence.* "If you were that close to death, how can you be so sure you weren't dreaming or hallucinating?"

"I felt someone going through my pockets. It was real, but if you don't believe me, read the police report. My cell phone was missing when my body was recovered."

"How am I supposed to get my hands on the police report?"

"You said you could be resourceful when the need arises. Find a way."

I was starting to get frightened again. This was absolutely the strangest night of my life, and that was saying something for me.

Was I really being blackmailed by a ghost? Did he truly expect me to conduct a murder investigation all on my own? If I failed, if I couldn't uncover his killer, would he haunt me for the rest of my life? Would he continue to devour my warmth and energy until I remained nothing more than a shell?

I tried to remain calm. "Assuming we somehow

manage to find this…whoever it was, how do you propose we make them talk? I'm not a cop. I know nothing about interrogations. And frankly, what you're proposing sounds incredibly risky. Not that you have to worry about it."

"I'm not out to get you killed," he said.

"That's reassuring."

"So long as you do as I say, you'll be fine."

And I was supposed to believe him?

Yet, even as I quivered in fear, an unexpected excitement coursed through me. All my life, I'd been sheltered and protected, not just from the ghosts, but from the world outside my cemetery gates. There was a time when I would have clung to that seclusion, to that safety, even to my loneliness, but the secrets I'd uncovered about myself in Asher Falls had made me reevaluate my ability and my very existence. I wanted to believe there was a purpose to my life, a reason why I saw ghosts. It wasn't just a dangerous legacy. I had been given a gift.

And now here was a ghost who offered me a way to attain a higher purpose. A reason to embrace that dark gift rather than hide from it on hallowed ground.

If I could help the Prophet move on, perhaps I could do the same for Shani and Mariama. And then Devlin would be mine—

I was a little shocked by the direction of my thoughts, and I told myself I wouldn't go there. It was too dangerous. Too foolish to even contemplate a time when Devlin and I might possibly be together. Besides, for all I knew he'd already moved on with the brunette. He might already have put *our* past behind him.

Then why had he sent a message on the day I'd left Asher Falls?

Why had his ghosts lured me into that woman's

garden tonight? Why did Mariama feel so threatened by me?

It wasn't over with Devlin. A part of me knew that, no matter what happened, no matter the passage of time or the miles between us, it would never truly be over. Devlin was my destiny. The one man I wanted above all others was the one man I could never have.

Unless I could somehow find a way to close that door.

I tried to tamp down that sinister glimmer of hope as I glanced at the ghost. "If I help you, we'll be even, right? My debt to you will be paid in full."

Robert Fremont smiled. "Never bargain with the dead. We have nothing to lose."

Four

Long after Fremont vanished, I sat there shivering in the falling twilight even though the evening was still quite warm. At some point, it occurred to me that Angus was barking in the backyard. Strangely, he'd been silent during the visitation, but now something had excited him. I called out, but my voice didn't quiet him.

I grabbed my shopping bag and hurried through the side yard to the back gate, contemplating the impact of my meeting with Fremont. In the space of a few short minutes, my whole life had changed. I'd knowingly entered into a relationship with a ghost. Talk about acknowledging the dead. Talk about tempting fate. I could only imagine what Papa would say about such an association.

Which made me wonder...had he ever encountered an entity like Robert Fremont?

I thought about the ghost of the old white-haired man I'd seen in Rosehill Cemetery, the hallowed place of my childhood. He had been my first manifestation and I'd only glimpsed him one other time since that long-ago day. My father had told me that ever since the initial sighting, he'd been afraid the old man's ghost had been sent to watch over me by something evil on the other side of the veil. But I had to wonder if Papa was still holding out on me. Despite everything he'd revealed about my birth and my heritage, I couldn't shake the notion that he kept things from me still. That he had secrets I'd yet to uncover.

Opening the back gate, I slipped inside. There was still light in the garden though the moon hadn't yet risen. Angus stood in the center of the yard, his gaze transfixed on the swing. It moved slowly back and forth.

Shani?

I didn't say her name aloud. I didn't think I needed to.

She didn't answer. I heard no sound at all except for the faint tinkle of the wind chimes and the pounding of my heart in my ears.

But the swing continued to move in the breeze.

Something was there. I could feel a chill in the air, and as I stood riveted, a scent drifted to me. Not the exotic fragrance from earlier, but the familiar scent of jasmine that harkened Shani's presence. Once again she had followed me home, but for some reason, she wouldn't or couldn't appear. Was she afraid of Mariama?

I didn't want to contemplate what that might mean. A child—even a ghost child—frightened of her own mother.

I was certainly afraid of Mariama.

"Shani?" Her name slipped out on a whisper.

Silence.

I watched the swing move back and forth, imagining the sway of the little girl's hair, the billow of her blue dress. The innocent peal of her sweet laughter.

How many times had Devlin remembered her that way? How many times had he roused from a dream, aching to hold his child in his arms only to recall his painful reality? He must have relived her death over and over in the two years since she'd been gone. A fresh despair every time he awakened.

My heart turned over. "I know you're there," I called softly.

I was playing with fire, and I could almost hear my father's condemnation. *What are you doing, child? Why are you flaunting the rules? Haven't you learned your lesson by now? The Others are still out there. Evil is still out there. By acknowledging the dead, you're inviting forces of which you know nothing into your world. Once inside, they'll have you at their mercy. Your life will never again be your own...*

Angus stood frozen just as I was, his gaze focused on the swing. He didn't growl as one would expect in the presence of a ghost. He seemed almost...enchanted. Mesmerized.

What's his name?

I heard the question as surely as if she'd spoken it aloud, but the only sounds in the garden were the gentle music of the wind chimes and the rustle of leaves in the live oaks.

"Angus."

My voice seemed to release him from his spell, and he came to my side, whining piteously as he nuzzled my hand with his cold nose. Even in the dim light of the garden, I could see the horrible scarring on his snout and the nubs where his ears had been cut off. I ran my hand along his back where the tan fur still bristled.

Did the bad man hurt him?

Was that a note of fear I detected? Or was I merely

projecting my own terror onto Shani? Onto a ghost. "The bad man?"

The trees seemed to shudder, and I heard a whimper. I continued to smooth Angus's fur with a trembling hand, but I didn't think the sound had come from him.

"Who is the bad man?" I asked carefully.

Another whimper.

"It's okay," I crooned, as much to reassure myself as to soothe Angus and Shani. "Everything will be fine."

But would it?

A line had been crossed tonight, and if Papa was right, I could never go back. For all my lofty ruminations of a higher purpose, I had no idea what I was getting into. What I was inviting into my life. Was I ready to accept the consequences of such a dangerous transformation?

Will you help me?

The question seemed to echo all my worries and self-doubt. All my midnight terrors. "What do you want me to do?"

The swing stopped, and I had a sense that Shani's spirit was already starting to fade back into the netherworld.

Come find me.

Five

The next day, I took Angus for a walk in the same neighborhood where I'd seen Devlin and the woman. And I even managed to convince myself that I had a legitimate motive for doing so.

I'd broken a statue in the garden and had then fled the scene without a word. The least I could do was extend an apology and an offer of compensation, even if the accompanying explanation would require a lie. A *white* lie, but an untruth nonetheless. After all, I could hardly confess that I'd been lured into her garden by a ghost and had then been accosted by another. And not just any ghosts, but the spirits of Devlin's dead wife and daughter. I could only imagine how that would go over with his…whatever the woman was to him.

Of course, the bigger lie was the one I told myself. My return trip to that neighborhood had very little to do with a guilty conscience. I wanted to find that woman's house and see her in daylight to assuage my curiosity.

I fully appreciated that my judgment in the matter wasn't what it should be. I blamed it on exhaustion. All those otherworldly visitations had wreaked havoc on my nerves, and I hadn't slept a wink. In the course of one evening, I'd been drawn into two disturbing mysteries—Robert Fremont's murder and Shani's need for me to find her. I had no idea what either search would entail and already I felt emotionally and physically worn out. But, as Angus and I strolled along the sidewalk, I told myself I wouldn't dwell on those unsettling contacts today, not even Shani's disquieting plea. The weather was just too gorgeous, so warm and mellow that the netherworld chill of last evening seemed like a bad dream. I had Angus on a leash, but that was a mere formality. He never strayed far from my side, nor did he rebel against the restraint, so I indulged him as much as I could, letting him take his time with whatever new sight or smell caught his fancy.

I used those frequent interludes to admire the gardens that I glimpsed through wrought-iron fences. The sweet fragrance of autumn clematis wafted from trellises, and now and then, I caught the spicier aroma of the ginger lilies that were just starting to open. I drew in a breath, letting the perfume of a Charleston morning wash over me.

I'd just stopped to admire the electric yellow of a ginkgo tree when the dark-haired woman from last evening suddenly came around the corner of her house. I recognized her immediately, though she looked somewhat different in daylight. A little shorter and curvier than I remembered, but by no means overweight. She had a round, pleasant face and an air of sweet gentility that conjured up images of lacy parasols and English tea roses.

Not at all the impression I'd been left with the night before.

Simultaneously, I noticed the burnish of auburn in her hair and the pink in her cheeks, neither of which I'd been able to detect in the waning light of her garden. She was dressed in faded cords and a droopy cardigan that hung past her generous hips, and judging by the stains on her knees and the large pair of pruning shears in one hand, she'd already been up to some gardening. If not for her ingénue-like countenance, I might have thought the gleam of those large blades a little sinister.

"Hello," she called, the husky timber of her voice taking me by surprise even though I'd heard her speak last evening. "May I help you?"

I realized that I'd been gawking and, in my embarrassment, blurted the first thing that came to mind. "I was just admiring your garden."

"Oh, thank you. I'm afraid I can't take any of the credit, though. I just moved in."

I noticed the Realtor's sign in the front yard then and the bright red "sold" sticker that had been slapped across the front. "I didn't even realize the house was up for sale." Of course, I wouldn't, seeing as how I rarely came down this street.

"It was a fast turnaround. Only on the market a few days. Luckily, I happened along at just the right time. The seller needed to move out quickly and so here I am." She set aside the pruning shears and walked over to the gate. Her hair was pulled back and fastened at the nape, but the breeze caught the loose tendrils at her temples and they floated about her face like sea anemones, giving her a lively animation. "Do you live in the neighborhood?"

I waved vaguely. "A few blocks over on Rutledge."

She peeled off her gloves and thrust a hand over the

fence. “I’m Clementine Perilloux.” She used the more exotic French pronunciation—Clemen-*teen.*

“Amelia Gray.”

We shook, and then she knelt and put out her hand to my dog. “And who is this?”

“Angus.”

She said his name softly, and he moseyed over to sniff her hand. Apparently impressed by what he smelled, he allowed her to rub his head and scratch behind the ear nubs. I tried not to begrudge his enjoyment.

“What a sweet face. Just look at those eyes.” She glanced up. “May I ask what happened to him?”

“I was told he was used as a bait dog.”

Her good humor vanished. “I assumed as much. I used to volunteer at an animal shelter when I was in college. We would see similar scars and mutilations from time to time. They cut off the ears to avoid unnecessary wounds.”

“So I’ve read.”

“Breaks your heart, doesn’t it? Although Angus seems to be in very good hands these days.” She gave him a few more brisk rubs, then stood. “Where did you find him?”

“Oh, he found me.”

“That’s always the best way.” Her eyes were hazel, I noticed, and as soft and limpid as Angus’s. Given what I’d seen last evening, I had been prepared to dislike her on sight, but I found it impossible to muster up even an ounce of animosity. She was so earnest and charming. So…wholesome. I would never have pegged her as Devlin’s type, but then if Mariama was the yardstick, I wasn’t even on the spectrum.

“Do you know what I think?” she said crisply as she dusted her hands on her gray pants. “I think you and

Angus should come around to the back garden and have some breakfast with me."

"We couldn't possibly impose," I protested.

"It's not at all an imposition. In fact, you would be doing me a huge favor. I don't know anyone in the neighborhood yet, and I would love having a friend nearby. My family lives here in the city, but they tend to smother, if you know what I mean."

I didn't, actually. My parents had always maintained a distance. Mama, because of the circumstances of my birth; Papa, because of his secrets. We were not a close family, though I had never once doubted their affection for me.

Clementine Perilloux opened the gate with a hopeful smile. "Please," she coaxed. "I've made scones. And there's a fresh batch of muscadine jelly from my grandmother."

Her smile was infectious, and I had no ready excuse, so I merely nodded and followed Devlin's brunette into the backyard with only a passing thought to the broken statue.

Six

A little while later, I sat on the patio and waited for Clemen*teen* Perilloux to return. She'd come out once to bring freshly squeezed juice and a pot of steaming coffee, and now I could smell something delectable wafting from the kitchen doorway.

"Are you sure I can't be of some help?" I called yet again.

"Everything's almost ready. Just relax and enjoy the garden."

Angus certainly was. He had explored and sniffed and pawed to his heart's content, and now he'd treed something behind the same azalea bushes that had hidden me the night before.

Like Clementine herself, the garden appeared very different from my first impression. By dusk, it had seemed a place of enchantment—dangerous and ethereal—but now I could see that she had her work cut out for her in restoring forgotten flower beds and taming overgrown bushes. The house was a charming two-story with a peaked roof and dormer windows, but a closer scrutiny revealed peeling paint and missing window screens. The whole place wore an air of gentle neglect.

The shards of the broken cherub still lay strewn across the stone pavers. I wondered if Clementine had even noticed. And I wondered why I hadn't yet said anything. The delay was just going to make my confession and apology that much more awkward.

Of course, deep down, I knew the real reason for my procrastination, and it wasn't one of my prouder moments.

She came out of the house just then carrying a basket of fresh scones and a jar of jelly the color of an antique garnet.

"My grandmother makes it every year," she said as she took a seat across from me. "It's a family tradition. When I was little, come fall, we would drive out to the country to pick the grapes. That trip with Grandmother was always the highlight of my autumn."

"You say your family lives in Charleston?" I asked, accepting a scone.

"Yes." She held up a piece of bacon. "Okay for Angus?"

I nodded.

She called to him and he came at once, gobbling the crispy strip right out of her hand. I might have felt a little betrayed by his gusto, but truth be told, I was quite taken with Clementine myself. I had to wonder, though, if she might not be a little too good to be true. Inviting strangers to breakfast, working in an animal shelter. A part of me wanted to believe that she wasn't quite as wholesome as she appeared. A part of me still wanted to hate her, but her childlike exuberance had charmed me.

My gaze strayed again to the back porch. Now that

I'd met her face-to-face, it was hard for me to imagine her in Devlin's arms. Hard for me not to imagine it, too.

She offered the last of the bacon to Angus, then straightened. "Where were we?"

"You were telling me about your family."

"Oh, yes. My grandmother has this wonderful old house on Legare just north of Broad near the Cathedral of St. John the Baptist," she said. "It's been in the family for generations. A big, old, rambling place with gorgeous piazzas and gardens. I grew up in that house. My father died when I was ten and pretty much left us destitute. Grandmother, bless her, took us in."

She offered me the jelly. "Thank you." I spread some on my scone and took a bite. The quick bread was warm, flaky and delicious. So she could also bake.

"She tried to get me to move back in after…that is, when I decided to settle in Charleston." A frown played between her brows. "I suppose it would have been the practical thing to do, but I need to prove that I can stand on my own two feet. I had some savings and I've always wanted to renovate one of these old places, so…"

"Here you are."

She drew a breath and released it. "Yes."

I couldn't help noticing a slight tremor in her hand as she lifted the cup to her lips and I glimpsed something in her eyes that made me wonder if there was more to the woman than the charming facade she presented to the world. "It's a lovely house," I said, feeling a momentary disquiet.

She glanced around proudly. "I can't wait to get started. My sister has offered to help, but I want to do as much of the work as I can by myself. Not that I'm completely self-sufficient, mind you. I did accept a job from Grandmother."

"What do you do?" I asked curiously.

"I work in her bookstore and tea shop. It's a little place on King Street called The Secret Garden. Do you know it?"

"I was in there not too long ago," I said in surprise. "It's a beautiful shop. The selection of teas is mind-boggling."

"I wonder if that's why you look so familiar to me," she murmured, her gaze searching my face. "I can't shake the notion that we've met before."

A sudden breeze gave me a slight chill as I glanced down at my plate. "I don't think so. Although I suppose it's possible you saw me in the shop. Or maybe we've passed on the street." *Or you spied me hiding in your bushes last evening.*

"That's probably it."

"How long has your grandmother owned the store?"

"Oh, forever. She came here from Romania as a young woman. Back then, she had a special room in the rear of the shop where she read tea leaves. She also had quite the reputation as a palmist. Some of her clients came from the wealthiest and most powerful families in Charleston. That's actually how she met my grandfather."

"She told his fortune?"

Clementine grinned. "To her advantage, no doubt. Grandmother is no one's fool."

"Does she still do readings?"

"Occasionally, but never for money these days. She gave it up after she married my grandfather. The practice was deemed unsuitable, borderline satanic in his circle, though many of his friends were her clients. She insisted on keeping her shop, though. She always said it was a foolish woman who relied solely on the discretion and generosity of a man, even one as wealthy and as smitten as my grandfather. She was quite the progressive in her day."

"She sounds like a very interesting woman."

"She certainly is. Drop by the shop sometime and I'll introduce you." She offered me another scone even though I'd yet to finish the first. "Oh, please eat up," she encouraged. "The leftovers will go straight to my hips."

I took another and I placed it on my plate.

"Well, I've certainly been the chatterbox, haven't I?" she said cheerfully. "I don't know what's gotten into me." A pause. "You're very easy to talk to."

"I am?" I would never have thought so. I'd spent too much of my life in my own company.

"You have a kind face and a soothing manner." She held out her hand. It was perfectly steady now. "May I?"

I felt myself immediately withdraw. "Oh, I don't know. I'm not much for fortunes. I've never wanted to see my future."

"Don't worry. I know little beyond the basics. Both hands, please. The future is shown in the left, the past in the right."

I placed my hands palm up on the table. She scrutinized both without touching either. "What do you do for a living, Amelia?"

"I'm a cemetery restorer."

She glanced up. "*Really*. How interesting. What does that entail, exactly?" She bent back to my palms.

"In a nutshell, I reclaim old graveyards that have been abandoned or fallen into a state of neglect."

"You mean like family burial sites?"

"And old public cemeteries, as well. Graves are forgotten and rarely visited after a generation or two. Neglect takes a rapid toll. The ground sinks. Headstones crack. Whole cemeteries get swallowed up by forests…." I trailed off. "Now I'm talking too much."

"Not at all. I love old graveyards. I've just never given much thought to the care of them. I imagine vandalism is a big problem."

"Vandalism, acid rain, moss and lichen. The problems vary. Every cemetery is unique. The time and attention required will vary from place to place, stone to stone. My motto is to do no harm."

"Like the Hippocratic oath," she said. "I suppose that's a good life's motto for any of us."

"Yes, it is."

"When I was little, my grandmother and I spent many a Sunday afternoon exploring churchyards all over Charleston. The Unitarian was always my favorite. I loved all the wildflowers and the story about Annabel Lee. She was supposedly the inspiration for Poe's poem, you know. I would beg my grandmother to tell her story every time we visited, even though I was terrified of running into her ghost. Luckily, I never did." She gave a little shudder as she fixed her gaze on my palms. "Hmm…that's interesting."

"Interesting good or interesting bad?" I asked with more than a shade of trepidation.

"You have water hands," she said. "I would have guessed earth."

"Because of my profession?"

"Among other things."

I curled my fingers and withdrew my hands to my lap. She didn't object.

"You have some unusual lines," she mused as she sipped her coffee. "But I don't know enough to give you a proper interpretation. You should let my grandmother do a reading for you sometime. Or my sister. She's very talented. Maybe the most gifted of us all."

"Thank you, but as I said, I'd rather not know what the future holds."

She leaned in. "I'll let you in on a secret. Chiromancy has very little to do with psychic ability. It's both an art and a science. A good palmist is more of a psychologist than a prophet. She bases her predictions on a particular set of factors she gleans from the client and then suggests a likely outcome. But my sister says that no one is interested in the actual methodology. People who visit palmists do so because they're drawn to the mystique. They want the show, in other words, and Isabel obliges in her own irreverent manner. She calls herself Madam Know-it-all."

"She's a professional palmist?" *Madam Know-it-all.* Why did that name ring a bell?

"She has a place right on the edge of the historic district, near Calhoun."

Something was starting to niggle. "Is it across the street from the Charleston Institute for Parapsychology Studies, by chance?"

Clementine's eyes widened. "Don't tell me you've been there. Now that *is* a coincidence."

Not coincidence, I thought uneasily. Synchronicity.

"A friend of mine is the director of the Institute," I said. "I notice your sister's place every time I visit. There's a neon hand in the front."

"Yes, that's it. But don't let the name fool you. Isabel takes her work very seriously."

The last time I'd been to the Institute, I'd spotted Devlin on the front porch with a shapely brunette who I had assumed was the palmist. Now I was sure of it, and I was equally certain that the woman I'd seen him with last evening hadn't been Clementine Perilloux, after all, but her sister, Isabel.

We both fell silent as we finished our coffee, and, given this new development, I wondered if I should just make a graceful exit and forget about the broken statue. I'd waited too long. Now a confession would be terribly uncomfortable. Still, Clementine had been nothing but gracious, and I felt I owed her the truth and some manner of compensation.

I nodded toward the garden. "I see your statue's been broken."

She followed my gaze. "Oh! Isabel said she and John heard someone in the garden last evening."

My heart skipped a beat. "John?"

"He's a police detective. He and Isabel…"

I leaned in.

"…are very close friends."

Friends? I was both hoping for and dreading an elaboration, but when none was forthcoming, I let out a breath. "You're not upset about the statue?"

Her eyes flickered. "There was one very like it in the garden at…where I lived before. I didn't care for that place so I'm happy to be rid of the reminder."

I felt a tiny prick of unease, that prescient tingle along my spine and scalp that made me say quickly, "This has been lovely, but Angus and I really should be going."

"I'll walk you around," she said. "Promise you'll come again. Next time I'll invite Isabel. I'd love for you to meet her. I know I'm biased, but she's…well, you'll just have to see her for yourself. I think the two of you would really hit it off. You have a lot in common."

Seven

That night I fixed a light dinner for myself, and after the dishes were washed and put away, I made a cup of tea and settled down to work. My office at the back of the house was a converted sunporch, surrounded on three sides by windows. By day, the sunlight shining in from the garden was warm and relaxing, but by night, the darkened panes spurred the imagination, especially on evenings like this when I sensed the nearby presence of restless spirits.

But I refused to give in to the sensation at my nape. I wouldn't look around. I wouldn't scour the garden for the telltale illumination of a manifestation. Instead, I powered up my laptop and opened a new document file.

For weeks, I'd been ignoring my blog, but now that I found myself in between restorations, the ad money generated by *Digging Graves* was an important source of revenue. I'd already come up with a new topic—"The Crypt Peeper: Communing with the Dead"—a piece about the popularity of graveyards during the Victorian era. Tonight, however, that subject seemed prophetic because I'd spent a little too much time lately conversing with ghosts.

I continued to work until I'd eked out a rough draft, and then I saved the file and logged onto the internet to do some research. If I was going to help Robert Fremont find his killer, I would need to study every scrap of information I could lay my hands on. I was still uneasy about my role as detective, but I'd always loved a good mystery and research was the backbone of cemetery restoration. I knew how to dig for the most obscure details, but unfortunately, I found precious little information about the murder. Fremont had worked undercover so I imagined that even after his death, cases and informants needed to be protected. I did run across the occasional mention of him on a site that archived old articles involving the Charleston Police Department and even managed to turn up a brief piece about the shooting and a sparse obituary.

Fremont had been thirty when he died. I'd already known he was close to Devlin's age because the two had gone through the police academy together. I'd seen a picture of them at graduation, along with a third man named Tom Gerrity, who was now a private detective in Charleston. He and Devlin made no bones about the contempt they held for one another. The bad blood had something to do with Fremont's death, but I knew none of the details, and the online article mentioned neither of them.

No witnesses to the shooting had ever come forward, and no information regarding motive or suspects had been released to the press. The case had apparently been kept under close wraps by both the Beaufort County Sheriff's Office and the Charleston Police Department.

Two items from the article and the obituary leaped

out at me. One, Fremont had grown up near Hammond, a small town in the coastal plain of South Carolina where Mariama had been raised. And two, the shooting had occurred the day after her accident. Fremont's time of death had been placed somewhere between two and four in the morning, several hours after Mariama's car had gone over a guardrail at dusk, trapping her and Shani inside the sinking vehicle.

I'd seen Robert Fremont's headstone last spring during the restoration of Coffeeville Cemetery, but I hadn't known who he was at the time so his date of death hadn't registered. Now, given what I'd learned of his connection to Devlin and possibly to Mariama, the proximity of their deaths intrigued me.

Grabbing a notepad and pen, I made a little diagram of names with arrows: **Devlin > Shani > Mariama > Fremont.**

Then I added **Clementine > Isabel > Devlin.**

As I stared down at the linked names, I became more and more convinced that nothing about the recent events was coincidental. Not Mariama's assault, not Shani's request and certainly not Fremont's haunting. All three ghosts had come back into my life for a reason, and the timing was important. Everything was connected, and the pieces of the puzzle were already starting to fall into place.

The stars have finally aligned, Fremont had said. *The players have all taken their places.*

I continued to search until the words on the screen blurred and a sharp pain stabbed between my shoulder blades. I got up and stretched, telling myself I should turn in early and try to get some rest. I was exhausted, drained, and who knew what the days ahead held for me, let alone the nights. I hardly dared contemplate them.

But after everything that had happened, I knew I would never be able to sleep. I was too wired, too certain that something dark was headed my way. And Devlin was somehow involved. I could feel it. That was why he'd been reaching out to me, why even now I could sense his irresistible pull.

The walls of my sanctuary started to close in on me, and not for the first time, I found myself resenting the legacy that kept me pinned to hallowed places. All my life, I'd followed Papa's rules, kept myself sequestered in loneliness, but now I felt an unaccustomed rebellion welling up inside me. The bloom of an unwise impulse that had very little to do with a noble purpose or a greater calling.

I wanted to see Devlin.

Not from afar as I had last evening and certainly not with another woman. I wanted him here with me, in my haven, where his ghosts couldn't come to us. I craved his touch, his warmth, the sound of my name on his lips.

Rising abruptly, I walked to the window and pressed my forehead to the cool glass. Why not go to him? I asked myself. Why not throw caution to the wind yet again? The rules had already been broken. The door had been flung wide. I'd seen the worst. What more could possibly happen?

Famous last words.

I glanced down at Angus. He was already in his bed and looked to be fast asleep, which reassured me that, despite my terrifying thoughts, all was well inside and outside the house. His ear nubs twitched, and I wondered if he dreamed about his dark past, about his time spent as a bait dog. I hoped with the passage of enough time, we might both leave our nightmares behind us.

As if sensing my attention, he opened his eyes and gave me a mournful look.

"Sorry," I murmured. "I don't like to be stared at, either, when I'm sleeping."

He settled more comfortably into his bed, snout on paws, and drifted off again. I turned back to the windows, my gaze searching the moonlit garden. The wind had picked up. The Spanish moss hanging from the old live oak billowed like gossamer curtains and the wind chimes jangled discordantly.

A storm brewed where only an hour ago the sky had been clear. For some reason, I thought of Mariama's wrath. Was this her doing? Just how much power did she wield from the grave?

I put a hand to my chest where I had felt the force of her anger. I'd experienced the touch of a ghost before, but mostly a chill breath down my back or the occasional trail of icy fingers through my hair. With Mariama, I felt physically threatened. She frightened me in a way that went well beyond my ingrained fear of ghosts.

She wanted to keep me away from Devlin. That much was obvious. From everything I'd heard about her, she'd been a volatile woman in life. Passionate and tempestuous. I was very much afraid that death had only intensified her anger.

As I turned away from the window, I caught a glimpse of my reflection in the glass. A pale, gaunt creature with wide eyes and sunken cheeks stared back at me. Hardly a match for Devlin's memory of the lush and exotic Mariama. Or for the mysterious Isabel Perilloux.

If I peered closely enough at my reflection, I could still see the scars from my time in the mountains, those thin, white lines that crisscrossed my face and arms where dozens of deep scratches had healed. I'd almost died in Asher Falls, but I was back in Charleston now, and like those scratches, the memory of that withering town was already fading.

My time with Thane Asher seemed like nothing more than a long-ago dream, distant and hazy. There were days when I would think of him suddenly and experience a pang of fleeting regret. I missed him, but I didn't ache for him the way I ached for Devlin. I didn't yearn for him in the middle of the night, didn't awaken to his conjured whisper in my ear, the phantom caress of his fingers along my spine. My time with Devlin haunted me as surely as his ghosts haunted him.

Doggedly, I went back to work, but I couldn't concentrate. My thoughts were too scattered, and the house felt claustrophobic. I told myself it would be foolish to go out after dark when I was already safely sequestered for the night.

But…maybe the fresh air would do me good, I reasoned. A short drive along the Ashley River might help to relax me so that I could finally sleep.

A few minutes later, I was still lying to myself as I turned down Devlin's street.

Eight

In all the months we'd been apart, I'd never once driven by Devlin's house, never once chanced to arrive at a place where I thought he might be or called his phone only to hang up when he answered. At twenty-seven, I was far too old to resort to such adolescent behavior, and truth be told, such tactics were foreign to me.

Growing up, I'd had very few friends, let alone boyfriends. My free time had been spent helping Papa groom graves or sequestering myself in the hallowed section of Rosehill Cemetery, away from the ghosts and alone with my books. Left to my own devices, I'd cut my teeth on the romantic classics: *Jane Eyre, Pride and Prejudice, Rebecca.*

Little wonder, then, when Devlin had appeared out of the mist that first night, so dark and brooding, so tragically flawed, the pump had been primed, so to speak. I never stood a chance.

But I'd had no experience in dealing with a real-life Byronic hero. My friend Temple had once pointed out that, until Devlin, I'd only ever been attracted to safe men. Scholars and intellectuals. Milquetoasts, she'd called them, and she'd warned me about getting too close too quickly to a man like John Devlin. Mariama, she'd said, would have known how to use her considerable wiles to control him whereas someone like me would only get her heart broken.

She'd been right about that, but it wasn't Devlin's fault. He couldn't help that he was haunted by his dead wife and daughter. He couldn't help that he wasn't ready to let them go.

So why had I come? What could I possibly hope to accomplish? Nothing about our situation had changed. Devlin's ghosts were still with him and Mariama's warning couldn't have been clearer. *Stay away.*

A warning I should have heeded.

But the adrenaline was already rushing as I pulled to the curb and parked down the street from Devlin's house. The clouds rolling in from the sea intermittently blocked the moon, and the neighborhood lay in deep shadow.

Thankfully, I saw no ghosts as I hurried along the sidewalk. It was just after ten, still early enough for the living. Up ahead, bicycle reflectors flashed around the corner and a young couple out for a pre-bedtime stroll murmured a greeting as we passed. It all seemed so normal.

But nothing about this night was normal. Certainly not my impulsive behavior. I could only imagine what my mother would say if she could see me slipping through the darkness. *No woman with a decent upbringing would ever arrive unannounced at a man's house in the middle of the night. I taught you better than that.*

She had. But here I was, anyway.

Of course, my mother had more important things to

worry about these days. Her battle with cancer had taken a toll, and, though her doctors had assured us that she'd made it through the worst of the treatment, she still had a long road ahead of her.

On nights like this, when I felt lonely and confused and out of my depth, I wanted more than anything to go to her and rest my cheek on her knee while I poured out my heart to her. I wanted to tell her about Devlin and have her smooth my hair while she murmured reassurances that everything would work out in the end.

Such comfort had been rare enough even before her diagnosis, even when I was a child. I loved my beautiful mother dearly, but she'd always kept me at arm's length. The circumstances of my adoption had created a chasm, one that she'd been too frightened to breach. And then there were the ghosts. My mother couldn't see them. That dark gift belonged only to Papa and me. It was our cross to bear, and the burden of our secret had also kept Mama at arm's length.

But I wouldn't dwell on my mother tonight when my own plate was already so full. Ghosts had invaded my world, phantom songbirds had serenaded me and the pieces of Robert Fremont's puzzle still swirled in my head. Where once my world had been narrow and ordered, everything now lay in chaos.

As I hurried along the shadowy street, something very strange happened to me. The night grew darker and colder, but I somehow knew it wasn't real. None of it was real. Not the nightingale, not the ghosts, not even my ill-advised trip to Devlin's house. I was home safe and sound in my bed, dreaming. How else to explain the sudden lethargy that gripped me? The shortness of breath and heaviness of limb that afflicted me in nightmares? How else to explain why the street before me now seemed endless, a frigid tunnel that cut through nothing but blackness?

Fear exploded in my chest, and my footsteps slowed, dragged. I could feel eyes all around me, staring and staring as arms reached out to grab me.

The sensation lasted for only a heartbeat. Then the arms morphed back into tree branches and the eyes vanished. I let out a slow breath. What had happened? I wondered. Had I just been warned?

Shivering, I continued down the street. There was a bite in the air that I hadn't noticed before, but the chill had nothing to do with the temperature. The first two weeks of October had been unseasonably warm, almost balmy in the afternoons, and the nights were mild. The icy draft came from beyond. The spirit world was suddenly very close. As close as I'd ever sensed it.

I cast a wary glance from side to side. I saw nothing in the darkness now, but I knew entities were all around me, floating down the murky walkways and alleys. Hovering within the walled gardens and historic homes. They sensed my energy just as I felt their coldness.

A gust of wind rattled the dry leaves in the gutter, and I could see the distant flicker of lightning over the treetops. Devlin's house was just ahead, a lovely old Queen Anne that he'd bought for Mariama. My steps faltered, and once again I felt spellbound. It was in that house that I'd finally succumbed to my feelings for Devlin. It was in that house that the door to the Others had been opened.

I told myself to turn back before it was too late, but I couldn't. Not yet. I was already flashing back to my night with Devlin, to the way he had held me so tightly, kissed me so deeply, and to the way that I'd kissed him. As if I could never get enough of him. I remembered so vividly the primitive rhythm of the African music playing in his bedroom, the heat of his skin as I placed my hand over his heart…sliding my lips downward, downward…and then a glance over my shoulder into a mirror where I'd seen Mariama's eyes staring back at me.

I forced the disturbing image from my head as I crossed the street. Thunder rumbled out in the harbor, and I could feel moisture in the air, the bristle of static electricity along my scalp. Clearly, a storm was headed this way. The signs couldn't have been more portentous.

But still I didn't turn back.

Whether I would have had the nerve to climb the veranda steps and ring the bell, I would never know. As I hovered on the walkway, hair rippling in that eerie draft, the door opened and I heard voices in the foyer.

I reacted purely on instinct, and, for the second time in as many nights, I ducked for cover in the bushes.

Nine

"Storm's coming," I heard Devlin say as I huddled in the bushes like the stalker I'd become.

"Seems fitting," another man replied. "Bad weather, bad juju."

"If you believe in that sort of thing."

"Of course. How could I forget? Nothing exists beyond the five senses, right, John?"

"I've learned to trust my instincts. Does that count?"

As always, the sound of Devlin's voice had a profound effect on me. My response was to shrink even deeper into the shadows beside the porch. But I couldn't resist peeking through the turning leaves to catch a glimpse of him.

Until last evening, I hadn't laid eyes on him since our final parting in Chedathy Cemetery months ago. I'd avoided his phone calls and email because I'd known the only way to get over him was to cut him completely from my life. During my short stay in Asher Falls, I'd almost managed to convince myself that I was ready to move on. I'd met a man whom I liked, a man whom I was attracted to, a man whom I might once have been happy with.

Now I knew better. Devlin was the only one for me, but so long as that door remained open, so long as he remained haunted, there was no hope.

So why couldn't I just accept my fate and let him go? I'd managed to keep my distance for months, so why was it getting harder to stay away?

Because I'd seen him with another woman. Because I was afraid he'd already let *me* go.

Maybe that was it. Or maybe Mariama had lured me here yet again for her own purposes. It was far easier to blame a ghost than to accept responsibility for my own questionable behavior.

Whatever the reason, I was stuck now until Devlin's guest left and he went back inside the house. I would be mortified if he caught sight of me cowering in the bushes.

As quietly as I could, I shifted my position so that I could get a better view. He stood on the veranda backlit by the chandelier in the foyer. I couldn't see his face, but I really didn't need to. His every feature—those dark eyes, that sensuous mouth—was permanently ingrained in my memory. I could even trace in my mind the line of the indented scar below his lower lip. That one tiny imperfection had always fascinated me.

The second man's voice sounded familiar, but he stood with his back to me, and I didn't recognize him until he turned to scour the shadows where I crouched. Light from the foyer fell across his face, and I drew a quick breath.

It was Ethan Shaw, a forensic anthropologist I'd worked with a few months ago. I'd first become acquainted with Ethan through his father, Dr. Rupert

Shaw, the director of the Charleston Institute for Parapsychology Studies. Dr. Shaw and I had been friends since I'd first moved to the city. He'd been intrigued by a "ghost" video I'd posted on my blog and had emailed to arrange a meeting. He'd even been instrumental in helping to secure my current residence from a former assistant of his who had moved to Europe suddenly.

I remained frozen as Ethan peered into the darkness. After a moment, he turned back to Devlin. "I thought I heard something."

"Probably just the wind."

"Or my imagination."

"Yes, there is that. Here." He handed Ethan a beer, and I heard the soft fizz as they each opened their bottles.

Devlin stepped out on the veranda then and stood with shoulders squared, feet slightly apart, as if bracing for something unpleasant. He was a tall man and lean to the point of gauntness from all his years of being haunted. But there was something very powerful about him just the same. Something almost menacing about the way he scowled into the darkness.

"I don't mind admitting I'm still a little jumpy," Ethan said with an uneasy laugh. He perched on the railing while Devlin leaned a shoulder against the porch wall. "Never in a million years did I expect to look across the street and find Darius Goodwine staring back at me. I'm telling you, John, it was the eeriest feeling. The weirdest coincidence."

"You don't really think it was a coincidence, do you?"

"I don't see how it could be anything else. I'm never in that neighborhood. I don't even have occasion to drive through it. Then today I was called out to an old house on Nassau to examine some bones that were unearthed beneath the porch. When I crawled out, there he was. He had on sunglasses and a hat, so I guess I could have been mistaken—"

"You weren't mistaken," Devlin said. "It was him."

"How can you be so sure?"

"Things are happening in this city."

"What do you mean?"

Devlin paused, his gaze lifting to the trees and for some reason, I thought of the nightingale and his strange insistence that I'd heard a mockingbird. "A woman was found dead on the east side a few nights ago. The toxicology screen turned up some interesting chemicals in her bloodstream. A cornucopia of botanical psychedelics, the coroner said, along with a substance that no one has been able to identify."

"What's that got to do with Darius?"

"Everything if that unknown substance turns out to be gray dust."

"*Gray dust?* Jesus." Ethan turned once again to scan the darkness. He looked pale and tense in the light that streamed through the doorway, and I could have sworn I heard a note of fear in his voice. "I thought that stuff disappeared years ago."

"Apparently, it's resurfaced just when Darius Goodwine returns from a long African sabbatical," Devlin said grimly. "There's only one source for gray dust and only a handful of outsiders that have ever been granted access. He's one of them."

"Yes, but he's not the only one."

"Come on." Devlin sounded impatient. "Today was no coincidence. He wanted you to see him just like he made sure those rumors about the gray dust got back to me. Just like he made sure the right chemicals turned up in that woman's body to create a mask. Every move he makes has a purpose." Again, Devlin tilted his head, as if trying to detect some distant sound. I glanced up, but the trees remained silent.

"What is it?" Ethan asked anxiously.

"Nothing. I guess I'm hearing things, too."

"Darius has that effect." Ethan rubbed the back of his neck. "It's hard to believe a man in his position would take such a risk. It's not like he needs the money these days."

"Money was never his motivation. Gray dust gives him the power to play God."

"The wielder of life and death," Ethan murmured. "Isn't that what he used to say?"

Devlin moved over to the steps and stood gazing out into the yard. If he looked down at just the right angle, he would surely spot me. I wanted to fade more deeply into the shadows of the porch, but I was afraid even a slight sound would draw his attention. Discovery would be the ultimate humiliation, but I was also fascinated by the conversation. Mariama's maiden name was Goodwine so I suspected she had some connection to Darius. What I didn't know was why the very utterance of his name seemed to invoke dread. I felt a tremor of something in the air that made my heart beat even faster.

"I used to think gray dust was a myth," Ethan said. "I always scoffed when Father and Mariama talked about it so reverently. I still say it's just a very powerful hallucinogen."

"It's more than that," Devlin said. "It stops the heart and people die. And the ones that come back…" As he moved down the steps, he turned his head away, and his voice became muffled. I couldn't make out the rest of his comment.

"You've seen them?" Ethan asked.

Devlin moved back to the steps. "They're still out there if you know where to look. Take a walk on the east side sometime, down along America Street. You can still spot one now and then among the crackheads and heroin addicts. Eyes frosted like a corpse, shuffling around all slumped over as if they'd dragged something back from hell with them."

Ethan was silent for a moment. "Father used to call them zombies."

"They're not zombies," Devlin scoffed. "Just fools that trusted Darius Goodwine."

Ethan rose and moved down the steps. I couldn't see either of their faces now, but their voices carried clearly to my hiding place.

"What are you going to do?" he asked Devlin.

"He'll have to be stopped."

"Not by you, I hope. He's a powerful man, John. From what I hear, he's got disciples all over the city. Some in very high places."

"I'm not afraid of him."

Something in Devlin's voice, a hint of excitement, sent a warning thrill up my spine.

"Maybe you should be," Ethan said.

"And why is that?"

"You know why."

"No, I don't. But I have a feeling you're about to tell me."

In the tense silence that followed, I was almost afraid the rapid thud of my heart would give me away. I hadn't a clue what they were talking about. I'd never heard of gray dust, but it made me think of what Fremont had said earlier about the place in between the Light and the Dark: *It's called the Gray.*

"I'm talking about the night of the accident…after

you found out about Mariama and Shani," Ethan said. "You went to see Father at the Institute, remember?"

"What of it?" Devlin's voice sounded terse and wary. Almost suspicious.

"You demanded that he help you contact the other side so that you could see them one last time. So that you could say goodbye. When Father couldn't help, you grew extremely agitated. Violent, even."

"I was still in shock," Devlin said in exasperation. "Out of my mind with grief. That's the only reason I went there. You know I don't believe in any of your father's nonsense."

"And we both know there was a time when you did. You were once Father's protégé. I've heard him say a million times you were the best investigator he ever had." Was that a note of jealousy I heard in Ethan's voice?

"That was a long time ago," Devlin said. "I was looking for a way to annoy my grandfather and Rupert's dog and pony show was a novelty to me."

"It was more than that. Even after you moved on…I don't think you completely let go. You married Mariama, after all."

"What are you getting at?" Devlin asked coldly.

"Some remnant of that belief must have remained. Grief and shock alone wouldn't have driven you to the Institute that night."

"Think what you want. I have no idea why you're dredging all this up now."

"After you stormed out, Father sent me to look for you, but it was as if you'd vanished into thin air. Where did you go that night?"

Devlin said nothing.

"You went to see Darius, didn't you? You asked him for gray dust."

Still, Devlin remained silent.

"I waited on this very porch for hours to make sure you were okay. You came home the next day looking like a corpse. Almost as if—"

"I'd just lost my daughter and my wife," Devlin cut in. "How did you expect me to look?"

"I didn't expect what I saw. You weren't just grieving, you were terrified. You couldn't stop shaking. I'd never seen you like that. That's why I gave you an alibi when the police came around asking questions about Robert Fremont's murder."

"I never asked you to lie for me."

"I was afraid not to," Ethan said. "You were barely able to drag yourself through that door, let alone handle a police interrogation."

"Interrogation? You make it sound like I was a suspect."

"You may well have been if they'd discovered your whereabouts that night. They already knew you and Robert had had a falling-out. Someone overheard the two of you arguing the day before he was shot."

Devlin's voice had gone quiet again. "Careful where you take this, Ethan."

"I'm only taking it to its logical conclusion. If Robert knew that Darius had supplied you with gray dust, he could have made things very difficult for you in the police department. A cop found using that stuff..." His voice trailed off.

"So you think I killed him." It was statement, not a question.

"No, of course not. But you do have a motive."

"And what about you?" Devlin asked, still in that same deadly quiet voice.

"What about me?"

"You told the police you were with me the whole night. You didn't just give me an alibi. You gave yourself one, too."

"What?" Ethan sounded taken aback. "Why would I need an alibi?"

"That's what I've always wondered."

A dog barked from someone's backyard, and I could hear the muffled roar of traffic over on Beaufain. But here in Devlin's front yard, everything was silent, the air so thick with tension I could scarcely draw a breath.

"You can't really think I had anything to do with Robert Fremont's death." Ethan sounded more hurt than outraged. "What possible motive would I have had?"

"Just forget it," Devlin said. "We need to stay focused."

I heard Ethan expel a breath. "You're right. We have to stick together. Even after all this time, there could still be questions about that night."

"I'll take care of any questions. You just call me if you see Darius again," Devlin said. "No matter the time."

Their voices faded as he walked with Ethan to the curb. A moment later, I heard a car door slam and the engine start up. I expected Devlin to go back inside, giving me a chance to slip away undetected, but instead, he sat down on the steps to finish his beer as he gazed out into the darkness.

He sat with shoulders hunched, forearms to knees, as if the weight of the world rested on his back. I wanted to go to him, but how would I explain my sudden appearance? What excuse could I give him for lurking in the bushes and eavesdropping on a private conversation? A very disturbing conversation. I was still reeling from the revelations and innuendoes, all of which seemed to lead back to Robert Fremont. *The stars have finally aligned.*

I also had a feeling the moment I showed myself, Mariama would materialize.

At the mere thought of her, the air grew colder. I shivered in the chill and braced myself in dread.

I must have made some involuntary movement because Devlin's head whipped around, and I saw his hand slide inside his jacket where I suspected he still wore his shoulder holster.

A cat darted out of a clump of bushes near the street and sprinted across the lawn to the house next door. Devlin's hand fell away. Slowly, he rose and scoured the yard before he turned to go inside.

As the door closed behind him, I started to emerge from my hiding place, but that terrible cold gripped me. I stood paralyzed as Shani's ghost manifested at my side.

Her hand was in mine, the frost of her existence chilling my whole being. She clung to me as she gazed out across the yard.

I was horrified by the contact, and my first instinct was to jerk my hand away. Already I could feel my strength waning. But, ghost or no, she was Devlin's daughter. I couldn't turn her away.

Her gaze lifted, and when she saw that she had my attention, she lifted a tiny hand and pointed to the cluster of bushes from which the cat had bolted. I almost expected to find Mariama's ghost swooping down on me.

Instead, I saw the gleam of human eyes in the darkness.

Ten

Someone was watching the house. Someone besides *me.*

My first instinct was to call and warn Devlin, but even the slightest movement or sound would alert the watcher to my presence. I remained motionless, hardly daring to even breathe as I shivered in the chill emanating from Shani's ghost.

The night was very dark. I could pick out little more than a silhouette until the moon peeked from a cloud, and in the sudden illumination, I got a clear view of him. He was black and uncommonly tall, though the shadows surrounding him may have added to the illusion. His gaze seemed transfixed on Devlin's house, and as I stood watching him, I heard the nightingale again. The trill was soft and mellow, like a dream. The man tilted his head to the sound, and I could have sworn I saw him smile.

Then he turned back to the house and lifted his hand to his mouth. Uncurling his fingers, he blew something from his palm. The shimmering particles hung suspended for a moment before they fell one by one to the ground and disappeared, leaving nothing but the faint odor of sulfur.

Throwing off the spell cast by those sparks, I cut my eyes back to the bushes. The man was gone. A moment later, I heard the thud of a car door down the street and the gentle hum of an engine. I waited until the vehicle was well away before I stirred. It was only then that I realized Shani had vanished, too.

Crawling from my hiding place, I hovered indecisively. I wanted nothing more than to head straight home to the safety of my sanctuary. Forget about this night, forget about the ghosts, forget about the troublesome connections to Fremont's murder that my eavesdropping had uncovered.

But I couldn't leave without warning Devlin, even if it meant giving myself away. For all I knew, he could be in terrible danger. His conversation with Ethan had certainly unsettled me. I didn't know what to make of any of it, but I knew that as soon as I was alone, I would go back over every word, dissecting nuances and inflections as I tried to figure out where these new details fit into the puzzle.

I hurried up the veranda steps, casting a wary glance over my shoulder. The wind had risen, rustling the palmettos, and already I could feel the aberrant cold seep from Devlin's house. I didn't want to go in there. Ghosts resided in that house. Not just Shani and Mariama, but entities from another realm, from beyond the Gray.

Minutes went by before Devlin finally answered. When he drew open the door, my breath escaped in a painful swoosh. He must have already been getting ready for bed because his shirt hung open and his hair was mussed as if he'd been running his fingers through it. Or as if someone had.

It hit me then that he might not be alone. That maybe Ethan and I had both interrupted his evening.

"Amelia?" He rested a hand against the door frame. "What are you doing here?"

"I…had to see you."

I tried to glimpse past him into the foyer, but I could see nothing beyond the doorway. My gaze flicked back to his and then, despite my best efforts, dropped. Where his shirt parted, I could see a strip of chest and against his pale skin, the gleam of his silver medallion. The talisman of the Order of the Coffin and the Claw, a secret society with a membership chosen from the city's oldest and most influential families. Devlin had shunned the constrictions of his upbringing, turned his back on his grandfather's legacy and expectations, yet, he still wore that symbol. He was still tied to his past in more ways than one.

All that strobed through my mind in a flash. In the next instant, I tossed another anxious glance over my shoulder toward the street.

He seemed to pick up on my urgency then, because he said sharply, "What's wrong?"

"I just saw something…I don't know what it means, but it frightened me."

"Come in." He took a step back so that I could enter.

Memories assaulted me the moment I stepped into the foyer, and my gaze went immediately to the staircase. I saw myself slowly climbing those steps, Mariama brushing by me, frightening me with her coldness, teasing me with a glimpse of her eyes in the mirror. I could almost hear the beat of those drums and the thud of my heart as I walked down the hallway to the bedroom. *Her* bedroom.

"What is it?" Devlin asked. "Tell me."

I turned. "Someone was in your yard just now. I saw him watching the house." I moved back to the door and pointed to the bushes where the man had been hiding. "He was there."

Devlin's demeanor instantly altered. "Wait here." He pulled open the drawer of a console in the foyer and removed a gun. I heard a series of snaps and clicks, and then he took another glance out the front door. But he didn't exit that way. Instead, he disappeared through the tall archway into the front parlor. I followed him, hovering just outside in the foyer as I watched him slip through the French doors into the side garden.

It was getting noticeably colder in the house. Devlin's ghosts were near. I could feel them. Fear shot through me.

An errant draft rustled paper on the console behind me, and the light in the foyer flickered, though the storm was still some distance off. I could feel a strange heaviness in the air and a pulse of electricity that tingled my nerve endings. Slowly, my gaze traveled through the parlor, probing dark corners.

I'd glimpsed this room once before when I came to see Devlin. I'd thought then as I did now that the weighty antiques and gilded frames were not at all to his taste. This room was Mariama's. I was certain of it. The lush decor belied the more common scent of lemon verbena stirred by that draft.

Over the mantel hung a portrait of Mariama dressed in a simple black dress that covered her arms and throat. The plain attire was no accident. Nothing detracted from those almond-shaped eyes, those cheekbones, that bewitching smile.

The only light in the room came from the chandelier in the foyer. It swayed gently, throwing shadows across the walls and over the painting so that Mariama's face alternated between dark and light. The movement was hypnotic, and it was only with some effort that I resisted the trance.

At one end of the room, a large window faced the street. Shani's ghost was there, motionless, as she peered out into the night. Watching for Devlin. Waiting for him to come back just as she had on the day of the accident.

Ethan had told me once that Mariama and Devlin had had a terrible row that day. *Shani kept tapping on John's leg to get his attention. I think she was trying to console him, but he was too angry...too caught up in the moment to notice. He stormed out of the house, and when he drove off, Shani was standing at the window waving goodbye. That was the last time he saw her alive.*

She was still at the window waiting for him, still trying desperately to get his attention. She must have sensed my presence—or felt my warmth—because she glanced over her shoulder with a finger to her lips.

My breath accelerated as I turned and lifted my gaze to the top of the stairs where Mariama's ghost hovered, the unnatural current stirring her hair and the hem of her gossamer dress. She was pale and cold, but her eyes were lit with an inner fire as she moved down the stairs, her feet floating inches from the steps. The papers swirled on the console, the light flickered and the air grew so frigid I could see the frost of my rapid breaths.

I looked down to find Shani at my side, nearly transparent save for the faint glimmer of her aura. She clung to my hand and I sensed Mariama's rage as she drifted ever closer.

Icy terror raced through my veins as my heart hammered against my chest. I wanted to back away, but I couldn't move, couldn't tear my gaze from the perverted beauty of her manifestation. I had no idea what she might be capable of, how much power she wielded from the other side. I thought of Devlin trapped in this house with her ghost, his energy waning, his youth stolen by a woman who had once claimed to love him.

Still loved him, it would seem.

She put out her arms to Shani, and my first instinct was to step between them. Despite my fear, I might have done exactly that, but when I looked down, the glimmer of Shani's aura blurred and then vanished, as if something had pulled her back into the ether.

Not so Mariama. With Shani's fading, she seemed to grow stronger, colder, hungrier. And I was already getting weaker. The place in my chest where I imagined my life force to be felt hollow.

Mustering the last of my strength, I backed away from the stairs, then turned to flee. Devlin had come in silently through the front door, and I ran straight into him. He caught my arms to steady me.

"Are you okay?"

"Yes…I thought I heard something," I said on a gasp.

"Inside?"

"I'm sure it was my imagination."

His gaze searched the stairs and the hallway behind me. "I left a window open upstairs. The wind may have knocked something over."

"That was probably it," I said shakily. "Did you find anything outside?"

"Not a trace. Whoever you saw is long gone."

"I heard a car start up and drive away. It might have been him."

"Can you describe him?"

"I only saw him briefly when the moon came out. He was black. Very tall and thin, although—"

Devlin's hands tightened on my arms. Something burned in his eyes. "How tall?"

"It was hard to tell. The shadows distorted him..." I trailed off, alarmed. "Why? Do you know who he was?"

"No."

He was lying, I thought. I wanted to ask him about Darius Goodwine, but I couldn't without giving my eavesdropping away.

"I heard the nightingale again," I told him. "It wasn't a mockingbird. I'm sure of it."

"There are no nightingales in Charleston," he insisted.

"Then why do I keep hearing one? Who was that man, John? Why won't you tell me?"

"I didn't see him. How would I know?"

"He blew something toward the house. It was like a shimmering blue powder. Don't you find that odd?"

He said nothing to that, but his hands fell away. He was still standing very close to me, gazing into my eyes. I had the strongest urge to lift my hand to his face, trace that scar with my thumb, assure myself that he was indeed real and this night was really happening. It wasn't another dream. We were here together. But Mariama was there at his side, stroking his arm, smiling at me over his shoulder. Taunting me because she possessed what I never could.

I glanced away.

"Why did you come here tonight?" Devlin asked. "Don't tell me you were just driving by."

"I came to see you."

He turned to glance out the door. "How did you get here? I didn't see your car outside."

"I parked down the street."

"Because you saw someone watching the house?"

"Because I didn't want you to see me," I blurted. "I wasn't sure I'd have the nerve to knock on your door."

"It takes nerve to knock on my door?"

I sighed. "Yes, and you know why."

It was all I could do to keep from reaching out to him, so magnetic was his presence. I let my gaze drift over him again. He'd buttoned his shirt while he was outside. The cut, as always, was perfection. He had an eye for clothes and the money to indulge his refined tastes. But there was an edge to the way he dressed, a hint of the rebellious nature that had driven him away from his elite upbringing and into the arms of Mariama Goodwine.

"So, why did you want to see me?" he asked carefully.

He was still staring out through the leaded glass panel in the front door. I focused my gaze on his profile and shivered. "I got your messages. I didn't have a chance to ask you about them last evening."

Slowly, he turned back to me. "What messages?"

"The ones you sent while I was away. The text came on my way back from Asher Falls."

"Asher Falls?"

"It's a small town in the Blue Ridge foothills near Woodberry. I had a restoration there, but then I had to leave suddenly, and I was on the ferry when I received your text."

Something flitted across his face. "I never texted you."

"But…the message came from your phone. I'm certain of it."

"I didn't send it," he insisted.

"Then who did?"

"I have no idea. Did you save it?"

"I had to replace my phone recently, and I lost everything. But it was sent from your number. I'm sure of it. And before that, I received an email from you. I suppose you didn't send that, either?"

"No."

"Well this is very strange." And more than a little unsettling. "I don't know what to say. I'm not making this up."

He smiled thinly. "I never thought you were."

I felt like bursting into tears. I'd been so certain the messages had come from him. And now to find out that he hadn't tried to contact me....

It was foolish to feel so devastated, I told myself. And yet I did.

"Who could have sent them?"

"I don't know," Devlin said. "But I intend to find out."

As I watched him, heart in my throat—and in my eyes—Mariama floated between us. I tried not to track her with my gaze.

How could he not feel the cold? How could he not flinch from her touch?

Go away, I thought.

I could hear her taunting laughter in my head. *You* go away.

Was I mad? I wondered. Had my years of living with ghosts finally driven me over the edge? Ever since Asher Falls, not only could I see specters, but I could hear them.

"What's wrong?" Devlin asked.

"I was just wondering why someone would go to the trouble of making me think the messages were from you. They must have somehow gained access to your phone, your email…" I trailed off as Fremont's cryptic words came back to me yet again.

"That's not likely," Devlin said.

Wasn't it?

Had Fremont somehow sent those messages from beyond in order to lure me back to Charleston?

We have to act quickly, he'd said. *Do you understand? It has to be now.*

Devlin was watching me closely. "You're trembling. Are you sure you're okay?"

"Yes. I'm still a little shaken and it's cold in this house. Haven't you noticed?"

He shrugged. "It's always been drafty."

Always? Or just since the ghosts came?

"What did the messages say?" he asked.

I was reluctant to reveal my intimate interpretation of the missives, particularly now that I knew they hadn't been sent by him. "In the email, you asked where I was."

"Did you answer?"

"No."

"Why not?"

"I don't really know," I said truthfully. "I was out of town, so I didn't think there was anything to be gained by telling you my whereabouts."

"What about the text?"

"It said 'I need you.'" My face warmed as he stared down at me.

Then he leaned in, his gaze dark and fathomless. "I need you," he drawled.

"Y-yes. That's what it said."

"Nothing more?"

I shook my head.

He looked pensive and slightly ominous. "When did you say you received the text?"

"A few weeks ago."

"And yet, you're just now coming to see me about it."

Yes, there was that. I couldn't explain my hesitance without giving away more of my feelings than I cared to reveal. "I couldn't come at once. I needed some time to recuperate when I got back. I wasn't well."

"Not well?" He placed his hands on my shoulders and turned me to the light. "You've been through something. I can see it on your face, in your eyes." His voice dropped. "What happened to you, Amelia?"

Don't, I thought miserably. *Don't say my name. Don't look at me that way. I'm only human. How can I not melt when you look at me like that?*

"I'm better now," I said.

He took my chin and gently tilted it. "What are those marks on your face? Who did that to you?" I heard something in his voice, a dark and dangerous undercurrent that made me shiver.

"Not who, what," I tried to say lightly. "I tangled with a briar patch. Occupational hazard. It was nothing."

"I don't agree."

I had backed away inadvertently, until I felt the wall behind me. Devlin moved with me, and now I started to feel panicky because he had that look again. He wouldn't try to kiss me, surely. Not after the way I'd run out on him.

But he was slowly leaning toward me, dark eyes glinting with something I didn't want to put a name to.

He said *Amelia* on a whisper, and my resistance weakened. I might have reached for him, despite my best intentions, but Mariama was there, as always. Floating between us. Touching Devlin. Touching me.

I drew a tremulous breath and turned my head away. "I should go. If you didn't send those messages, I suppose there's nothing more to talk about."

"Actually, there's a lot that needs to be said."

"It's getting late and I have to be up early—"

He lifted a hand to my hair and let the strands sift through his fingers. "Don't go."

I closed my eyes and sighed. "I have to."

He placed a hand on the wall above me, trapping me. He didn't touch me again, but I could feel the heat of his skin mingling with the cold of Mariama's presence. She'd drifted away, but not too far. She was somewhere in the shadows, watching us.

"Are you ever going to tell me what happened that night?" He glanced toward the stairs, and I shuddered as memories assailed me. *His lips pressed to my pulse, his fingers skimming my thigh...*

"Please let me go," I whispered.

"I'm not holding you. I just want to know what happened that night. The way you looked when you ran out of the bedroom...it's haunted me. I've been over it a million times in my head. What did I do to frighten you? Did I hurt you somehow?"

"No. No! It wasn't anything you did. Please believe me. The timing was all wrong. And you said yourself, you weren't ready to let go of the past. You didn't want to let *them* go...." My babbling trailed off. "I'm sorry I couldn't explain it better at the time. I don't think I really understood it myself until later. Until I had time to think—"

I never had a chance to finish that lame excuse. A loud crash from the parlor startled us both, and Devlin's hand flew to his back where he'd slid the gun into his waistband. He drew it now and motioned for silence as he eased across the foyer, me at his heels. Taking a quick sweep of the parlor, he dropped his arm and turned on the light.

Mariama's painting lay facedown on the floor.

"What happened?"

"Damned if I know. The wind couldn't have knocked it off. That thing weighs a ton."

"Then what caused it to fall?" Dumb question. I already knew the answer.

"The fasteners must have loosened."

"The glass is broken," I said inanely because I didn't know what else to say at that moment. Mariama's message was perfectly clear.

"It can be repaired," he said. "I've been meaning to take it down, anyway. I just never got around to it. I rarely come in this room. It's always so cold in here, even in the summer. I've never been able to figure out where the draft comes from." He looked up as the chandelier stirred. "See what I mean?"

I was standing in the archway and could feel that same current sweeping down the stairs. I looked up, expecting to see Mariama once again, but instead, the darkness on the galley pulsed and throbbed with shimmers, like tiny strobes, where the Others were trying to come through.

I stared wide-eyed and terrified as the flickers intensified. I had to get out of that house, away from Devlin, away from the emotions that drew those ravenous entities like moths to flame.

"I have to go."

"Amelia, wait."

I was out the front door and all the way down the

veranda steps before he caught up with me. Once again he took my arms and turned me, searching my face in the darkness. "What's wrong? Why did you run out like that?"

"Just let me go. Please."

I tried to wrench away, but his grasp only tightened. "What is it about this house that frightens you? What is it about *me?*"

My gazed went past him to the house. I could see Shani in the window and Mariama hovering in the doorway. Maybe it was my imagination, but I thought I saw the glimmer of faces in every other window. "You know why," I said breathlessly.

"What are you talking about?"

"You *know,* John. You just refuse to admit it."

He dropped his hands and took a step back from me. Even in the dark, I could see the look of horror that flashed across his face.

Eleven

As soon as I got home, I let Angus out into the backyard. Then I poured myself a glass of wine and gulped it. Poured another and gulped it, wishing I had something stronger. The third glass I carried out to the garden and sipped while I waited for Angus to get on with his business. He took his sweet time as he always did, and as impatient as I was to get to my computer, I didn't have the heart to rush him. He'd spent most of his life cooped up in cages and kennels, suffering horrors that I could barely comprehend. The least I could do was indulge his curiosity.

A mild breeze stirred the wind chimes, but I felt no ghostly presence in the garden. Thankfully, Shani hadn't followed me home tonight.

Shivering, I zipped my jacket all the way up to my neck. The night had turned chilly, but at least the storm seemed to have passed us by. Or maybe the clouds had only gathered over Devlin's house. Here, a few blocks away, the moon was out and the thunder had faded. I even saw a few stars peeking out.

I wondered if the hazy ring around the moon was an omen. Fishing for the talisman I wore around my neck, I rubbed my thumb across the smooth surface. The polished stone had come from the hallowed hills of Rosehill Cemetery, my childhood playground. How many afternoons had I spent curled up in the shade of an old, drooping live oak or with my back pressed against the warm granite of a weeping angel, devouring the pages of my favorite Gothic novels, fueling an imagination already primed by the ghosts? Back then, I'd dreamed of someone like Devlin. A darkly charismatic man with even darker secrets. As a lonely teenager, nothing had seemed more romantic than doomed love, nothing more beautifully melancholy than unrequited passion.

How stupidly naive I'd been. There was nothing remotely beautiful or desirable about being denied the love of one's life, as I had been so cruelly reminded tonight. Even without the threat of the Others, Mariama would always find a way to keep Devlin and me apart.

The wine was going straight to my head, making me slightly hysterical and borderline maudlin. Hovering just outside the door, I watched Angus amble around the yard as my thoughts raced and images flashed in my brain—the almost kiss…the falling painting… Mariama in all her dead glory.

Shani clutching my hand.

In some ways, the ghost child's attachment to me was the most disturbing development of all. Not because I was actually scared of her—at least, not the way I feared Mariama—but because it seemed a direct manifestation of Papa's broken rules, a terrifying reminder that I had inadvertently crossed a threshold from which there would be no return.

I'd brought all of this on myself, of course. How many

times had Papa warned me? By allowing a haunted man into my life, I'd made myself susceptible to his ghosts. And those ghosts had drawn other ghosts. By letting down my defenses, I'd opened myself up to an invasion. Not just from Shani and Mariama and Robert Fremont, but possibly from spirits that had yet to make their way to me.

It was all well and good to contemplate a higher purpose, but when delusions of grandeur became stark reality, I didn't know what to do. I had no idea what would be expected of me, what lay in wait for me. I didn't have an inkling of where all this would lead me, but I thought perhaps it was a very good thing that Clementine Perilloux hadn't been able to tell my fortune. More than ever, I had no wish to see my future.

With another fortifying sip of wine, I tried to shepherd my thoughts from ghosts to the overheard conversation between Devlin and Ethan. Robert Fremont's murder investigation had taken an unexpected turn tonight and Devlin's involvement was an added complication. Suddenly, something Fremont had said came rushing back to me. *We follow the clues no matter where they lead. Understood?*

Even if those clues led to Devlin? Had that been his implication?

I played that conversation over and over in my head because it was easier to dwell on what I'd learned from my eavesdropping than to delve more deeply into what had happened in Devlin's house.

Finally, Angus finished his business, and we went back inside. He prowled through the rooms for a while before settling down in his bed. I took a shower and changed into my pajamas before returning to my desk.

Wineglass within easy reach, I ignored all those dark windows and opened my laptop. I typed in Darius Goodwine, almost expecting the same sparse results yielded by my previous search. But instead, a dozen or more links popped up. Excited by the prospect of immersing myself in a project, I began to click through the pages.

Whatever I expected to learn about Darius Goodwine certainly wasn't what I found. The way the two men had spoken of him earlier had spawned images of a dangerous criminal living on the fringes. But Darius Goodwine had quite the impressive résumé. For starters, he had a doctorate from the University of Miami in molecular biology with an emphasis on ethnobotany. I only had a vague idea of what that entailed so I looked up the Wikipedia definition—*the study of how people of a particular culture and region make use of indigenous plants.*

Dr. Goodwine had done most of his fieldwork in the Gabonese Republic where he spent years studying as an apprentice to a *Bwiti* shaman. His sojourn to West Africa had inspired several books that delved into the complex relationship between certain cultures and plants, specifically those used in divination. Having resigned both his professorship at North Carolina State and a seat on the board of a large pharmaceutical company headquartered in Atlanta, Dr. Goodwine now spent most of his time in West Africa, writing and researching.

He, too, had grown up in Beaufort County, in a tiny Gullah community near Hammond, which made me all the more certain that he was related to Mariama. She and a male cousin had been raised together by their grandmother.

Darius was in his late thirties, so he was only a few years older. Strangely, the only photograph I could find was one blurry snapshot taken in Gabon. He appeared extremely tall, but I couldn't be certain he was the same man I'd seen watching Devlin's house.

I moved on to gray dust. Here, I did run into a wall. One link led to a Cornell University piece about quasar environments and another to an online fantasy game. Nothing at all about a powerful hallucinogen that stopped the heart and caused people to die.

Gray dust exhausted, I returned to Darius Goodwine, clicking through the rest of the articles in the hopes of turning up a clearer photograph. As I scanned the information, I copied and pasted and made copious notes on my legal pad as my chart evolved:

Devlin > Shani > Mariama > Fremont
Darius > Mariama > Devlin > Ethan
Clementine > Isabel > Devlin

Devlin was clearly connected to all the players, but it was hard for me to imagine that he'd ever been involved in drugs or the occult. He'd never made a secret of his disdain for Dr. Shaw's work and had gone so far as to advise against an association with the man or the Institute.

Yet, he had once been Dr. Shaw's protégé. A gifted paranormal investigator according to Ethan. Devlin had married a woman with strong ties to her Gullah heritage, and he appeared to have some sort of relationship with Isabel Perilloux, a palmist. Which only served to remind me of how very little I knew of the real John Devlin. In so many ways, he was still a stranger to me, but rather than discouraging my affection, his secrecy only intensified my unrealistic fantasies.

The office had grown cold as I sat there absorbed in my research. I'd cut off the air-conditioning when the temperature began to drop at night, and I wasn't yet ready to turn on the heat. It was only a slight chill. Something on my arms was all I needed.

I got up to grab a sweater, and as I walked down the hallway to my bedroom, I became aware of a subtle, yet unsettling background noise. I stopped in midstride to listen. The house was very quiet at night without the coming and going of my upstairs neighbor. I wondered briefly if he might have returned, but the dripping—as I had now identified the sound—was definitely coming from my own apartment. Despite the age of the house, I'd never had a problem with leaky pipes or faulty plumbing, so a dripping faucet caught my attention.

Tracing the sound to the bathroom, I turned on the light and glanced around. The scent of rosemary lingered from my bath as I walked over to check the faucets in the shower and then at the sink. The beveled mirror was fogged over, and without thinking, I reached up to clear it. My hand froze.

A pattern had formed in the mist. The barest trace of a heart.

Shani. The ghost child's basket name meant "my heart."

She'd chosen to communicate with me this way once before. She'd traced a heart on my office window to let me know she was there. To let me know who she was.

I stared at that heart now as a dark dread descended. Never before had I seen evidence of a manifestation *inside* my house, *inside* my sanctuary. Hallowed ground had always been my safe haven.

Was she still there?

I resisted the urge to whirl and scour the shadowy spaces behind me as I warned myself to remain calm. That was always the key to dealing with ghosts. When I was little, my father had taken me to the cemetery every Sunday afternoon so that I could become accustomed to the specters that floated through the veil at dusk. He'd always stressed the importance of controlling my reaction. *Show no fear, child, even when they manifest near you. Never acknowledge the dead even when they touch you.*

I'd developed quite the poker face over the years even when apparitions suddenly appeared before me. Even when they ran their icy fingers through my hair or down my spine. I knew how to suppress shudders and shivers and how to look through ghosts without looking at them.

But this was different. Never had one invaded the sanctity of my protected space.

I dropped my hand casually to my side and turned, bracing inwardly for what I might see. Nothing was there. No Shani. No aura. Not even a lingering shimmer.

But as I moved back into the hallway, I couldn't shake the notion that something trailed me. I went from room to room, making sure doors and windows were secure. Not that locks would keep out phantoms. I had to do something, though, because if my sanctuary had truly been violated…

Mentally, I shook myself. I couldn't allow myself to think about that. The heart traced on the mirror might have been there for ages and was only now showing up in the frost. I hadn't noticed it before, but the outline was very faint. Of course, I'd cleaned that mirror any number of times since moving into the house….

Resisting the temptation to glance over my shoulder, I went back to my office. Angus had risen from his bed and stood growling at one of the windows. I'd heard him make that guttural sound once before when he'd been in the presence of a ghost. And in the presence of evil.

The glass was so fogged, I couldn't see outside, couldn't see the entity that lurked in the garden, but just like Angus, I sensed an unnatural presence.

He growled again and eased himself over to my side. I reached down and put my hand on his back, stroking his ruffled fur as I took comfort in his warmth.

The scent of jasmine came to me then, so strong I might have opened a window. But this time of year, the starry blooms had long since faded. The perfume came not from my garden, but from Shani's ghost. She wanted me to know she was there.

"You're here," I whispered. "Now what do you want?"

The computer screen cast an eerie glow on the frosted windows, and for one split second, I thought I saw something outside, a featureless face peering into my office. It was there one moment, gone the next as another scent drifted in, almost masked by the jasmine. Sulfur.

The knock of my heart was so painful at this point I could scarcely breathe. My hand stilled on Angus's back as a terrible revelation came to me.

Shani wasn't alone. Something had followed her to my house. Something dark and malevolent. I could feel it out there in the garden even now.

I heard a whimper as Angus pressed himself against me. I wanted to cry, too, but I didn't make a sound. Instead, I just stood there clutching the polished stone at my throat, my thumb working frantically over the smooth surface. My gaze was riveted to the windows where a message began to appear. Not a heart this time.

Not a request or a plea, but a bold, angry demand that repeated over and over in the frost:

HELP ME HELP ME HELP ME HELP ME HELP ME HELP ME

Twelve

Needless to say, I slept very little that night. Long after the frost on the windows melted, I'd remained in my office reeling from this new development. Never had I felt threatened by a ghost in my home. Never had the boundaries of my sanctuary been breached by any entity, and yet, somehow Shani had traced a heart on my bathroom mirror.

Why on the mirror and not on the window? Did she want me to know that she had found a way into my haven? Was she making sure that I couldn't ignore her?

And what of that other presence?

I really, really wanted to believe the face I'd glimpsed outside my window had been nothing more than a manifestation of my fear or a wine-induced hallucination. I hadn't been sleeping or eating properly, and by Fremont's own admission, he'd been haunting me. Plus, after my trip to see Devlin, I'd hardly been in the most stable frame of mind, so it wasn't hard to conclude that in such a state, my imagination could have played tricks.

But on Angus, too?

I kept a tense vigil in my office until well after midnight. Exhaustion finally drove me to bed where I tossed and turned for hours.

Despite a restless night, I arose the next morning at my usual time even though I had no particular place to be. I didn't have a restoration scheduled until the following month and, other than a few headstone repairs, nothing much else on the books. But between my savings and the ad revenue generated from *Digging Graves,* I was certain I could manage for a while.

Actually, I could do more than manage. An unexpected legacy had provided me with a generous nest egg, but that money was safely tucked away until I could decide how and when I wanted to use it. Considering the circumstances of my birth, I'd wanted no part of any inheritance from my blood family, the Ashers, but then I reminded myself that my mother's illness had likely depleted her and Papa's savings. If I could help them out financially, perhaps everything I'd been through in Asher Falls would be worth it.

Dressing for my morning walk, I donned a track jacket over a UNC T-shirt and then let Angus out into the backyard. The horizon glowed as I headed down Rutledge toward the harbor. I performed a few warm-ups and then picked up the pace. The morning was crisp and clear, and the jacket felt good all the way to Broad Street before I finally had to shed it.

Tying it around my waist, I turned left on Meeting Street, striding past the parade of historic churches and grand old homes with barely a glance. Another left and I found myself on Tradd, the most scenic of all avenues in a city known for its beautiful boulevards and thoroughfares. It was the only street in Charleston where one could glimpse the Ashley and Cooper Rivers at the same time, but this morning, I looked neither right nor left as I made my way to East Bay Street, where the colorful row homes and stately mansions were still bathed in misty gray.

I passed only a few early birds on the Battery. Migrating to my favorite spot, I stood facing the harbor as the sun broke the horizon and the sea burst into flames. It was a sight I never tired of.

Against the background of tiny Fort Sumter, a formation of pelicans glided low across the water, searching for the telltale shimmer of silver beneath the surface. It was very quiet where I stood. I could hear the gulls out in the harbor and the murmur of voices from the tourists that had risen early to watch the sunrise, but the sounds were muted and easy enough to tune out.

Someone appeared beside me at the railing. My gaze was still glued to the light show over the water, but I knew who he was. I slanted a glance at Fremont's ghost. Right here on the Battery was where I'd first seen him months ago. Only then, I'd still thought he was a flesh-and-blood man. Perhaps even a murderer.

"You don't look so good," he commented.

"I just walked all the way from my house. I'm a bit winded."

"No, that's not it. You look ill. What's wrong with you?"

I cut him a glance. "Oh, I don't know. Could it be that you're haunting me?" I asked with more than a shade of sarcasm.

I couldn't see his eyes behind the dark lenses, but I felt the frost from his gaze. The sensation was eerie and unsettling. "I'm not doing that to you."

"Really? Because as I recall, you admitted to draining my energy so that you could sustain your presence in the living world. That's what you said, isn't it?"

"That was then. I needed a way to get your attention. I had to make sure you would agree to help me. But now that we've come to an arrangement, I've backed off."

I merely lifted a brow.

"I've purposely kept my distance so that you could build your strength back up." He paused, and I felt that icy stare yet again. "You'll need every ounce of it."

"Is that a prediction?"

"You can take it as such."

Ignoring his ominous tone, I leaned against the railing. "If you're not draining me, then who is? Or should I say what?"

"Another ghost would be my guess."

Another ghost. I didn't know why, but it struck me as significant that, despite his humanlike appearance, he thought of himself as a ghost. He was under no delusions of remaining in the living world. Far from it. He just wanted to solve his murder and move on.

I tucked a strand of hair behind one ear. "You don't look like any of the other ghosts I see. You have no aura, no transparency. How do you manifest after dawn and before twilight? Don't you have to wait for the veil to thin? How are you here now, when the sun is coming up?"

"It takes a lot of energy and concentration."

"If you're not draining me, where do you get your energy?"

"Why does it matter?" he asked tersely. "It has nothing to do with you."

"Everything about our arrangement concerns me. You came to me, remember? And for all I know, you brought something with you that *is* draining me." I thought of that lurking shadow outside my window and shivered. "I know you're probably tired of answering all my questions, but this is important. My house is built on hallowed ground and yet you were sitting on my front porch. You were able to breach my sanctuary and now something else has, too."

"I told you it wasn't me."

"I know that's what you said, but assuming you wanted to, *could* you manifest inside my house?"

"No, not inside."

I paused in relief. Then glanced at him doubtfully. "Is that the truth or are you just telling me what I want to hear?"

"The real truth? I've never tried."

"Why not?"

"Because, believe it or not, I'm not looking to inconvenience you any more than I have to."

Inconvenience me? That was certainly an interesting way of putting it.

"I appreciate your consideration," I said. "But unfortunately, my sanctuary has been violated. A heart was traced in the frost on my bathroom mirror. I don't see how it could have been done unless a ghost entered my home."

"Psychokinesis," he said.

"You can do that?"

"On occasion. If you're worried about a visitation, try burning some sage in the house. You can use the ashes to smudge the mirrors and windows."

"That actually works? Sage will repel you?"

I saw a thin smile. "Me? No. But it might discourage a lesser manifestation."

"Like a ghost child?"

He shrugged.

"If you're not draining me, then it must be Shani," I mused.

His voice sharpened. "Shani?"

"John Devlin's daughter. She seems to have latched onto me."

"She drowned," he said.

I whirled in surprise. "Have you seen her?" A woman walking by on the Battery slanted me a curious glance, and I turned back to the harbor, lowering my voice. "You've seen Shani Devlin?"

"I told you I keep my distance from the other ghosts."

"Then how do you know about the drowning?"

"Someone must have told me."

I was silent for a moment. "You say you have no recollection of the shooting or of the time preceding it. You don't even know why you were in the cemetery or the identity of the woman you met sometime earlier, the one whose perfume you still wear. Yet you know about a death that occurred just hours before yours. The accident happened at around twilight. The car Shani was riding in went through a guardrail into a river, and she and her mother were trapped inside. You were shot sometime between two and four in the morning. In the hours in between, you somehow learned about Shani's death. This could be important because it would help establish a timeline. Did someone call to tell you about the accident?"

"I remember nothing," he said.

"Not true. You remembered she drowned. That must mean something."

"I was a cop, remember? It wasn't unusual to hear about accidents, especially one involving another detective's kid."

A man sidled up to the railing to admire the bloodred sunrise. "Beautiful, isn't it?"

"Yes, lovely," I murmured.

"I've watched sunrises all over the world," he said. "Nothing beats the one over Charleston Harbor."

I smiled noncommittally as I watched one of the pelicans break formation and dive, emerging from the sea a moment later with a flash of quicksilver in its beak.

"Have a nice day," the stranger murmured and sauntered away.

I glanced over to make certain Fremont was still beside me. He was.

"Something about that girl's death," he muttered.

"What?" I asked anxiously.

"I don't know. Tell me more about her ghost. You say she's latched onto you?"

"Like you, she can't move on. She wants my help, but I'm not sure what it is I'm supposed to do."

He said, very softly, "You still don't know who you are, do you? You still don't understand why we come to you."

His ghostly voice swept over me. "You come because I can see you." *And because I broke Papa's rules.*

He nodded vaguely as he turned back to the harbor. "Why can't the child move on?"

I took a deep breath, trying to quell a rising foreboding. "I can't say for sure. She was only four years old when she died. She doesn't converse with me the way you do, but she can communicate."

"You mean the heart?"

"And sometimes I hear her in my head. I think she can't move on because her father won't let her go."

"That makes sense. I saw them together a few times. They were very close."

"Her mother was trapped in the car, too, but I doubt she's ready to move on. She has John right where she wants him."

"That sounds like Mariama," he said, his gaze still on the horizon.

The sound of her name startled me, and I turned to stare at his profile. "You knew her?"

"We grew up together," he said, in that strangely hollow voice.

"Were you friends?"

"Friends? Hardly…."

"Lovers?"

"Every man who crossed Mariama's path loved her."

"Including you?"

"For a time. Then I moved to Charleston and discovered that the world didn't revolve around Mariama Goodwine."

"How did she take that revelation?"

"Not well."

"Are you the reason she came to Charleston?"

"She came because she saw an opportunity and seized it. A man named Rupert Shaw offered to finance her education."

"I know Dr. Shaw. He's a friend of mine." Fremont paused and I could feel a facture in the air as if something unseen had moved between us. "He used to spend a lot of time in Beaufort County."

"Doing what?"

"Research," he said. "He was particularly interested in Essie Goodwine, Mariama's grandmother. She was the most prominent root doctor in the area. He wanted to learn about medicinal conjure, but knowing Essie, she only taught him a few harmless incantations and spells. She wouldn't cotton to anyone's use of the root for evil."

"Evil? I hardly think that criteria would apply to Dr. Shaw," I said, remembering my own visit with Essie Goodwine. She'd given me a packet of Life Everlastin' and an amulet to ward off evil spirits.

She'd also told me there would come a time when I would need to tell Devlin about Shani's ghost because he would have to choose between the living and the dead. I couldn't imagine revealing such a thing to him back then, but last night I had come very close.

He knows, Essie had said, touching her heart. *In heh, he knows.*

He probably did know on some level. The draft, the cold spots…the inexplicable sounds in the middle of the night. The spiny hair at his nape, the icy shiver along his spine…

I forced my attention back to the ghost at hand.

Robert Fremont gazed down at me so intently, I wondered for a moment if he could read my thoughts. He had the power to pass himself off as human. What else could he do?

"Do you know anything about rootwork?" he asked.

"I only know what I've read here and there. You don't grow up in South Carolina without some knowledge, no matter how rudimentary. It originated in West Africa, didn't it?" Which naturally made me think of Darius Goodwine.

"Devotees believe that all things have spiritual essence, a soul even. A knowledgeable root doctor can tap into that universal power through the spirit world and use it for good or ill. Mariama was raised to respect the root. She was meant to follow in Essie's footsteps. I think that's why Shaw really brought her to Charleston."

"So that he could use her to tap into the spirit world? I suppose that makes sense. He's always had a keen interest in the afterlife, but not for personal gain or power. His wife was ill for a long time before she died. He tried to make contact through séances, but according to Devlin, Mariama wanted no part of it. She was afraid of what Dr. Shaw was trying to do."

"She had a healthy fear of the dead as anyone with her knowledge would."

"Because a person's power isn't diminished by death?"

"Because she knew you can't always control what you bring back," he muttered.

A chill wind feathered up my spine. "Did you see a lot of Mariama after she moved here?"

"Some, but she wasn't in town long before she met someone new."

"John?"

"He was taboo and that made him all the more irresistible to her."

"Why was he taboo?"

"Old resentments run deep in these parts. Distrust of the white man is still alive and well, and a union with John Devlin was considered a betrayal by some. He wasn't just white, he was rich. Old-money, Charleston rich."

"So, Mariama's family didn't approve of the relationship?"

"It was deeper than disapproval. And much more complicated."

I was very curious about Devlin and Mariama's relationship, but reluctantly I moved on to a new subject. "She lived with Dr. Shaw when she first came to Charleston, didn't she? Did you know Ethan Shaw?"

"Well enough to realize that he was in love with Mariama, too."

My brows shot up in shock. "Ethan?"

"It's like I said—"

"Every man who crossed paths with Mariama loved her." But *Ethan?* "Did Devlin know?"

"He may have, but most men had blinders on when it came to Mariama."

"Do you think anything went on between them?"

His gaze was scornful. "She wouldn't have given someone like Shaw the time of day. But she wasn't above using him if the need arose."

"Using him how?"

He took a moment to answer. "Mariama had an unnatural power over the living. Whatever she wanted… whatever she needed…she could always find someone willing to do her bidding."

That didn't exactly answer my questions, but I suddenly remembered something Devlin had said to Ethan the night before. *You told the police you were with me the whole night. You didn't just give me an alibi. You gave yourself one, too.*

He couldn't have been doing Mariama's bidding that night, though, because she was already dead.

"What's wrong?" Fremont asked.

"I'm just wondering why so many smart men fell in love with her. I understand she was beautiful and charismatic, but from everything I've heard, she was also selfish and cruel."

"She wasn't always like that. She was wild and impulsive and more than a little dangerous. But not cruel. Not until Darius changed her."

I marveled that, even dead, he was still quick to

defend her. "Darius Goodwine? What was their relationship?"

"First cousins, but they were raised as siblings."

"How did he change her?"

"He knew how to use her Achilles' heel against her."

"What do you mean?"

"John Devlin was her weakness. There was a part of him that Mariama couldn't touch, couldn't own. His resistance drove her mad. She would have done anything to weaken *him.* So Darius exploited her vulnerability."

"How?"

"He persuaded her to run off to Africa with the child. It took Devlin weeks to find them. He brought Shani back home, but Mariama stayed on with Darius. By the time she finally returned, Darius had made the transformation."

"What kind of transformation?"

"From shaman to *tagati.*"

"What's a *tagati?*"

"The closest translation would be sorcerer. Or witch. Someone who uses medicinal conjure for evil purposes."

Medicinal conjure as in gray dust? I wondered.

"The most powerful *thakathi* are female and Darius convinced Mariama that with his knowledge and her power, they could be an invincible force. He followed her back to Charleston and his influence had a profoundly negative effect on her."

"Because she started to believe him?"

"Because she knew it was true. It's not easy for an outsider to grasp, but in our community, the concept of magic is as accepted as the concept of God. There is an old saying that we practice one religion openly on Sundays and another in secret every other day of the week." He'd been gazing out over the water, but now he turned to stare at me. "A lot of people don't believe in ghosts, but that makes me no less real to you."

I could hardly argue with that logic. "You say Darius followed her back to Charleston. Is that when he brought in gray dust?"

Fremont said in a hushed voice, "What do you know about gray dust?"

"It's a hallucinogenic powder that stops the heart."

He glanced around as if afraid someone might eavesdrop. Which, when I thought about it, was pretty strange. The only one who could be overheard was me, and people would likely take me for a nutcase and keep their distance.

"Who have you been talking to?" he demanded.

"No one. I've just been doing some research. That is what you expected of me, isn't it? That I should be more resourceful?" I didn't give him a chance to reply. "If you were investigating Darius at the time of your death, then he's our most likely suspect."

"I wasn't just investigating him," Fremont said. "I was trying to stop him."

"From drug smuggling?"

He paused. "Yes."

Something in his voice drew another shiver. "Were you working with Devlin?"

He murmured something so low I couldn't make it out. I had the troubling notion it was a chant or incantation.

"What are you doing?"

He didn't answer.

"Why is everyone afraid of Darius Goodwine?" I demanded. "He can't possibly be a threat to you now."

The ghost didn't reply. He was already starting to fade and in another moment, he was gone. I stood at the railing alone and trembling as a cold gust cut through me. My foreboding grew with the wind. The harbor sparkled with sunlight but somewhere in the distance, darkness gathered.

Thirteen

Normally, I would have continued along the Battery to Murray Boulevard and then up Rutledge Avenue past Colonial Lake Park to my house. This morning, however, I cut through White Point Gardens, striding past the Civil War monuments and cannons and giving a wide berth to the lovely white gazebo where a sunrise wedding had just taken place.

Casting a longing glance at the happy couple, I stopped briefly to admire a bed of purple asters, then headed up King Street where the restaurants and bakeries were just starting to come alive. The smell of fresh coffee and pastries wafted on the cool breeze, and I was sorely tempted to stop at one of the outdoor eateries and treat myself to a leisurely breakfast. The streets were filling up, too, and I could sit there and people watch while I nibbled on vanilla French toast or a peach almond muffin and reflect on my conversation with Fremont's ghost. But I'd done enough dwelling and obsessing over the past two days. What I needed was a diversion.

So I continued on past the trendy cafes and gourmet coffee shops and didn't break stride until I reached Cumberland. Then I slowed, searching for The Secret Garden. I spotted it just ahead on my right, a quaint little shop with a metal awning over the front door and, as I remembered, a walled garden and fountain in the back where one could sit with a book and a cup of tea.

I was disappointed to find the shop closed, though I could have hardly expected otherwise at this early hour. Still, a cup of exotic brew and a pleasant chat with Clementine Perilloux would have been just the thing to take the chill off my meeting with Robert Fremont. I had to admit that, despite the circumstances, I'd enjoyed my visit with her. And I was glad that I'd felt that way even before I discovered that she was the sister and not, in fact, Devlin's brunette.

I supposed my impromptu trip to the shop so early in the morning was a testament to my loneliness. I'd had so few close friends over the years. There really was no one I could call on the spur of the moment to have coffee or lunch. No one I could talk to about books or movies or Devlin.

Devlin. No matter how much time or distance I tried to put between us, my thoughts always came back to him.

I didn't believe for a moment that he'd had anything to do with Fremont's murder, but he was somehow connected. Everything was connected. I was more certain of that now than ever. Shani's drowning, Devlin's disappearance after the accident, Ethan's alibi to the police.

I could only imagine how Devlin must have been suffering that night. Out of his mind with grief, he'd said. It would have been understandable if he'd turned to drugs to numb the pain. But gray dust wasn't a tranquilizer or a sedative. It was a powerful psychedelic. How could something like that help him cope with his loss?

But according to Devlin, gray dust wasn't just any hallucinogen. It stopped the heart and people died. And some of the ones who came back suffered terrible side effects. *Eyes frosted like a corpse, shuffling around all slumped over as if they'd dragged something back from hell with them.*

The images conjured by that piece of the conversation were disturbing and way too macabre for a sunny morning. I tried to shove the grimness aside as I peered into the shop window. A cup of tea really would have hit the spot.

I don't know how long I'd been standing there when it came to me that I was being watched. Not by a ghost this time. I felt no frigid breath at my collar, no icy fingers skimming along my spine. No, this was the sensation that anyone might experience when being secretly observed.

Turning, I surreptitiously scanned the sidewalk as I pretended to check the time on my phone. From my periphery, I took note of a man across the street. I couldn't tell much about his appearance, only that he was white, a little shorter and wider than Devlin. He wore khakis with a madras blazer and a straw fedora pulled low over his face. Typical attire for Charleston. The nondescript appearance would blend seamlessly with tourists and locals alike. But the sidewalks here were still sparse, and so he stood out.

When I lifted my head to casually view the traffic, he turned away quickly and strode through the open gateway of a private alley.

I didn't panic. For all I knew, he might have been nothing more than an admirer. I didn't attract attention the way a woman like Mariama would have. I was hardly the type to inspire such passion. But I was young and blond and in good shape from the physical labor of my profession. I caught a male eye now and then.

Still, I couldn't shake the notion that he hadn't just been staring at me, but watching me.

Turning back to the bookstore window, I pretended to peer inside the store. Another face appeared in the glass, that of a handsome black man. He stood right behind me, but when I turned, no one was there.

Palmettos rustled in the rising wind and a paper cup rolled along the sidewalk in front of me. I had the notion once again that a storm brewed on the horizon even though the sky was clear. I lifted my face as something dark scuttled across the sun. A bird, I told myself. Nothing more ominous than a raven or a sparrow.

Across the street, the man in the hat emerged from the alley and I could have sworn I saw him cast his gaze in my direction. His lips were moving, but there was no phone to his ear and no one else was around. No one that I could see.

Fear blossomed, but was I just being paranoid? I'd yet to pose a single question about Fremont's murder to any living person. No one could possibly know of our investigation and I was certain the man outside Devlin's house last night hadn't seen me. So why would I be under surveillance?

I started walking, slowly at first, pretending to window-shop so that I could keep track of him. But either he soon realized I was on to him or he really was just some innocent pedestrian because he turned on Market Street, losing himself in the traffic, and I didn't see him again.

Stopping at an open-air market, I purchased a bundle of fresh flowers and some sage and headed straight home. Angus, as always, was excited to see me. I put him on his leash and gave him a quick stroll around the block, and then we had breakfast together in the garden.

For the rest of the day, I puttered around the house, cleaning out summer closets, working on *Digging Graves,* chatting with my mother and my aunt Lynrose on the phone. The busywork distracted me for a few hours, but by mid-afternoon, I was starting to get antsy. After a phone call or two, I made sure Angus was settled in the house and then I drove over to the Charleston Institute for Parapsychology Studies to meet with Rupert Shaw.

The Institute was located on the ground floor of a beautifully renovated antebellum on the fringes of the historic district. It was a plantation-style house with long, graceful columns and fern baskets swaying from three stories of shady piazzas. I parked in the back, and as I came around to the side entrance, I noticed as I always did the house across the street with the neon hand hanging from the porch. Madam Know-it-all's.

I'd always been curious about the place and secretly amused by its proximity to the loftier Charleston Institute for Parapsychology Studies. Now that I knew the palmist had a connection to Devlin, I was even more fascinted. Clementine had said Devlin and Isabel were very close friends, but I'd seen the way he'd held her in the twilight. I'd heard the intimacy of their soft murmurs. They were more than friends. But how much more?

As I stood gazing over at the house, a blue Buick pulled up to the curb and sat there for a moment, idling. The driver wore aviator glasses that covered the upper portion of his face. That and the angle of the sun made his features nearly indistinguishable, but a glimmer of familiarity had me wondering if he was the man I'd seen earlier.

He didn't get out of the car but sat there gazing up at one of the balconies. I didn't think he spotted me. I was concealed by a thick rhododendron bush. My heart accelerated as I watched him. *Was* I being followed?

"Amelia?"

Years of living with ghosts had schooled my nerves, and I turned casually at the sound of my name. Ethan Shaw had come up behind me, so stealthily I hadn't heard his footfalls.

"I thought that was you." He smiled then, his eyes crinkling with genuine pleasure as he closed the distance between us. He was a tall man, well-dressed and well-spoken, with an easygoing demeanor that I'd always found attractive. But I'd glimpsed another side of him last night at Devlin's house. As the overheard conversation reared its ugly head, I felt a disquieting ripple along my spine. Had he really been in love with Devlin's wife? Had he really been willing to do her bidding?

"Ethan, hi. I didn't hear you come up."

"I just came around from the back," he said. "Father and I had a nice visit in the garden."

"Oh, he's in, then?"

"Yes." Another puzzled stare. "Why are you in the bushes?"

"I'm not hiding, just observing."

"What are you observing?"

"Do you know that blue car?" I asked anxiously.

His gaze moved beyond me to the street. I saw something flicker in his eyes, but he shrugged. "No, why?"

I paused. "I thought I might have been followed here."

His brow lifted. "Why would you think that?"

I could hardly tell him about the Fremont investigation, so I muttered, "I don't know, paranoid, I guess."

His smile turned sympathetic. "That's understandable after everything you've been through."

"I suppose."

He flicked another glance toward the street. "So what brings you to the Institute today?"

"I'm here to see Dr. Shaw. I don't have an appointment so I hope he has time for me."

"He always has time for you. As do I," Ethan said politely, but the compliment sounded rote, as though his mind were occupied elsewhere.

I resisted the urge to glance over my shoulder. "Can I ask you something?"

"Of course."

"I've always been fascinated by the house across the street."

"Bodine's Tattoo Parlor?"

I laughed. "The house next to it. Madame Know-it-all's. Do you know anything about her?"

"Her real name is Isabel Perilloux. She has an excellent reputation if you're in need of a palm-reader."

"I'm not. The last thing I want is to know about the future. I'm curious, is all."

He gave me a look that made me wonder if he knew about Isabel and Devlin.

"Anyway…I don't mean to keep you."

"You're not. I'm glad I ran into you. Temple is in town. We're having dinner tomorrow night and we'd love to have you join us if you're free."

Temple Lee was my former employer. I'd worked for her for two years at the Office of the State Archeologist before moving to Charleston to open my own business. We kept in touch via email and texting, and

I considered her my closest friend, which, considering how infrequently we saw each other face-to-face, was a little sad.

"I'd love to if you're sure it wouldn't be an intrusion."

"It's just a friendly dinner," he said. "A chance to catch up since she hasn't been down this way much lately. I'll call you later with the details."

"Thanks."

I waved as I left him to go inside the Institute. I assumed he was headed for the parking area, but as I stepped through the side door into the foyer, I caught a glimpse of him through the front window that looked out on the street. He was peering in the Buick's windshield. Then slowly hc circled the now-empty car, his head lifting now and then to scan the area as if looking for the driver.

He seemed agitated, almost angry, which triggered my curiosity. I watched him for a moment longer, then turned away from the window.

Fourteen

The wooden floor creaked beneath my shoes as I stepped from the foyer into what had once been the front parlor. Now it was the reception area, and a new assistant had taken over the front desk and phones.

She looked up with a curious half smile as I walked in, her chocolate-brown eyes disdainfully sizing me up from ponytail to sneakers. She was dressed much more stylishly in a silky blue top that looked gorgeous with her dark skin tone.

"May I help you?" she asked, with a trace of an accent I couldn't place.

"I'm Amelia Gray. I don't have an appointment, but I'm hoping to see Dr. Shaw."

"He's very busy today."

"Could you at least tell him I'm here? If he doesn't have time to see me, I can come back later."

She hesitated, not at all receptive to my request.

"We're friends," I added, which did not impress her.

"Wait here," she coolly instructed as she rose from the Charleston-style desk and disappeared down the hallway. I heard a door open, the murmur of voices and then thc brisk click of her heels on the wood floor as she returned.

"This way," she said, her lips pursed in disapproval.

"Thanks."

I'd been to the Institute many times before, so, of course, I knew where the office was located, but I followed her silently down the corridor to where she opened a set of pocket doors. She said nothing, merely stepped aside for me to enter, and then slid the doors closed behind me.

I stood glancing around at what appeared at first to be an empty office. It took me a moment to spot Dr. Shaw balancing precariously at the top of a ladder as he pulled a dusty volume from the highest shelf of an overflowing bookcase. I didn't speak for fear of startling him, even though I'd already been announced and he'd undoubtedly heard the door.

His office was as crowded as ever, a treasure trove of ancient tomes that begged to be explored from cover to cover. The furnishings were sparse, but the room itself was lovely with a cozy marble fireplace for winter evenings and a set of French doors that led out into a well-kept garden. The oak floors were covered with faded rugs and stacks upon stacks of books. I inhaled deeply the scent of leather bindings and a hint of tobacco, although I had never seen Dr. Shaw smoke. But it wasn't hard to imagine his teeth clamped around the stem of some great, curved pipe as he pondered the complexities of this world and the next.

"Hello," he called from his lofty perch. "Have a seat, won't you? I'll be with you in a moment."

"Take your time."

I placed my bag on the floor beside the chair opposite

his desk and walked over to glance out at the garden. The doors were ajar, and a mild breeze blew in the fresh talcum scent of the heliotrope that grew in clay pots on the patio. A fat calico sunning on the stone pavers observed me through slitted eyes. Then something at the gate caught her attention, and her ears pricked as she turned. I saw nothing suspicious, although the trail of salt across the threshold piqued my curiosity.

Dr. Shaw descended the ladder and came to greet me. He was even taller than Ethan, with an unstudied elegance that suggested a life of affluent gentility. He had thick, white hair and the most piercing blue eyes I'd ever encountered. Despite his old-money air, he wore his usual attire of threadbare flannel and houndstooth, both trousers and jacket hanging loosely on his lanky frame.

I smelled something faintly musty and herbal as he took my hand in both of his and smiled warmly. "It's been a while."

"Yes, too long. How are you, Dr. Shaw?"

"I'm very well, Amelia. And you?"

"Just fine, thank you."

He cocked his head, observing me. "What have you been up to lately? Forgive me for saying so, but you look a little worse for the wear."

"I've been under the weather," I said. "Nothing serious." Unless you counted a near-death experience serious. Unless you counted being haunted serious.

But I wouldn't mention any of that to Dr. Shaw because, as much as I appreciated his knowledge of all things paranormal, I'd never opened up to him about the ghosts. The sightings were personal and private and talking about them would be yet another way of acknowledging the dead.

"Let's sit, shall we?" He gestured to the chair across from his desk. "Would you like some tea?" he asked as we settled in.

"No, thank you. I won't take up too much of your time. I've stumbled across something that I'd like to ask you about."

His ears seemed to twitch with the same mild inquisitiveness as the calico. He leaned forward, eyes gleaming. "Let me guess. You've encountered another shadow being."

"No, it's not that."

"Psychic vampire?"

"Not that, either."

He folded his hands on the desk, and I noticed once again the ring he wore on his pinkie. A snake curled around a claw. It was the same emblem Devlin wore around his neck—the talisman of the Order of the Coffin and the Claw. That secret society for the Charleston elite.

I glanced up into those vivid blue eyes and shivered.

"Is the breeze too much?" he asked in concern and started to rise.

"No, no. I'm fine. The reason I wanted to see you…"

He held up a graceful hand to silence me. "As eager as I am to find out what brought you to me this time, I need to get some business out of the way first if you would indulge me. Otherwise, it may slip my mind entirely. I tend to be overly forgetful these days," he said, a shadow fleeting across his distinguished features. That shadow worried me. I hoped his memory problems weren't symptomatic of an illness, but on closer inspection, he did look a little frail.

"What business would that be?" I asked.

"I need to ask something of you and I'm afraid it will dredge up a lot of unpleasant memories."

"What is it?" I asked nervously.

"Have you heard about Oak Grove?"

Another shiver but one of a very different nature. The very mention of that old graveyard invoked dark feelings. "What about it?"

"The police have finally finished their investigation. The cemetery has been turned back over to Emerson University, and the Committee has decided to go ahead with the restoration. I've been asked to approach you about our plans, but considering your history with the cemetery, no one will hold it against you if you'd like to be released from the original agreement. But make no mistake. You're still our first choice."

Return to Oak Grove? After everything that had happened there? I drew a breath as the faces of dead women flashed before my eyes. "When would you want me to start?"

"As soon as possible. Emerson's bicentennial is well underway, so we would like to have the restoration completed before the end of the year. It would be a nice way to close a very unpleasant chapter. You'd be working with Temple Lee for a time. I believe the two of you are acquainted?"

"Yes. She's a friend of mine."

He nodded. "Given the age of the disturbed graves, the remains fall within her jurisdiction. But since you know each other, the arrangement should be amicable. No territorial disputes, I trust. That is...if you decide to come back. Take a couple of days to think it over and let me know by the end of the week."

"That won't be necessary," I said. "I started the restoration and I'd like to be the one to finish it."

"Are you sure?" He gazed at me kindly. "As I said, no one will hold it against you should you decide otherwise, and it will in no way affect my future recommendations."

"I appreciate that, but I really would prefer to finish what I started." It was a matter of professional pride, but it would also be good for me to have something with which to occupy my mind other than Devlin and his ghosts and Robert Fremont and his murder. I had a tendency to obsess.

Dr. Shaw sat back in his chair with a nod. "That's settled, then. I'll let the Committee know that Oak Grove is once again in your capable hands."

"Thank you."

"Now to your business," he said with a slight lifting of his brows.

"Oh, I'm not here on any real business," I said. "I've stumbled across something and I'm hoping you may be able to answers some questions for me."

"Not shadow beings, not psychic vampires…hmm," he mused. "I can't imagine."

"Have you ever heard of a substance called gray dust?"

The moment I uttered the words, I could have sworn the breeze blowing in through the French doors grew stronger. Pages ruffled in an open book on Dr. Shaw's desk, but my gaze remained fixed on his face. I saw something flash across his features that made my blood run cold. Surprise, yes, and maybe even a hint of fear. But what lifted the hair at my nape was a look of malevolence that I would never have believed had I not witnessed it with my own eyes. Not from the refined and elegant Dr. Shaw.

As he put out a hand to close the book, I remembered

something Robert Fremont had said only that morning about Essie's relationship with Dr. Shaw. She would never divulge her secrets to a man with evil intent.

"Where did you hear about gray dust?" he asked almost casually. His tone was so completely devoid of malice, his eyes so mildly inquisitive, that I might have imagined his momentary agitation.

"I take it you know what it is, then?" I asked with my own practiced calm.

"I've heard of it, yes."

"Can you tell me about it?"

He picked up a silver letter opener and ran his thumb along the blade. "To understand gray dust, you need to understand where it comes from."

"It comes from Africa, doesn't it?"

"Gabon, to be precise. Are you at all familiar with the country?"

"Only that it appears tiny on the map and is bordered by Cameroon, the Congo and Equatorial Guinea." And that Darius Goodwine had spent a lot of time there writing, researching and apparently studying with a shaman. And had then made the transformation to *tagati.*

Dr. Shaw grew pensive. "It's been said that Gabon is to Africa what Tibet is to Asia…the spiritual epicenter of an entire continent."

I felt the bite of the wind again as it blew in through the French doors. Dr. Shaw got up to close them, taking his time with the latch as he glanced anxiously into the garden. I had a feeling he was biding his time while he figured out how he wanted to proceed with the conversation. His hesitation, not to mention the look that had crossed his face, was very unsettling.

He came back over to the desk and lowered himself stiffly to the chair. His faltering mobility seemed odd considering that only moments earlier I'd seen him balanced effortlessly atop a ladder.

"Gabon is one of the most mysterious countries in the world," he said. "The area has long been a source of fascination to researchers and adventurers alike. Much of the area is covered in a forest so impenetrable as to provide a natural deterrent to undesirable influences. Religious beliefs have been preserved for generations without corruption from the outside world, including the integration of certain plants into their rituals and ceremonies."

He paused as the pocket doors slid open and the assistant stuck her head in the office. "It's three o'clock, Dr. Shaw. You wanted me to remind you."

"So I did. Thank you, Layla."

"I've made you some tea," she said as she carried in a silver tray that held a single demitasse cup and saucer and placed it on the corner of his desk.

"Are you sure you won't join me?" Dr. Shaw asked me as he reached for the cup.

Layla shot me a dark look, one that seemed to dare me to acquiesce, so I said quickly, "I'm fine, thank you. But…should I go? Do you have another appointment?"

He put up a hand. "It's a small matter that requires my attention. Thank you for reminding me, Layla."

"Not at all. That's why I'm here." She exited the room without a backward glance.

Opening a desk drawer, Dr. Shaw withdrew a tiny plastic packet, unzipped it and sprinkled the contents into his tea. I smelled that same musty, herbal odor as he stirred, then sipped.

I said nothing during this interlude, but I was curious to know what manner of herb he'd used to doctor his tea. Once again, I hoped his frailty was more a matter of working too hard than any ill health.

He took another taste, closed his eyes, and after a moment, I began to think that he'd drifted off. The silence lengthened until it became awkward. Should I say something or quietly slip away? I wondered. Just when I thought I might need to summon Layla, his lids fluttered open, and he sat very still until his eyes gradually came back into focus.

"Where were we?" he asked.

"Gabon," I said hesitantly. "But are you sure I'm not taking too much of your time? I can always come back another day."

He didn't answer, but instead picked up precisely where he'd left off as though there'd never been an interruption. "You see, in most African religions, there remains a strong belief that life doesn't end with death, but continues in another realm. In some cultures, it's a rite of passage for a young initiate to enter the spirit world and converse with dead ancestors before he's accepted into the sect."

"How does he go about entering the spirit world? Or conversing with dead ancestors, for that matter." And why would one want to? In my world, ghosts were to be avoided whenever possible.

"He's able to pass through into another realm by consuming plants with magical properties. Or, in other words, by ingesting a powerful hallucinogen."

"Like gray dust?"

His eyes flickered, and I couldn't help noticing that his pupils had dilated after sipping the tea. "Like the root bark of *Tabernanthe iboga,* which is a plant that forms the very foundation of the *Bwiti* religion."

"What does it do?"

"A mild dose can cause anxiety and sleep deprivation. A high dose produces hallucinations and a state of lethargy that can last for as long as five days."

"*Five days?* That's potent stuff. Is it dangerous?"

"A massive dose can cause paralysis of the respiratory muscles and death."

"So, this iboga plant…" I pronounced the name carefully. "Is that where gray dust comes from?"

"No. Gray dust is a derivative of a plant that no one outside of a certain sect has ever been able to identify. The effect is different from ibogaine."

"How?"

He settled back in his chair. "The hallucinations, for one thing. After iboga bark is chewed, the initiate falls into a deep sleep and has no real consciousness of the outside world. In his vision world, he's faced with a series of obstacles that must be overcome before he can enter the spirit world. Once he's allowed to pass through the barriers, a guide, usually a long-dead ancestor, will accompany him on his spiritual journey where he'll witness many fantastical sights. Legions of the dead, typically with painted faces and open bellies from ritual autopsies. Here, he's able to look upon the gods and speak with his deceased ancestors. When the effects of the iboga wear off, consciousness returns and he's expected to recount his journey to the elders."

"And gray dust?"

"Gray dust has nothing to do with hallucinogenic visions," Dr. Shaw said. "It has a property that literally stops the heart. The initiate flatlines. In a medical environment, he would be considered clinically dead anywhere from seconds to minutes. During that interval, his spirit is able to leave the body and enter the realm of the dead, not through visions, but because his life in this world has ceased. And because he is dead, there are no obstacles to overcome. No barriers to cross. He can move through the spirit world as freely as his ancestors, traveling into realms unimaginable even through visions and hallucinations. The danger, of course, is wandering too far and becoming lost. After a certain amount of time passes, the physical body can't be resuscitated. The shell withers and dies or, in some cases, is invaded by another spirit. At least…that's the claim."

I found myself shivering again. This whole conversation was bizarre and unsettling. Not that I didn't believe it. I knew better than anyone that the spirit world existed as surely as the living world, but the notion of someone purposely traveling through the veil was unfathomable to me. I hadn't yet thrown off the shackles of my father's rules even though I had apparently embraced my arrangement with Robert Fremont. It was as though I once again found myself suspended between two worlds, only now the tug-of-war was being waged between my past and my future. Between the safety net of what I knew and feared, and my desire to attain a higher purpose. But I couldn't remain in this limbo forever. The ghosts wouldn't let me. Already they were seeking me out.

"What about the ones who make it back from the spirit world?" I asked. "The ones who are resuscitated. Do they suffer from any side effects?"

"Some report a spiritual enlightenment and feelings of euphoria, while others suffer from episodes akin to PTSD. And still others undergo drastic transformations both mentally and physically from what they saw on the other side. Or from what they brought back."

"Brought back? You mean like ghosts?" I thought about Shani and Mariama. Had Devlin brought them back from the Gray? Was that what Shani seemed so desperate to tell him?

"If gray dust makes it easier for the living to enter the realm of the dead, it stands to reason the reverse would also be true, would it not?"

"Yes, I suppose so."

Idly, he stirred his tea. "There are those among the Gullah even today who believe something as simple as an improper burial can allow the dead to come back and control the lives of the living. If a root doctor has enough power, he can enter the spirit world and bring back the dead himself. He can also attack his enemies in the dream realm, when they're most vulnerable."

Once again, I thought about Fremont's insinuation that Dr. Shaw's interest in rootwork stemmed from some evil intent. I still couldn't buy it. Everything I knew of Rupert Shaw pointed to a man of good character. "Did rootwork originate in Gabon?"

"Like most of the Southern conjure arts, it's based upon the beliefs and practices of a number of religions in west and central Africa. A sort of spiritual soup seasoned with Christianity. The foundation of rootwork, like *Bwiti,* is the mystical and medicinal quality of certain plants. A smear of blood root paste will cure your skin irritations, a pinch of goldenseal will help your digestion." He stared down into his cooling tea. "A little celandine will ward off evil spirits and the law. And anything else that may hound you…"

He seemed to drift off again, and I leaned toward him in concern. "Dr. Shaw? Are you okay?"

He roused from his lethargy and rose to claim another book from a nearby shelf. Blowing dust from the cover, he handed it to me. I glanced down at the title: *Sticks and Stones—Roots and Bones.*

"That'll get you started," he said. "If you still have questions, come back and see me. I can even arrange a consultation with a root doctor, if you'd like."

"Essie Goodwine?"

A brow lifted. "If you feel up to taking a drive. Otherwise, we can walk down the street and talk to my old friend, Primus—"

He swayed, and I laid the book aside as I jumped to my feet to take his arm. "Are you all right?"

"It's nothing. Just a little dizziness," he murmured.

He tottered again and my grip tightened. "What should I do?"

"Help me to my seat, if you would." His voice sounded strained, and I could see the sheen of perspiration on his face. "It'll pass in a moment."

I led him back to his chair and waited until he was safely settled. The hand he lifted to cover his eyes trembled.

"Do you have these episodes often?" I asked worriedly.

"Every now and then."

"It's none of my business, but do you think it wise to climb ladders? Especially when you're alone?"

"I usually have some warning before a spell comes on," he said, dropping his hand from his eyes. "At any rate, it's passing already. I feel fine now."

"Are you sure I can't get you something? Call someone?"

"Please, don't trouble yourself. It really is nothing. But perhaps we could continue our conversation at another time?"

"Of course. I'll get out of your hair." I went around the desk to retrieve my bag.

"Before you go…" His voice lowered, and I saw his

gaze dart to the French doors as though he were afraid someone lurked out in the garden. "There's something I must tell you."

I glanced down in alarm. "What is it?"

His blue eyes looked troubled and very intense. Frightened, I would say. "You must be very careful who you talk to about this. And don't repeat any of what was said here today."

My pulse quickened as my hand tightened around the strap of my bag. "Of course, but may I ask why?"

"Gray dust is an innocuous name for a sacred substance that is used sparingly even by the most powerful shamans and witch doctors. An unseemly interest by someone outside the sect might be taken as blasphemy and could put you at considerable risk."

"At risk? You mean someone might try to harm me?"

"Not physically perhaps, but…tell me, my dear, do you keep bay leaves in the house? Citronella candles, perhaps? Or some eucalyptus? Dragon's blood under your pillow would be even better."

"Why do I need them?"

He didn't seem to hear me. He'd drifted off yet again, and after a moment, I quietly slipped away.

Fifteen

As I exited the Institute, I heard my name called from across the street. It was the cautious hail of someone who thought she knew me but had some doubt. That still happened on occasion. I was sometimes recognized as The Graveyard Queen from an online ghost video that had gone viral months ago. Now that the clip had run its course, my notoriety was fading. More common were the puzzled glances from fellow taphophiles who recognized but couldn't place me.

Clementine Perilloux had pulled up in front of the house next door and was just getting out of her car. She waved gaily when she had my attention and motioned for me to join her on the sidewalk. I walked down the drive and crossed the street to speak with her.

"Fancy meeting you here!" she exclaimed, lifting a hand to swipe back her windblown hair. She was dressed in jeans and an olive sweater that did lovely things to her eyes and picked up the auburn highlights in her curls. "Although you did say you visit this place from time to time." Her gaze roamed over the graceful columns and generous piazzas of the Institute. "I've always loved this house. It looks as though it's straight from the pages of *Gone with the Wind,* doesn't it? What's it like on the inside?"

"It's pretty well-preserved for the most part. Lots of books and antiques." I followed her gaze. Yes, the house was beautiful, but now my worry for Dr. Shaw's health had cast a pall over the Institute. In the space of only minutes, the charming, absentminded professor I'd become so fond of had morphed into a fragile, doddering old man whose symptoms—I would swear—had been exacerbated by whatever herb he'd stirred into his tea.

And what of Layla? She was neither fresh-faced nor fervent, neither Goth nor Southern like so many of her predecessors. She was polished and sophisticated, and I found her territorial behavior as intriguing as it was unsettling.

"Of course, I've only seen the ground floor," I told Clementine. "The upper stories are Dr. Shaw's private quarters."

"What's *he* like?"

"Dr. Shaw?" I heard the usual description slip through my lips. Elegant. Refined. Professorial. But now I couldn't help wondering about the look on his face when I'd first mentioned gray dust. That malevolent shadow, no matter how fleeting, chilled me even now in memory.

"What goes on in there?" Clementine's little shiver mirrored my own disquiet. "Séances? Experiments? Secret rituals?" She widened her eyes in exaggeration. *"Sacrifices?"*

I smiled dryly. "Hardly. At least not to my knowledge. Dr. Shaw's work is primarily focused on research.

He leaves the fieldwork up to his team unless a particularly juicy case crosses his desk."

"And just what constitutes a juicy case?" Clementine asked with another shudder. "Or do I even want to know?"

"I'm not personally familiar with his criteria. If you're interested, you should go over and talk to him sometime. I'm sure he'd love to hear about your family's history of palmists."

"Maybe I will." She slanted a doubtful glance at the Institute. "Anyway, speaking of palmists, I've just come to drop off a goody basket for Isabel from Grandmother. If you're not in too much of a hurry, why don't you come in with me? I'm dying for you to meet her."

A dozen excuses flashed through my head, but I really did want to meet Isabel Perilloux. I'd been curious about Madam Know-it-all before I'd ever seen her with Devlin—before I even *knew* Devlin—having long been an admirer of the irony and wit that had come up with such a moniker.

But...what if Devlin was with her right now? The very idea made me cringe. Such a scenario had the makings of a terribly awkward moment, one that I wanted to avoid at all costs. Our last meeting had taken a lot out of me. I needed time to regroup before I dealt with Devlin and his ghosts again.

Quickly, I scanned the street. I didn't see his car, but I did spot the blue Buick pulled to the curb a few houses down. The driver stood leaning against the front fender, feet crossed, arms folded as if waiting for someone. His head was turned so that I still couldn't see his features. But there was something about him that niggled. I knew him. I couldn't place him, but somehow, somewhere our paths had crossed. I was certain of it.

Was he the same man I'd seen on King Street that morning? Had he followed me here?

I rubbed the back of my neck where a warning had started to tingle.

"What's wrong?" Clementine asked.

"That man leaning against the blue car…have you seen him around here before?"

She lifted a hand to shade her eyes as she stared down the street. "Nope, never. Why? Do you know him?"

"He seems a little familiar, but I can't place him."

She shrugged. "I wouldn't worry about it. He looks harmless enough. Of course," she said cheerfully, "that's what they said about Ted Bundy. Or was it Jeffrey Dahmer?"

At least she hadn't mentioned a killer that hit more closely to home.

As my gaze moved away from the Buick, I glanced across the street at the Institute. Layla stood at the front window looking out at me. She didn't melt back into the shadows when I caught her staring but instead boldly held my gaze until I finally turned back to Clementine.

"So, anyway," she was saying. "Do you have time to come meet my sister?"

"She wouldn't mind me just dropping in like this?"

"Of course not. Why would she mind? She's used to drop-ins, and she's forever badgering me about making new friends. Come on. It'll be an experience."

An experience? I was a little afraid of that.

Reluctantly, I followed her up the walkway, glancing back once at the Institute and once at the man in the dark glasses. Why couldn't I remember where I'd seen him?

Telling myself to relax about the whole matter, I tried to tune out those nagging anxieties as Clementine chattered away. I used the diversion to scope out her sister's place, a white cottage with green shutters and a wrap-around veranda. As we climbed the porch steps, I noticed the calico from Dr. Shaw's garden stretched out in a cane rocker, watching us curiously.

"Hello, Ursula," Clementine greeted as she reached down to rub the feline's head.

"Beautiful cat," I murmured.

"And she well knows it. You're quite the princess, aren't you, my lovely?"

Ursula yawned.

"Is she polydactyl?" I hadn't noticed the six toes earlier. "She reminds me of a storybook illustration. There's so much character in that face."

Clementine laughed. "You almost expect her to speak, don't you? Although I can only imagine what she'd have to say. She's so above it all. Actually, she and Isabel do carry on conversations, it's just that no one else can understand them."

Clementine straightened and knocked on the door. When no one answered, she took out her own key. "Isabel said she might be running late." She held the screen door for both Ursula and me. The cat pranced in first, and I followed meekly behind her.

"I'll go make some tea," Clementine said as she hung up her scarf and bag in the tiny foyer. Then she gestured toward the parlor on the left. "Make yourself at home. I'll be right back."

I glanced curiously through the archway. It was a small space, but stylishly decorated in chartreuse and cream with touches of black and lots of pillows. A row of windows looked out on the veranda, and I walked over to take a peek through the blinds to see if I could still spot the Buick. Then I told myself I was being ridiculous. *Just let it go.*

Across the foyer, another arch led into what must have once been the dining room but now appeared to be the space where Madam Know-it-all conducted her readings. I couldn't resist a closer inspection. The decor was so much more dramatic than the parlor, with red fringed scarves, beaded curtains and scented candles strategically placed for ambient lighting. Slowly, I walked around the room, admiring a collection of vintage postcards that had been framed and mounted on the wall. A small table and four chairs were placed in the center of the room. On the table were a deck of tarot cards, a deck of Zener cards used to test clairvoyance and a crystal ball.

A more sophisticated eye might cringe at the odd little kickshaws displayed about the room, but I appreciated the whimsy.

A shadow fell over me, and I caught the whiff of some delectable perfume, a scent that was lush and hypnotic. Haunting, I would even say.

An unpleasant sensation whispered along my nerve endings as I turned. There she was, leaning against the door frame watching me. Devlin's lovely brunette.

For whatever reason, Robert Fremont chose that moment to come creeping into my head. *All I remember is the scent of her perfume. The smell was still on my clothes when I died.*

Sixteen

Outwardly, I showed no reaction, but my pulse jumped as our gazes met. I tried to assess her without the ghost of Fremont in my head or the specter of Devlin's arms wrapped around her, but that was impossible. I could see him even now slipping up behind her, murmuring in her ear.

She was gorgeous. Naturally, she would be, and I wasn't a big enough person to stifle the needle of jealousy that nicked at my poise. She was tall, with dark hair that spilled over her shoulders in windblown spirals and hazel eyes fringed with thick, curly lashes. Her lips were tinted with a light-colored gloss, but I thought the roses in her cheeks were natural. She looked a good deal like Clementine but without her sister's effervescence. Isabel was much more subdued, much more guarded, as she stood there returning my stare.

In the split second before either of us spoke, it occurred to me that she must have come in another way because I hadn't heard the front door or her footsteps. She'd just appeared there in the archway. Despite the mild weather, she wore a coat in a chic military style that complimented her lean lines. She unbuttoned it now as she took a step into the room.

"I hope you don't mind my having a look around," I said awkwardly. "I was just waiting for Clementine."

"Not at all. You must be Amelia. I've heard a lot about you."

From who? I wondered.

She came forward and offered her hand. "I'm Isabel."

"Clementine has told me a lot about you, too," I said.

The handshake was brief, but her grip was warm and firm, and she looked me directly in the eyes when we spoke. I appreciated that.

"So, you're Amelia," she murmured again, and I thought she studied my face a shade longer than was polite.

Discomfited by the scrutiny, I turned. "This is such an interesting room."

"I'm glad you like it. It's a little over the top, but it serves the purpose." She slipped out of her coat and tossed it onto the back of a chair. As she moved about the table, her scent came to me again, dreamy and exotic, and now it reminded me of the fragrance I'd smelled on the walkway just before I'd entered Clementine's garden. On anyone else, such a heady perfume might have been cloying, but somehow it seemed as much a part of her as the green-gold eyes and dark hair.

Picking up the deck of tarot cards, she idly tossed out a few face up on the table. I saw Justice, the Page of Swords, the Moon and one that might have been lovers before she quickly scooped them up. A little shiver went through me because I had the notion she'd just done an impromptu reading, and judging by the speed with which she'd returned them to the deck, she hadn't liked what she'd seen saw.

Clementine appeared in the doorway with a tray just then. "I see you two have already met. Come in to the parlor and have some tea. Grandmother sent over your favorite macaroons."

"Bless her heart," Isabel murmured as we exited the room.

I took one last look at the tarot cards, then followed the sisters into the next room where I perched on the edge of a black leather chair as they seated themselves side by side on the cream chenille sofa. Ursula came in and made herself at home on Isabel's lap while Clementine poured out the tea and passed around the cups. "This is a brand-new blend," she said. "It has the most luscious flavor."

"Oh, it's peach," I said, after sampling the tea. "You're right. It's delicious."

"The single origin makes all the difference," she said. "That's hard to find these days except in specialty shops like ours."

"I'll have to pick up some next time I'm in."

Isabel grew weary of Ursula and our small talk. She shooed the cat away and picked up her cup, eyeing me over the rim. "Tell me again how you two met? You're neighbors, you say?"

"No, we're not neighbors," Clementine corrected. "I saw Amelia and Angus out walking one morning and invited them to breakfast."

"Angus is…?"

"My dog."

Clementine turned to face her sister. "You have to meet him sometime, Isabel. He's such a sweetheart and he has the most beautiful eyes."

"I'm sure he does, but you know I'm a cat person." Was that the tiniest bit of reproach I heard in her tone? "No offense," she added.

"None taken. Ursula is a real beauty."

"She's certainly the queen bee around here," Isabel said. "She's a very special cat." She took another sip of her tea. "My sister tells me you're a cemetery restorer. She's quite impressed, aren't you, Clem? She and Grandmother have always loved poking about in old graveyards. How did you come by that line of work?"

Why did I have a feeling she already knew more about me than I would ever voluntarily reveal? "My father was a caretaker. I grew up in a house at the edge of a cemetery. I always loved playing there as a child. I thought it very peaceful and beautiful."

Clementine leaned forward. "Have you ever seen a ghost?"

"Why, yes," I said benignly. "Old graveyards are full of them."

She looked horrified. "Really?"

"She's pulling your leg, Clem." Isabel laughed, a deep, throaty, sultry sound that made me think of her with Devlin. "I'm sure if you took a midnight foray into an abandoned cemetery, you'd be in far more danger from criminals and drug addicts than from ghouls."

"Crime in cemeteries can be a problem," I agreed, my mind on Oak Grove. It was just a matter of time before I would be going back there, to the place where it had all begun. I pictured Devlin that first night, standing among the headstones, stoic and professional in the face of such a brutal discovery.

I felt Isabel's eyes on me and took another sip of my tea to suppress a shiver.

"I don't like to think that someone could come back

from the dead," Clementine said uneasily. "The very idea makes my blood run cold."

"Don't worry," Isabel murmured, placing her hand on her sister's arm. "*No* one is coming back from the dead."

I had no idea why, but her words troubled me, and I thought again of Robert Fremont. *Her scent is still on my clothes,* he'd said. *I can smell it even now.*

My gaze went from sister to sister. They made such an attractive pair, sitting there side by side on the sofa. Almost like bookends, with the same dark hair, the same hazel eyes. The same polite smiles.

Maybe it was my own uneasiness with the circumstances or the specter of Devlin still hovering in the background, but I had a feeling there was more to the Perilloux sisters than met the eye. I couldn't help remembering that fleeting hesitation when Clementine had mentioned buying her house and settling in Charleston. I'd sensed then some unpleasantness that had driven her decision. And now her references to ghosts…to her fear of someone coming back from the dead.

It probably was my imagination, I decided. I'd been charmed by her that first day, and as far as I could tell, nothing had changed except my own attitude.

I tried to bury my discomfort as I glanced at Isabel. "I hope you don't mind my asking, but your perfume… it's so haunting. Almost hypnotic."

Hypnotic indeed. What with the heat of the tea, my imagination and Isabel's perfume, I was starting to feel a little woozy.

"What a gratifying description," she said. "A fragrance should haunt, don't you think? Like an elusive memory."

Did her scent haunt Devlin? I wondered. "I've been

sitting here trying to identify the top notes. Tuberose? Freesia? Orange blossom?"

"She'll never tell." Clementine gave her a sister a dark look. "I've been asking her to share for years."

"It's an unsuitable scent for you," Isabel scolded. "You know that." To me, she said, "Our mother is a perfumer. She created signature fragrances for us on our eighteenth birthdays."

"What a lovely gift," I said.

"Yes, it was. But Clem never wears hers anymore."

"And you know why."

Another look flashed between them. It was evident that they were able to communicate volumes with just a glance or the brush of a hand. My mother and aunt Lynrose were like that. They often spoke in little riddles and sister shorthand, and as a child, I hadn't understood much of their conversations. I'd only listened in because I was soothed by the sound of their voices, mesmerized by their lovely, Lowcountry drawls. It was only in looking back that I realized I had often been the subject of their hushed talks.

I was feeling warmer and more uncomfortable by the moment. I wanted nothing more than to throw open a window and let a blast of fresh air dilute the effects of Isabel's perfume. Where earlier I had thought it lush and dreamy, now I found it positively suffocating.

Was that my feeling or was Fremont trying to communicate with me?

I had no reason to think that either of the Perilloux sisters had even known Robert Fremont, but for whatever reason, I couldn't wait to be away from their company. The urgency was almost overpowering.

I set aside my cup. "Thank you so much for the tea, but I really should be going. I still have work to do this afternoon." I turned to Isabel. "It was very nice meeting you."

"The pleasure was mine, I'm sure. As I said earlier, I've heard so much about you." Her phone rang and she rose to answer it. "Will you excuse me?"

"Of course."

Clementine stood, as well. "If you'll wait a moment, I'll get you that peach tea."

"Oh, no, that's fine. I can pick some up in the shop. Please don't bother."

"No bother at all. I can always bring Isabel another tin."

Despite my protests, she disappeared down the narrow hallway to the kitchen. I was left standing alone in the parlor. I could hear Isabel's voice in the next room. She was speaking in a low tone, but the house was so quiet, her voice carried easily.

"No, it's fine. She's just leaving."

A pause.

"By the way, you were right."

She listened for a moment longer, then said, "Come over whenever you want. I'll be waiting…"

Seventeen

I hurried down the steps of Isabel's house, happy enough to be out in the fresh air. The breeze revived me at once and cleared the vestiges of her rich—yes, cloying—perfume from my nostrils. But as I headed down the walkway, I had a notion the scent clung to my clothes. Shrugging out of my jacket, I tossed it onto the backseat of my car even as I recognized that my behavior was unreasonable and perhaps even childish.

Clearly, the woman had made an impression, and I had enough self-awareness to recognize that my jealousy played some role in the case I had begun to build against her. A case entirely without merit because there wasn't a shred of evidence that connected her or Clementine to Robert Fremont. Unless one counted Devlin. And, honestly, wasn't he at the root of my suspicion?

All those meaningful glances and subtle inflections had probably been nothing more than the bond between two close sisters, like the one my mother and aunt shared. That I had read so much into a very brief conversation was surely a testament to my current frame of mind. As much as I liked putting together puzzles, maybe I wasn't cut out to be a detective, after all. Obviously, I lacked the necessary objectivity when it came to matters involving John Devlin. And all the snooping, the paranoia, the jumping to conclusions, was exhausting. I'd even imagined that I was being followed before I had ever uttered a word about gray dust or Darius Goodwine to anyone but a ghost.

None of this rationalization was at all a comfort to me. It wasn't as if I could ring up Fremont and tell him I'd changed my mind, our arrangement just wasn't working out for me. He'd promised to keep his distance so long as I helped him, but if I broke our agreement, I had no doubt he'd do whatever he deemed necessary to coerce my cooperation. He needed to move on and I needed to get a grip.

Forget about the Perilloux sisters, I told myself. They weren't a part of this. I needed to forget about Devlin, too, for the moment and concentrate on what I'd learned from Dr. Shaw. He'd been a fount of information, and now I was anxious to get home to my computer to follow up. But first I needed to retrieve the book he'd loaned me from his office. I'd laid it aside when I rose to help him to his chair, and I'd left without it.

As I hurried up the drive to the side entrance, I resisted the urge to glance over my shoulder at Isabel's house. My curiosity had been assuaged, and that was the end of it. My path need never cross hers again. Clementine might be harder to avoid since she lived so near me, and I felt a momentary guilt at my willingness to discard her so easily. Maybe I wasn't cut out for friendship, either. Being a loner was too deeply ingrained.

Layla was away from her desk, but I decided not to wait for her. Instead, I went straight back to Dr. Shaw's office and knocked. The doors were slid back, and I hovered on the threshold, searching for him.

He wasn't at his desk or atop the ladder. I didn't think he'd gone far, though, because the French doors were open, and I could hear voices in the garden. I went over to let him know I'd come back for the book.

Just as I started to step through onto the terrace, his voice lifted. "You have some nerve!"

I withdrew immediately, startled by his anger. He didn't appear to notice me, nor did his companion, the man from the blue Buick. He'd removed his sunglasses, and for the first time, I caught a glimpse of his face. It finally came to me who he was, and my heart thudded anxiously. Tom Gerrity. The private detective who had once been a cop. I'd met him months ago when I'd gone to his office. Of course, at that time, Robert Fremont had posed as Gerrity. His ghost had deliberately deceived me so that I would still think him human. But in Gerrity's office, I'd seen a picture of the three men—Gerrity, Devlin and Fremont—on the day they'd graduated from the police academy. Only one of them remained a cop, but I believed them to still be connected by circumstances revolving around Fremont's death.

"I told you never to come here," Dr. Shaw said coldly.

"That's what happens when you don't return my phone calls," Gerrity said. "Or show up for our meeting."

"Something came up."

"Too bad. You don't keep your end of the bargain, I don't keep mine. Simple as that."

"What are you talking about? You're the one who reneged. This was over a long time ago. Why did you have to come back?"

"Times are hard, doc. In a downturn like this, fat gets

trimmed. People in my line of work become expendable."

"Your line of work? You mean dealing in filth?"

Gerrity laughed. "I've heard worse. At least no one can accuse me of murder."

Murder? I shivered as his implication sank in. Dr. Shaw?

He withdrew an envelope from his pocket and handed it to Gerrity. "This is the last of it. Do you understand me? Don't ever come back here again."

Gerrity took the envelope, glanced inside, then tucked it away. "Pleasure doing business with you, as always."

He gave a mock salute as he turned toward the gate and disappeared.

Dr. Shaw sat down heavily on a nearby chair and buried his face in his hands.

I didn't know what to do. I backed away from the door as quietly as I could. The book I'd come back for had fallen to the floor beside the chair I'd vacated a little while ago. As I bent to retrieve it, I noticed a small iron bolt on the floor beneath Dr. Shaw's desk. I started to reach for it when a hand fell on my shoulder.

Eighteen

I turned to find Layla standing behind me, and I wondered how long she'd been there and whether she, too, had overheard the argument between Dr. Shaw and Gerrity.

"May I help you?" she asked coolly.

"I just came back for a book Dr. Shaw loaned me." I held it up, but she barely glanced at the cover. "Would you mind telling him that I was here?"

"Perhaps you should tell him yourself," she said and nodded toward the garden.

Dr. Shaw stood silhouetted in the doorway, staring into the office as if he'd seen a ghost. His face was pale, his eyes glazed and riveted on something just beyond my shoulder. It was all I could do not to look back.

"Sylvia…" he muttered and put out his hand.

I did glance back then, but there was no ghost. Not even the chill of an invisible presence. Whatever he'd seen must have been inside his own mind.

"Dr. Shaw, are you okay?"

"You didn't see her?"

"See who?" I asked anxiously.

His gaze moved to his assistant, and I could have sworn I saw a flash of fear. Then his knees buckled, and both of us dashed across the room to catch him. "It was her…I swear it was her…."

"No one else is here," Layla said. "You're imagining things again. You've been working much too hard. You really must listen to me when I tell you it's time for a break."

Her stern voice seemed to raise his ire. "Don't treat me like a child. It was *her*, I tell you."

We helped him to his chair. "Just relax," Layla soothed. "I'll go make you some tea."

"I think we should call a doctor," I said.

"No, no doctor." He laid a weak hand on my arm. "It's good of you to be concerned, but I'm just feeling a little under the weather. It's nothing to be concerned about."

"At least let me call Ethan," I said.

"No, please…" His grip tightened on my arm. "I don't want to worry him."

"But he'd want to know if you're not feeling well."

"It's nothing a good night's sleep won't cure," Layla said firmly.

"Yes, quite right," Dr. Shaw murmured. "I'll have that tea now, if you don't mind."

"Of course." Her gaze met mine. "May I show you out, Miss Gray?"

I glanced down at Dr. Shaw. He was still clinging to my arm. "Are you sure I can't be of some help?"

I could feel the tremble of his hand, but his eyes were clear now as he turned and lowered his voice. "Just remember what I said earlier. Don't repeat what we spoke of in this office. Tell no one what you heard here today."

* * *

The blue Buick was in front of me as I turned on Rutledge.

I certainly had no intention of following Tom Gerrity. Earlier, I'd come to the conclusion that I'd had enough of all this snooping and sleuthing and jumping to conclusions, but then I'd overheard yet another conversation, and here I was back in the thick of things.

It didn't take a genius to deduce that Gerrity was blackmailing Dr. Shaw, but why? And had he really implied that Dr. Shaw could be involved in murder? Or had I misinterpreted what might have been nothing more than a snide comment?

Evidently their association went back a long way. I racked my exhausted brain trying to recall everything that Devlin and Temple Lee had told me about Rupert Shaw before I knew him. He used to be a professor at Emerson University, but he'd been dismissed when concerns for his stability and unfounded rumors began to circulate. Rumors about recruiting his students to participate in midnight séances and his overall preoccupation with death. Some of the students had talked, and the powers-that-be had let him go. That's when he'd opened the Charleston Institute for Parapsychology Studies.

I'd always found Dr. Shaw to be of sound mind if a bit distracted at times. But today he'd seemed genuinely confused by something—or someone—he thought he'd seen in his office. I was pretty sure he'd only imagined it, though. I would have known if there'd been a ghost, but hallucinations were an entirely different matter.

The Buick made a turn onto Canon, and, rather than continuing toward home, I followed Gerrity to the city's east side. Dipping down King Street to Mary, we cut back up America, which had once been considered the most dangerous street in Charleston. Gentrification had curtailed some of the crime, at least by day, but come nightfall, a seamier element came calling.

It was not yet dusk, so the streets were still teeming. Old men in lawn chairs gossiped in front of the corner grocery, while mothers kept watchful eyes on their children from shady front porches. The air was filled with the usual traffic noises—gunning motors, blaring music and the occasional screech of brakes. Despite the din, there was a homey camaraderie about the neighborhood that belied a recent rash of midnight shootings.

I made sure my doors were locked as I pulled into a parking place a few spaces back from Gerrity. He climbed out of his car and crossed the street to a sagging, three-story Victorian. The house had once been glorious, but the blue paint was faded and peeling, and much of the spindle work and gingerbread trim had long since rotted away. Two young men in baggy jeans and Panthers jerseys reclining on the porch steps tried to hassle him. He brushed off their taunts with barely a glance, and I heard their guffaws even through my closed windows as he disappeared inside the house.

He'd been gone for maybe ten minutes when I decided this wasn't such a great idea. I couldn't wait around here forever. I'd start to attract attention. The least I could do was circle the block a time or two.

I started the engine and was just about to pull onto the street when I glanced up at the Victorian's third-story balcony. A man stared down at me. Even though he leaned against the railing, I could tell that he was very tall, with skin the color of rich mahogany. He had on slacks and a loose white shirt that billowed in the breeze, and I saw a necklace dangling from his throat. He was looking right at me. I had no doubt about that.

Even from this distance I could feel the power of his gaze and—I could have sworn—the strength of his will. A shiver chased up my spine as our gazes held for the longest moment. He was smiling. I had no doubt about that, either.

I felt certain I was staring into the eyes of Darius Goodwine.

How I could be so positive about the man's identity, I didn't know. Maybe it was his height, the power of that gaze. Maybe it was because Ethan had said he'd seen Darius in this part of town at a house where human bones had been uncovered.

Maybe it was because I could feel him inside my head, creeping around in my memories.

I was almost relieved when something smashed into my passenger window, breaking the spell of that probing gaze. I whirled to find one of the young men from the porch leering at me. The other one popped up on the driver's side, and I heard him say something obscene through the glass. I put the car in gear and shot forward, making them both jump back from the tires. I didn't glance in the mirror as I drove away, but I knew they were laughing at me.

So was Darius Goodwine.

Nineteen

I dropped by my aunt's house on the way home to check on my mother. She was napping, so I promised my aunt I'd come back in a day or two for a visit. Now that I was back in Charleston, I tried to have dinner with them at least twice a week, and sometimes we'd all go shopping or to a movie if Mama felt up to it.

Occasionally, Papa would come by while I was there, but as always, he kept pretty much to himself, puttering around the Trinity house while Mama was gone and keeping himself busy at the cemetery. He was retired from his caretaker position, but he still lent a hand now and then, and he was forever working on the Rosehill angels.

Mama was nearing the end of her chemo treatments, and she seemed to be getting some of her old spark back—despite everything that had happened in Asher Falls. Papa and I had kept most of the details from her, but like Devlin, she'd only had to glimpse my face to know that I'd been through an ordeal.

I didn't want to think about my time in the mountains, though. I didn't want to dwell on a legacy that would haunt me forever. Things were complicated enough right here in Charleston. I'd unwittingly stumbled upon what appeared to be a blackmail scheme, and I'd overheard a conversation between Devlin and Ethan that connected them both to Fremont's murder. Devlin had disappeared the night his wife and child had died—perhaps to acquire gray dust from Darius Goodwine—and Ethan had given a deceptive alibi to the police. And Ethan may or may not have been in love with Devlin's wife. All these suspicious goings-on whirled inside my brain, but none pointed conclusively to a motive, let alone to the murderer. I still considered Darius Goodwine a suspect, but I was not at all anxious to confront him. Whether he had real supernatural power or merely the power of persuasion, I had felt something truly terrifying in his presence.

My head ached from too much thinking, too much tea and that cloying perfume that I could still smell on my jacket. As soon as I got home, I tossed it into the washing machine, and then Angus and I went for a short walk. After that, I took Dr. Shaw's book out to the terrace to read while I still had light. I wouldn't have been surprised to see Robert Fremont or Shani appear out of the shadows, but all was quiet in the garden.

I sat there for the longest time caught up in the pages of that book. I'd heard about rootwork all my life. It was a practice prevalent in the Sea Islands and the Georgia-Carolina coast, but even as far inland as Trinity, there'd been a woman who kept various powders sprinkled around her doors and claimed she could charm away warts with a special incantation. Some of the local kids swore they'd seen her kill a chicken and bury it in her front yard, but I personally had never witnessed her do anything more sinister than hang some bundled peppers from the rafters of her porch. Although once Papa and I had found a strange altar near a grave in Rosehill Cemetery with candles and pictures of saints and tiny pieces of paper with scribbled notes to the deceased.

All of that seemed fairly tame compared to the practices Dr. Shaw had told me about. Ritualistic autopsies. The ingestion of hallucinogenic substances. Entering the spirit world to converse with ancestors. Attacking enemies in the dream realm.

I thought about Darius Goodwine gazing down at me from that balcony. If, in fact, that very tall man had been Darius. He was one of only a handful of outsiders who had access to gray dust, a substance so powerful that it could stop the heart and allow one to enter the spirit world without the crutch of hallucinations. A powder so sacred that it was used sparingly even by shamans and witch doctors.

I still couldn't imagine why anyone would willingly pass through the veil, but then I had no great yearning to tap into the power of the spirit world, and I certainly had no desire to bring back the dead. Enough of them were already here.

"Amelia?"

Speaking of ghosts…

A shadow stood at my garden gate. A mirage, I told myself. An illusion called up by memories and loneliness and the dreamy smell of the angel trumpets.

And then Angus growled.

"You have a dog," Devlin said.

I got up from my chair, aware suddenly that we were on the brink of twilight. The shadows had deepened in the garden, and I could see the telltale glimmer behind Devlin where his ghosts would soon come through.

My breath quickened, and I felt a little light-headed, as if I'd been walking for miles in thin air. How many times had I dreamed of seeing him at my garden gate? How many nights had I lain awake, thinking about what I would say to him? Now that he was here I found myself awkwardly speechless, my heart beating entirely too fast inside my chest.

A thousand thoughts raced through my mind, none that I dared share with him. How could I when even the smallest chink in my armor could bring down every last one of my defenses?

When he moved to open the gate, Angus growled again.

"Is it safe to come in?" he asked.

No, it wasn't safe. Not for me, not for him. His presence in my life was a danger to us both. Mariama had made that abundantly clear. She would do whatever she could to keep us apart. I had no idea how much power she wielded from the other side, but the last thing I wanted was to provoke her.

Finding my voice, I tried to say calmly, "You'll have to forgive Angus. He's very protective of me."

"I can see that," Devlin drawled, his voice sending shivers up and down my spine. I could feel his gaze on me, dark and probing, and a jolt of electricity thrummed along my nerve endings, lifting the hair at my nape.

"Should I stay out here, then?" he asked.

"No, just come in slowly. Give him time to get used to you."

Devlin did as I instructed, and I heard the gate click behind him. He stood quietly inside while Angus sized him up. After a moment, Devlin knelt and put out his hand. Angus ambled over for a closer inspection. He nuzzled and sniffed, and then stood very still and allowed Devlin to pet him.

"Do you think I pass muster?"

"It would seem so." I still couldn't believe he was here, but I didn't know why I was so surprised. I'd gone to see him last night. Why shouldn't he drop by my house without warning? Why wouldn't he want an explanation of why I'd run out on him yet again?

If I were smart, I'd send him away before his ghosts had a chance to manifest. Mariama would not be happy to see me, and she'd already proven that she could hurt me. It was madness to tempt her.

But I said nothing, merely stood there taking him in. He must have come straight from headquarters, I thought. He had on his usual work attire of black sports coat, black pants and a gray shirt open at the neck. All beautifully tailored and trim-fitting. I sighed in spite of myself.

"He's been used in fights?" Devlin asked, tentatively scratching behind Angus's ear nubs.

"Yes. He's had a hard time."

"Poor guy. Where did you get him?"

"In Asher Falls. He'd been left in the woods to starve. He came out of the trees one day and just stayed."

"Asher Falls," Devlin said. "That's an interesting little place, isn't it?"

"You've been there?" I asked in surprise.

"No, but it sounded familiar when you mentioned it last night. That made me curious, so I looked it up after you left. The town has a history, but that's not how I knew the name. It's been in the news recently because of all those mud slides."

"Why would you go to the trouble of looking it up? Why didn't you just ask me about it?"

"Because we had other things to talk about. Or so I thought." Slowly he rose, his gaze meeting mine in the fading light. "Something happened to you in that town, didn't it?"

"I don't know what you mean."

"I read the news reports. People died in those slides, and I think you must have somehow been affected by the tragedy. Or by something."

I tucked a loose strand of hair behind one ear. The breeze had risen, and I could feel a chill through my shirt, but I knew the wind wasn't the reason for the shivers up my spine. "It doesn't matter. It's over. I'm home now."

"But I don't think it is over," he said, and I heard something in his voice, a proprietary edge that quickened my breath. "Whatever happened there changed you. I can tell just by looking at you."

I tried to make light of it. "I told you I got caught in a briar patch."

"I'm not talking about those scars on your face. They're almost healed, but something inside you hasn't. You're different. Tell me why, Amelia."

God help me, I melted at the sound of my name. I didn't want to. I wanted to be strong and pragmatic and wise enough to know that his dead family would always be there between us. But when he said my name like that. When he looked at me as though I were the only woman in the world, how could I not just…dissolve?

Thankfully, his ghosts hadn't manifested yet. Angus could sense them, though. He left Devlin to stare through the pike fence, fur bristling in agitation. I sensed them, too. They were there just beyond the gate, shimmering softly as they waited for twilight.

"Maybe we should go inside," I said and rubbed a hand up and down my arm. "It's getting chilly out here."

"I can't stay long."

Because he had other plans?

I wouldn't think about that. Baseless speculation would drive me crazy. I wouldn't think about his arms around Isabel Perilloux or that murmured invitation I had heard her issue on the phone. *Come over whenever you want. I'll be waiting....*

Gathering up my book and sweater, I headed for the gate. I couldn't completely drown out those taunting voices in my head or the unwelcome images they painted, but at least I would be safe inside from Mariama's wrath, though no sanctuary could ever protect me from Devlin.

We went in through the side door and I took him back to my office where I could keep an eye on Angus and watch out for the ghosts. Devlin walked restlessly around the room, hands in pockets, studying the books in my shelves and the photographs on my walls. He seemed aimless and edgy, like a panther stalking his cage.

I said a little too breathlessly, "Do you want something to drink? Some tea or coffee? A glass of wine, maybe?"

"I'm fine. I'm just on my way to dinner. I saw your car out front so I took a chance that you'd be home."

I nodded, fighting the urge to fling myself at him. He was so close, and I'd been so lonely without him. But already Mariama lurked in the shadows. Watching us. Taunting me.

"I've always been intrigued by these images." He nodded toward the double-exposed photographs I'd taken of old graveyards superimposed over cityscapes.

"The first time I saw them, I knew they were an insight into your world. I found them lonely and unsettling, but I was drawn to them just the same."

My heart still thudded. "And I told you they were just pictures."

"Revealing pictures." He pinned me with those brooding eyes. "That bothers you, doesn't it? You don't like to let anyone in."

"I could say the same about you."

"My world is sometimes a pretty bleak place," he murmured, moving over to the bookcases and then to the windows.

I could see his reflection in the glass, and I watched him there, the hollow in my chest growing deeper by the minute. He had no idea what he did to me. No clue that here in my sanctuary, away from his ghosts, he had unwittingly replenished his siphoned energy with mine. Already my knees had gone weak.

"This room brings back a lot of memories," he said.

For me, too. It was here that we had pondered an investigation together, here that we had shared our first kiss. Here that I had fallen in love with him. No, that wasn't quite right. I'd fallen for Devlin the moment he'd stepped out of the mist on the Battery. It was only in my office where we'd worked on a case together that I'd finally been able to admit it.

He turned. "I've missed you," he said softly.

I closed my eyes on a tremulous breath. "I've missed you, too."

"Then why did you run away from me last night?"

"I was frightened."

"Of what?" When I said nothing, I saw a fist clench at his side. "You have no idea how I've racked my brain, trying to figure you out. When you came to my house that night last spring…I would have sworn you wanted me as much as I wanted you. Or did I read you wrong?"

"You weren't wrong."

"Then what happened?"

"Your ghosts happened."

He stared at me for the longest time, something flickering behind his eyes. Doubt? Fear? Disbelief? "My ghosts?"

"Your memories. Your guilt. They're still there, aren't they?"

"Yes," he said, and I thought I heard him sigh. "They're still here."

It was a long time before either of us spoke after that. He gazed out into the gathering darkness as I stood there gazing at his reflection. I'd wondered over the months since I'd last seen him if my memory had dramatized his features—those fathomless eyes, the perfect nose, the tiny imperfection of a scar beneath his lower lip. I still dreamed about that face, about those eyes, about that sensuous mouth and what it could do to me.

There was a time when I'd thought I could move on without him, but that moment was long gone. All he had to do was look at me, say my name in that devastating drawl, and I knew it would never be over. I would always be trapped in this limbo. Suspended in the in-between space of what was safe and what I desperately wanted.

He finally turned from the windows. "This conversation isn't going at all the way I planned it," he said with a trace of irony.

I lifted a brow. "How did you plan it?"

"I never meant to come over here and badger you for answers or dredge up old grievances. The time for airing all that is long past. I actually came here to tell you that you were right to run away last night. Somehow I got sidetracked." His gaze searched my face, lingered on my lips, and I felt a flutter of awareness deep down in my stomach.

"When did you come to that conclusion?" I asked coolly, even though I knew it was ridiculous to feel hurt and rejected when, in fact, I was the one who had bolted like a frightened colt. With good reason, of course, but he couldn't know that.

"Something's come up. I'm involved in a matter that could get a little dicey. I don't want it touching you."

So…his rejection wasn't personal. He wasn't being driven away by his ghosts or even by another woman. I felt a rush of unreasonable relief until dread pricked my bubble. That overheard conversation on his porch came rushing back, and suddenly I knew why he was so wired. I recognized the source of all that nervous energy. He was going after Darius Goodwine.

I walked over to the window, resisting the temptation to place my hand on his arm. To draw comfort from his warmth even as he sustained himself with mine. "This involvement…has to do with a police investigation?"

"Unofficially."

"What does that mean?"

He gave a slight shrug. "I'm looking into something that isn't exactly by the book. But that's all I can say. The less you know the safer you'll be."

"What does any of this have to do with me?" I asked in confusion.

"It doesn't, except that someone might try to use you to stop me."

"How?" I asked in alarm, my mind on Darius Goodwine.

"It doesn't matter because I won't let it happen."

I stared at him for the longest moment, trying to intuit

his emotions from his stoic demeanor. "Whatever it is, it sounds dangerous."

"Not if you do as I ask."

"I wasn't talking about me."

His features softened, and I saw the hint of a smile that made my knees go even weaker. "You don't need to worry about me. I know what I'm doing."

Of course, he did. I'd never known anyone so competent, so utterly focused when he needed to be. But that glimmer of excitement in his eyes troubled me. That pent-up tension worried me even more. He wasn't at all frightened. He relished the prospect of going after Darius, a man Ethan said had devotees all over the city. A man Fremont said had made the transition from shaman to sorcerer.

"How can I not worry?" I asked sharply. "You're telling me just enough to *make* me worry."

"I'm sorry. That wasn't my intent. I just wanted you to understand why we have to keep our distance."

"I'm getting that message loud and clear."

My wounded tone seemed to take him aback. "When I can tell you, I will."

"That really isn't much comfort."

He still looked bemused and not a little intrigued by my reaction. "It's the best I can do for now. But there's something else I need from you. It's very important."

"What is it?"

He put his hands on my shoulders and gazed directly into my eyes. "If I disappear, don't come looking for me."

"What?" Panic skittered over me as my anger fled. "What do you mean, if you disappear?"

His grip tightened ever so slightly. "If you don't see or hear from me, just let it go. Don't call my phone, don't go by my house, don't ask any questions. And for God's sakes, don't notify the police."

I had to fight to keep a terrified tremor from my voice. "If you disappear…how can I just let it go? That's asking too much."

"You have to." His dark stare impaled me, besieged me. "Promise me."

"Now you're really scaring me."

He touched his hand to my face. "Don't be frightened." His soft drawl invoked forbidden images, and I shivered as his hands slipped into my hair. He brought his mouth down on mine, lightly at first, and then with growing heat until I clutched his arms for support. My eyes closed, my lips parted and I didn't hold back, nor did he. I had been starving for that kiss, and in spite of Isabel Perilloux, in spite of his ghosts, it seemed as though he had, too.

He lifted his head and whispered my name on a ragged sigh as he pulled me to his chest. I melted into him, and he held me for the longest time in silence. I pressed my cheek to the thud of his heart and savored the scent of him, the feel of him, while I still could.

Then all too soon, his arms fell away, and it was time for him to go. The whole scene had a sense of finality that I refused to accept. Whatever happened, I had to believe that Devlin and I were a long way from over.

I stood on the veranda and watched him go. He didn't look back. Not even once. He strode down the walkway, and by the time he reached the garden gate, his ghosts were with him. Mariama floated at his side, her hand skimming his arm, touching his shoulder, dashing that glimmer of nascent hope that had sprouted from his kiss.

Shani trailed behind them, her blue dress blowing

delicately in a nonexistent breeze. She glanced over her shoulder and pressed a finger to her lips before she quietly vanished.

A moment later, I felt a numbing cold, a paralyzing fear, and glanced down to find her at *my* side. She clung to my hand as we stood there watching Devlin walk away into the twilight.

I waited until the little ghost faded before going back inside. Shani was coming to me more and more frequently, her manifestations increasingly bold. There was little doubt now that she haunted me and she would not be leaving until I found a way to help her move on. I was equally certain that Mariama would do everything in her power to make certain that didn't happen. Shani was her tie to Devlin.

The house was very quiet and my nerves were already unsettled. I went to the door to call for Angus. He came at once, as eager for my company as I was for his. I saw nothing out of the ordinary in the dusk, but I had a strange sense that spirits were close. Whether Shani had led them to me or my own transformation had attracted them, I didn't know. But they were out there, searching for me even as I scoured the shadows for them.

I stood there on the threshold as nightfall deepened and the vanilla scent of the phlox awakened. A three-quarter moon peeked over the treetops and the lamb's ear and sage took on a silvery glow. The garden became a fairyland, delicate and ethereal, and the song of the nightingale that drifted down through the leaves might have seemed perfectly suited to such a dream world. But there were no nightingales in Charleston. *It was a mockingbird you heard.*

I saw him then, just beyond the swing, in the deepest shadows of the yard. Not a ghost, but a flesh and blood man, uncommonly tall and mesmeric even in the dark. He lifted a hand and the wind rose, I could have sworn it. Born on that unnatural breeze, the scent of sulfur drifted across the garden, mingling with the night-blooming datura. The perfume enveloped me like a cocoon. Trapped in his spell, I couldn't move or breathe. The sensation should have been terrifying, but I felt no fear. Just a strange fascination.

Then it was over. The scent evaporated and the man disappeared. I told myself he must have been a ghost or a conjure of my imagination. No human could simply dissolve into the shadows. Not even a *tagati.*

But I couldn't shake the notion that I had just been paid a visit by the infamous Darius Goodwine.

Twenty

My night was filled with the strangest dreams and I awoke with a splitting headache. If I hadn't known better, I would have sworn I suffered from a hangover, but I'd gone to bed early without so much as a sip of wine. I could barely even remember Devlin's visit, let alone the incident in the garden. Both visits had joined the surreal parade of visions that had marched through my sleep.

As per Dr. Shaw's wishes, Temple and I had arranged to meet at Oak Grove Cemetery that morning at nine, but I arrived early and was sorely tempted to remain in my locked vehicle until she got there. I didn't relish entering that abandoned graveyard alone. My memories of Oak Grove were still too fresh.

This was my first trip back since the police had sealed the cemetery late last spring. After months of tedious and methodical excavating, all the bodies had been recovered, and the investigation had finally come to an end. But my nightmares would linger for years. I wasn't yet sure how I would cope, but it was too late to back out now. I'd given Dr. Shaw my word.

I took my time lacing my boots, pulling on my jacket and checking my camera. Even after all that, Temple still hadn't arrived. I got out of the car and glanced around, uneasy in spite of the sunshine. It was so very quiet out here. Quiet…and isolated. I'd forgotten the completeness of that silence, the profound stillness that settled heavily over the overgrown landscape.

Oak Grove had always been an unnerving place. Surrounded by woods and accessible only by foot, the cemetery was owned by the prestigious Emerson University, but for years it had been allowed to languish behind crumbling walls, with no visitors to speak of except for students looking to party and a killer anxious to bury young women's bodies.

Being all too familiar with *that* recent history, I kept a watchful eye as I made my way through the tall grass toward the gates. Briars clutched at my jeans, and despite the cooler weather, I swatted a couple of annoying mosquitoes buzzing around my face.

At least I didn't have to worry about ghosts, I told myself. Oak Grove was one of those cemeteries where even the dead feared to tarry. But I'd seen something far more disturbing than a restless spirit at the edge of the woods late one afternoon. From my description, Dr. Shaw had called the entity a shadow being, and he'd almost had me convinced that those periphery glimpses were nothing more than my imagination or tricks of light and shade. I knew better now. Shadow beings were real, but unlike ghosts that awaited twilight, they seemed to prefer the shifting light of pre-dusk.

I threw off that memory and lifted my face to the sun. The morning was bright and cool, perfect weather to begin a restoration. The prospect of getting back to work, of immersing myself in my own little world, excited me even if it did mean a return to Oak Grove.

But that budding anticipation withered the moment I walked through the gates. The cemetery's dark past hung like a pall over the blackened headstones and moss-shrouded statues, and I stood there shivering as I glanced around.

Oak Grove had once been the site of a large plantation with underground slave quarters still echoing with misery. Aboveground, it was lush and Gothic, the once parklike setting typical of the Rural Cemetery Movement that had migrated here from England during the Victorian era. The gravestone symbolism was some of the finest I'd ever encountered—willow trees and urns signifying sorrow and the soul's mortality, hourglasses depicting the fleeting passage of time, roses in various states of bloom that denoted age at time of death.

A dove marked a tiny grave near the gates, the bird of peace a symbol often found on the headstones of children. As I bent to pull back a tangle of weeds from the site, I thought of Shani's little grave in Chedathy Cemetery, decorated with nothing more than a simple headstone and seashells shaped in a heart. Her visit, too, seemed a part of some half forgotten dream.

Her ghost had remained at my side last evening only until Devlin had been out of sight. Then she, too, had vanished, leaving nothing of her presence behind. No hearts on frosted glass. No jasmine. Nothing but the memory of that little ghostly hand in mine. Instinctively, I knew it was important that she'd drifted from Devlin to me. So significant, in fact, that I almost couldn't bear to think about her motive. No matter how hard I tried to resist, her persistence chipped away at my resolve.

With each manifestation, her determination became more obvious. She wasn't going away until I found a way to help her move on.

Keeping to the cracked pavers, I worked my way to the back. Most of the graves in the front section of the cemetery ranged from mid-nineteenth to early twentieth century, hence the prevalence of weeping angels and grieving saints, but graves in the older area dated back to the early 1700s. Headstones from that era were adorned with more gruesome images of death: the grim reaper, winged skulls, skeletons in open coffins.

The deeper I walked into the cemetery, the thicker the canopy. Only a spangle of light shone through here and there, and the temperature dropped. I could see the spires of the Bedford Mausoleum peeking through a tangle of kudzu and, everywhere I looked, ivy. The ubiquitous vines curled around statues and monuments and snaked along the limbs of the old live oaks, snuffing the life from the centuries-old trees.

As I approached the first excavated grave, I became aware of a slight sound and cocked my head to listen. I heard what I thought was the crunch of dead leaves underfoot and assumed that Temple had arrived just after me. I started to call out to her, but something held me back. Cemetery etiquette precluded loud voices, and the need for caution had long become a habit. I didn't exactly feel the urge to hide, but neither did I bother stepping out into the open. I had on dark clothing. Unless someone knew I was there, I blended seamlessly into the shadows of the monuments.

After a moment, a man emerged through the drapery of Spanish moss and grape vines and stood gazing around. He was average height, with an athletic build that had gone soft. I could see the outline of a paunch over his belt and, despite the distance between us, the telltale sag of his jaw line. Or maybe that was only my imagination because I could determine nothing of his other features. The brim of his hat was pulled too low over his eyes.

The man on King Street instantly came to mind. I told myself there was no way this could be the same person, and yet, I had a sinking feeling that he was. And since he'd been tailing me before I'd ever spoken a word about Darius Goodwine or gray dust to Dr. Shaw, I could only assume he was here because of Devlin. A connection had already been made, and now someone wanted to use me to get to him.

My first instinct was to ease the phone and a can of mace from my pocket. But I didn't dare move for fear he would spot me. I stood there with suspended breath and pounding heart praying he'd move on so that I could call for help.

He lingered for what seemed an eternity. Then I heard my name shouted from the front of the cemetery. Temple had arrived, and thankfully she had no compunction about raising her voice. The man whirled and strode back along the path the way he had come. My relief was followed instantly by a dart of panic that had me bolting from my hiding place. If he kept on the path, he would run straight into Temple.

I cut through the graves hoping to head him off. Stumbling over roots and broken stones, I burst from the old section only to stop dead in my tracks. Temple and the stranger stood talking on the path. When they heard me approach, he turned nonchalantly, giving me the sleaziest grin I could ever imagine.

"There she is," he drawled with a wink. "The infamous Graveyard Queen."

Twenty-One

"Amelia, this is—" Temple turned with a narrowed gaze. "I'm sorry, what did you say your name is again?"

"Ivers. Jimmy Ivers." He fished in his pocket and handed me a business card.

"Mr. Ivers is a reporter for the *Lowcountry Chronicle*. It seems he's doing a story about Oak Grove Cemetery."

He glanced around appreciatively. "This place is creepy as hell. You ladies don't get spooked working out here all by your lonesome?"

The way he looked us over made my skin crawl. I tried to commit his features to memory just in case I ever needed to pick him out of a lineup. Other than pale eyes and that flaccid jaw line, his appearance was completely nondescript. "I'm sorry...how do you know who I am? And how did you know we'd be here today?"

"You've heard of having sources, right? With enough incentive, anyone will talk. You'd be surprised," he said, and I thought to myself that if he winked at me again, I wouldn't be responsible for my actions. "As to the first question, I know who you are because I've done my homework."

"Then you must know that without written permission from the university, you're trespassing on private property," I said. "If you don't leave of your own accord, I'll alert the campus police and have you escorted out of here."

He looked affronted. "No call for that. I'm just trying to do my job."

"As are we. Now if you don't mind..." I nodded toward the gate.

"You can't just answer a few simple questions for me? It won't take a minute." He turned to Temple. "How about you?"

"How about no." She handed him her card. "Call my office next week, and I'll see that you get a statement."

"I guess that's better than nothing," he grumbled. "You ladies have a *great* day."

He sauntered off, snapping a few shots with his phone, and I glanced at Temple. "That was weird."

"No kidding. That guy's about as much of a reporter as I am." She glanced at his card. "Probably had these printed up on his way over here."

"What do you think he really wanted?" I asked nervously.

She shrugged. "I've seen people like him before. I call them gore junkies. He was probably hoping for a look at an open grave. Maybe even to glimpse some remains."

"He knew who I was, though."

"Well, you were in the news last spring during the heat of the investigation. I must say, everything considered, you handled that extremely well." An errant curl fell across Temple's face, and she tucked it back.

She was dressed much the same as I—cargoes, dark jacket and boots—but she'd left her hair down to blow artfully in the breeze while I'd scraped mine back into a ponytail. "I've never seen you so assertive."

"Maybe he just caught me on a bad morning." I watched Ivers—or whoever he was—disappear through the entrance. "I should probably go lock the gates," I said on a shiver.

"Good thinking. I'll come with you just in case Mr. Creepypants gets any wild notions."

"There is no excuse for such wanton neglect," Temple said a little while later as we gazed down a row of overturned headstones. "I'm ashamed something like this happened on my watch."

"It's not like you could be here every second of every day," I said. "The excavations went on for months."

"I realize that, but the blatant disrespect is like a slap in the face."

"I wouldn't call it disrespect. The police tried to observe proper protocol, but after the scope of the investigation became evident, priorities shifted."

The killer had been very clever about hiding the bodies of his victims in old graves marked with meaningful inscriptions and images. Once the perpetrator had been identified, it then became a matter of recovering the remains. Dozens of sites had been exhumed, disturbing original interment. After the dirt had been sifted for evidence, the graves had been hastily filled in to prevent further exposure to the elements. As the state archeologist, Temple had authority over any human remains older than a hundred years. Her job at Oak Grove was to ensure the reburials had been conducted properly and that any artifacts such as personal mementoes,

The Reader Service – Here's How it Works:

Accepting your 2 free books and 2 free gifts (gifts valued at approximately $10.00) places you under no obligation to buy anything. You may keep the books and gifts and return the shipping statement marked "cancel". If you do not cancel, about a month later we'll send you 4 additional books and bill you just $21.42 in the U.S. or $23.46 in Canada. That's a savings of at least 21% off the cover price of all 4 books! It's quite a bargain! Shipping and handling is just 50¢ per book in the U.S. and 75¢ per book in Canada.* You may cancel at any time, but if you choose to continue, every month we'll send you 4 more books, which you may either purchase at the discount price or return to us and cancel your subscription.

*Terms and prices subject to change without notice. Prices do not include applicable taxes. Sales tax applicable in N.Y. Canadian residents will be charged applicable taxes. Offer not valid in Quebec. All orders subject to credit approval. Credit or debit balances in a customer's account(s) may be offset by any other outstanding balance owed by or to the customer. Please allow 4 to 6 weeks for delivery. Offer available while quantities last.

If offer card is missing write to: The Reader Service, P.O. Box 1867, Buffalo, NY 14240-1867

NO POSTAGE
NECESSARY
IF MAILED
IN THE
UNITED STATES

BUSINESS REPLY MAIL

FIRST-CLASS MAIL PERMIT NO. 717 BUFFALO, NY

POSTAGE WILL BE PAID BY ADDRESSEE

THE READER SERVICE
PO BOX 1867
BUFFALO NY 14240-9952

scraps of clothing and bone had been returned to the appropriate graves.

I went over to kneel beside one of the fallen headstones. Using a soft-bristle brush, I cleaned away dirt and dried moss to reveal the artwork—a winged face symbolizing the flight of the soul. "I don't see any fresh cracks or chips. Maybe they were afraid of breaking them, so they left them where they fell. Which was a good call, actually. You know how fragile these old stones are."

Temple's eyes snapped. "You're far more charitable than I am. I think it more likely that in their zeal to dig up the next headline, they just got careless. But I'll admit my contempt for the Charleston Police Department may have something to do with the speeding ticket I got on my way over here. That's why I was late."

I squinted up at her. "And you couldn't talk your way out of it? That doesn't sound like you."

"I know. I must be slipping. Old age is hell," she said with a grimace.

"Oh, yes, you're so decrepit."

"Speaking of..." She cocked her head, giving me a sharp scrutiny as I straightened from the marker. "I didn't want to say anything earlier in front of that creep, but you don't look so good this morning."

"Why does everyone keep telling me that?" I asked with a frown.

"Could be those dark circles under your eyes. Or those hollow cheeks. And you look like you've lost weight since the last time I saw you. What on earth is going on with you?"

I'm being haunted by Devlin's dead daughter. "I haven't been sleeping well."

"Nightmares about this place?" Her tone was sympathetic. "I have to admit, I was a little concerned when I heard you'd agreed to come back."

"Why? It's just another cemetery."

"Your stoicism is admirable, but you don't fool me one bit. You and I both know that Oak Grove isn't just any cemetery. It's a place where some very bad things happened. And some of those bad things happened to you."

"I'd rather not think about that."

"But you will think about it. How could you not? I saw how shaken you were by Ivers." Her gaze traveled over the murky terrain. "Oak Grove may be small compared to contemporary cemeteries, but you still have a lot of ground to cover here. It'll take weeks just to clear away the brush and debris. Are you prepared for all those long days when you'll be working out here alone?"

I gave her a hard stare. "Why do I get the feeling you're trying to scare me away?"

"I'm not at all. I'm relieved a historic cemetery will be in such capable hands. But you went through an ordeal here. It must have taken a toll. You can't just will away those memories. Something like that can haunt you forever."

"I'm fine," I insisted. "Or I was until you brought it all back up. Can we please change the subject?"

She gave me a benign smile. "We could talk about your love life, but I have a feeling that would be even more depressing."

"Ha-ha, very funny. How about we just get to work?"

"You don't want to hear about my running into Detective Devlin at dinner last night?" She gave me a sidelong glance as I pretended to study the site map. Butterflies danced in my stomach as they always did at the mention of Devlin's name.

"He was with the most gorgeous brunette," she added.

"Where was this?" I asked casually.

"A little Italian place I discovered on King Street. I stopped by their table to say hello. Naturally, Devlin pretended not to remember me at first. He does like to play his little games, doesn't he?" It was unfathomable to Temple that Devlin or anyone else would ever forget her, even if only momentarily.

"That's nice." I turned to look out over the headstones and monuments. "The next excavation is over by the mausoleum. We should get all the photographing out of the way, and then you can tell me how you want to proceed."

"Wait a minute. Don't you want to know about the brunette?"

"Let me take a wild guess. Was her name Isabel?"

Temple gave me a wide-eyed look. "You know about her? Well, I guess Ethan was right, then. Things didn't work out between you two."

"You talked to Ethan about Devlin and me?"

"Is the subject taboo?" she asked innocently.

"It makes me a little uncomfortable," I admitted. "I'd rather not be the subject of gossip."

"Well, you know Ethan. He's worse than any old woman. He was positively salivating to give me all the juicy details."

"What on earth did he say?"

She made a face. "Not much, unfortunately. I guess Devlin isn't the kiss-and-tell type."

I shrugged, but the nerves in my stomach were still bunched. "There's really nothing to tell, but I don't know why that should surprise you. You're the one who warned me about him, remember?"

"Did I?"

"Yes. I believe the implication was that I could never live up to Mariama."

"No one can ever live up to the dead wife," she said dryly. "But Mariama was…"

"Yes, I know."

Temple shivered as we headed toward the mausoleum. I kept my eyes on the ground because those gothic spires invoked a very different kind of chill in me.

"She really was something," Temple said on a blissful sigh. "I've never met anyone quite like her. She was so extraordinarily beautiful and so blatantly self-indulgent."

I turned in surprise. "You talk as if you knew her, but you only saw her that one time, right? At a crime scene, I think you said."

She looked a little flustered and fanned herself. "Well, yes, but that one time made an impression."

"Because of the argument?"

Confusion flashed in her eyes, and then she said quickly, "Oh, right. The argument between her and Devlin. Heated and very passionate. The whole blowup was extremely titillating."

My gaze strayed to those spires in spite of myself. "Did Ethan ever mention why his father brought Mariama to Emerson?"

"I'm sure he saw potential in her. As I said, she was extraordinary, and Rupert used to be quite the philanthropist before he got so caught up in the occult. Then all his time and energy and, I would assume, money went into the Institute."

"When's the last time you saw him?" I asked.

"Rupert? A day or so ago. Why?"

"I went by the Institute yesterday. He was acting very strangely."

"How could you tell?" she asked dryly.

I folded the site map and tucked it away. "I know he's always been eccentric, but this was different. And he has a new assistant."

"Layla?"

"So you've met her, too."

"Beautiful woman," Temple murmured. "I found her quite fetching."

"Really? Because I found her a little strange. I got the impression she's definitely taken charge of the office. She gives off this sort of territorial vibe that's extremely unsettling."

"I didn't notice anything strange about her," Temple said.

"No, you wouldn't," I grumbled. "Maybe territorial is the wrong word. She's more like Dr. Shaw's caretaker."

"He's always needed someone to look after him, if you ask me," Temple said. "I'm as fond of him as you are, but I've always been concerned about his stability, particularly after his wife died. That's when his interest in the afterlife became an obsession."

"He seemed perfectly fine when I first arrived. Then Layla brought him tea and he stirred something into it. An herb of some kind, I think. That's when he started zoning out."

"How do you mean, zoning out?"

"He just drifted off in the middle of our conversation. Then later, he had a dizzy spell. If I hadn't been there, I think he might have collapsed."

"That doesn't sound good," Temple mused. "At his age, one worries about strokes and heart attacks. Have you talked to Ethan about it?"

"No, I thought I might mention it at dinner tonight. Dr. Shaw asked me not to say anything, but I'm really worried about him. I've never seen him like that."

"What else was going on when he had this episode? Did something happen to upset him?"

"No, I don't think so. At least not while we were talking. We had this long discussion about rootwork."

"Rootwork?" She gave me a look. "Don't tell me he thinks someone has put a root on him."

"A root? You mean like a spell or a hex?"

"Did you notice anything else out of the ordinary about him? Any peculiar smells in his office?"

"Now that you mention it, I did notice a sort of musty, herbal odor even before he had his tea. And someone had sprinkled a line of salt outside the terrace doors. I assumed it was to keep the garden slugs away from the plants."

"Did you see any iron or silver lying around?"

My mind flashed back to the iron bolt beneath his desk and the silver letter opener in his hand. "Yes, as a matter of fact. Why? What does all this mean?"

"The herbs he put in his tea? The salt line at the door? He's trying to protect himself."

"From what?"

"Probably nothing more than his imagination. Rupert can seem perfectly reasonable at times, but he has always had strange notions."

"Just for the sake of argument, if someone did put a root on you, how would you go about removing it?"

"You'd go to a root doctor for a protection spell. In essence you'd be buying nothing more than illusion, but in the hands of a true believer, the power of persuasion can be a potent tool," she said. "I once had an interesting experience with a root doctor."

"What happened?"

"We were called out to move an old cemetery where a highway was going through. There was a woman… I'll never forget her…Ona Pearl Handy. She lived just down the road from the property and her ancestors were buried in that cemetery. She was convinced they'd come back to haunt her if she allowed those graves to be disturbed. Our first day on the job and there she was, planted in a lawn chair at the entrance with this white powder sprinkled all around her. She'd put it on the graves, too. Called it law-keep-away dust." Temple chuckled.

"Did it work?"

"Of course not. But she was convincing enough that it played with our heads. All sorts of weird things happened on that job, and it really started to freak people out. Phones wouldn't work. Car batteries died. Equipment malfunctioned. The worst thing, though, we dropped one of the coffins. The lid popped open, exposing the remains, and Ona Pearl went into hysterics. She was terrified that once the remains had been desecrated, her great-aunt Bessie would come back at night and try to mount her."

"Eww."

"Sounds kinky, but in that context she meant possessed."

"Did you get the graveyard moved?"

"Eventually, yes. Her roots weren't strong enough to keep us from doing our job, albeit shoddily. But she had us all wondering there for a while."

"Sounds like an experience."

"Oh, it was." Temple shook her head on another chuckle. "Poor Ona Pearl. Last I heard, she got busted for drugs and was doing some time. So much for her law-keep-away dust. Which proves my point. Rootwork is all about smoke and mirrors. I wouldn't be at all surprised if Rupert's affliction turns out to be nothing more serious than the power of suggestion."

"I hope you're right," I said.

But I didn't think the scene I'd witnessed between Dr. Shaw and Tom Gerrity had anything to do with perception. From what I'd heard, it was straight-up blackmail. And *that,* I had a feeling, was the real source of Dr. Shaw's affliction.

Twenty-Two

Temple had just left that afternoon when Regina Sparks, the Charleston County coroner, dropped by. I hadn't seen Regina since the first two exhumations the previous spring, but I would have recognized her red hair anywhere. Like me, she wore it pulled back in a ponytail, but curls had popped loose all over her head, and the tiny bronze corkscrews shimmered charmingly in the dappled light.

I had lingered at the gate, perhaps to prove to Temple and to myself that I wasn't afraid to be alone in Oak Grove. The sun was just sinking below the treetops, but there was still plenty of daylight left. Even so, my heart had tripped when I first spotted someone plowing through the weeds toward me, so it was a relief to recognize the flaming hair, as well as the logo of the coroner's office emblazoned on her navy shirt.

She gave a pleasant wave as she approached. "A little bird told me you might be out here today. I found myself in the vicinity, so I thought I'd stop in and say hello, see how everything is going."

I eased the mace back into my pocket. "Who is this little bird? I only found out myself yesterday afternoon that I'd be here."

She shrugged as she swiped back those wiry curls. As always, she seemed tightly strung, as though it were a struggle to keep her restless energy constrained. "This is Charleston. The one thing you can count on is that everybody knows your business before you do. It's annoying, but what are you going to do?"

"I'm just surprised that anyone would care enough to talk about it," I said.

"Are you kidding? After everything that happened here? There was even an article about it in the online edition of the paper this morning."

"That was fast."

"It ran with lots of photographs, including one of you, and a link to your blog. You'll be happy to know they spelled your name right."

"That is good to know." Someone on the Committee had obviously pulled strings to get a story planted so quickly. I could hardly blame them for wanting to shift the lurid publicity associated with Oak Grove to something more positive like a restoration, particularly since Emerson was in the midst of its bicentennial celebration.

"I emailed the story to my aunt," Regina said. "She's still over the moon about our having worked together last spring. You're a celebrity in Samara, Georgia, you know. They think that ghost video put them on the map."

"Even after it's been so ruthlessly debunked?"

"They don't care. They believe what they want to believe."

The video in question had been shot by a news crew that had come to interview me during a restoration, and for months the clip had made the rounds on ghost-hunting sites. Paranormal aficionados were convinced that lights floating over the cemetery behind me were otherworld entities. I'd known better, of course. There were no ghosts in Samara Cemetery, but it had taken a digital imaging analyst to convince the diehards that the lights were, in fact, reflected glare from embedded glass in one of the headstones.

"I thought everyone had pretty much forgotten about that video," I said.

"Not in Samara. My aunt was so excited when I mentioned your name, she and her Bunko cronies actually talked about catching a bus to Charleston just so they could meet you. No worries, I put the kibosh on that little scheme. Bless their hearts, they mean well, but I can only take Aunty Bitty in small doses and Loretta is a dipper. The whole crew reeks of Bengay and Youth-Dew. Need I say more?"

"I get the picture."

"Anyway, I don't mean to keep you. Looks like you're heading out."

"You aren't keeping me. I still need to lock up."

She stepped up to the gates and peered through the rungs. "I don't mind saying, I'm happy to have seen the last of this place."

"I can imagine."

"Helluva way to spend a summer," she muttered.

"At least it's over now."

"Is it?" I saw a shudder go through her. "I don't know what it is about Oak Grove. This place still gives me chills."

"There's a rural cemetery in Kansas known as one of the seven gateways to hell. I've been there. The atmosphere in and around that graveyard feels a lot like Oak Grove."

"Remind me never to go there," she said. "A gateway to hell is just asking for trouble."

We were both silent as we gazed out over the cemetery. The sun hovered just at the horizon, and the shadow of one of the angels fell sharply across our faces. The breeze died away, and there was no movement in the trees or among the graves. No darting silhouettes or gathering mist, but somehow the absolute stillness unnerved me far more than a manifestation.

The days, weeks, months of working in that cemetery alone unfolded before me, and I experienced a moment of intense panic before I quickly squelched it. I wouldn't let myself dwell on the nightmarish claustrophobia of Oak Grove or the dark haven of the surrounding woods. I had other things with which to occupy my mind, Devlin foremost among them. But I was also fixated on Shani's visitations and, of course, the Fremont murder investigation.

As we stood there peering through the wrought-iron bars at that shadowy necropolis, it occurred to me that Regina might be able to help me. Even though the murder had happened in Beaufort County, I felt certain she would have access to the autopsy files. How I could convince her to allow *me* access, I had no idea, but the longer I stood there thinking about it, the more convinced I became that something important could be gleaned from those records.

"It's a coincidence that you stopped by today," I began tentatively. Not that I believed in coincidences these days. Everything happened for a reason, even a seemingly random visit by the Charleston County coroner.

"How's that?" she asked.

"I'm hoping you can help me with a problem I've run across on one of my other jobs."

"Don't know much about cemetery restoration, but shoot."

"It's a small graveyard down in Beaufort County. Some of the headstones were stolen, and now there's a dispute over the gravesites. Everyone I've talked to seems to have differing opinions as to who is buried where, not to mention disagreements over birth and death dates. And so far, I haven't been able to locate a cemetery registry or site map."

"What about death certificates?"

"They weren't even filed in some cases, and others have been amended so extensively as to be useless. It's a real mess."

"Sounds like more than a mess," she said. "I would say someone is going to a lot of trouble to create all that confusion. If official records have been altered or destroyed, you're dealing with someone who is seriously motivated and probably well-connected. Have you talked to the sheriff down there?"

"The legalities aren't really my concern. I'm just trying to sort out those graves. It occurred to me that autopsy reports would be indisputable evidence as far as date of death is concerned. I was wondering how someone like me would go about getting copies? Aren't they a matter of public record?"

"Depends on the state, and within the state, it varies county by county. In Charleston, we tend to operate under the same guidelines that govern the privacy of medical records. But having said that, there are ways to obtain copies. If you're next of kin, you can submit a request online. If you're some yahoo looking for gory details, you could always try filing a claim under the

Freedom of Information Act, although—a word of warning—we tend to frown on that sort of thing. Since you're neither, you can always plead your case directly to the coroner. I happen to know Garland Finch pretty well. He's a good guy but he's a stickler."

"You don't think he'd be willing to help me?"

She shrugged. "You won't know until you ask him. I'd be willing to give him a call and see if I can soften him up a little for you."

"You'd do that? It would be a huge help."

"On one condition."

"Yes?"

"You have to tell me something." She turned, her eyes glinting with what I could only interpret as suspicion. "Anyone ever mention what a terrible liar you are?"

"I…don't know what you mean."

She cocked her head. "Come on. That story has about as much credibility as the two-headed gator that ate my fifth-grade science project."

I sighed.

"What's really going on?" she asked.

"It's a personal matter."

"This personal matter wouldn't involve a lawsuit or infringement on an ongoing investigation, would it?"

"No, nothing like that. I'm just trying to help out a friend. It's been two years since someone close to him died and he still can't move on. I thought a look at the autopsy records might put some questions to rest. Give him closure."

"Is there some dispute about cause of death?"

"Not really. But seeing it in black-and-white…" I trailed off. "I realize I'm grasping at straws, but I don't know what else to do."

"If this friend is a relative of the deceased, why don't you file a request online like I suggested?"

"How long do you think it would take to get an answer?"

"Anywhere from weeks to months."

"I was afraid of that."

"Your friend can't go to the coroner himself?"

"No. That wouldn't be a good idea."

Her stare was very direct. "And would this friend happen to be anyone I know?"

Since Fremont had been a cop and Regina was the county coroner, I felt it safe to assume they had at least been acquainted. "I wouldn't be at all surprised."

"If I stick my neck out, I need your assurance that none of this will come back to bite either of us on the butt."

"I don't see how it could."

She gave me a stern look. "I wouldn't do this for just anybody."

"I appreciate that."

"It goes against my better judgment."

"I understand."

"Here." She took out a card and scribbled a note on the back. "If Garland gives you a hard time, and he probably will, show this to him. He'll know what it means."

"I don't know how to thank you."

She gestured toward the cemetery. "If it hadn't been for you, that psycho might still be out there. Consider this payback from Charleston County. And everything considered, I'd say we're getting off pretty damn easy. There is one thing I'd like to know, though."

"What's that?"

"How long did it take you to come up with that ridiculous story about stolen headstones and altered death certificates?"

I smiled. "It's not so ridiculous. It really happened on one of my restorations."

She looked highly dubious. "Not in Charleston. Not while I've been coroner."

"No. Actually, it was in Samara."

"Oh, well, that figures." She shrugged. "That place is more corrupt than a tin-pot dictatorship. I should know, seeing as how my ex is the county sheriff down there."

Twenty-Three

Almost as if my thoughts had summoned him, Fremont's ghost appeared by my car when Regina and I emerged from the overgrown path a few minutes later. He looked the same as ever. Dark glasses obscuring his dead gaze. Arms folded, feet crossed as though he had all the time in the world. Which, in a sense, he did, although there seemed to be some urgency to our investigation.

I kept my gaze carefully averted from his dead form.

When I was younger, I'd learned not to give too much thought to the how or where or why of manifestations, other than to keep a watchful eye come twilight. Papa had not been one to talk about the ghosts, and I'd followed his rules so stringently that to question or wonder—even to myself—had seemed like too much of an acknowledgement of the dead. I'd always tried to keep my mind otherwise occupied so as not to court their presence. But clearly Robert Fremont's ghost had a connection to me. Some sort of telepathy, perhaps.

I would never get used to his humanlike appearance—not to mention his pre-dusk materialization—and it was only with every ounce of self-control I could muster that I didn't give myself away to Regina when I first spotted him.

We said our goodbyes, and I lingered over storing my tools and camera, then took out my phone and pretended to check messages in order to give her ample opportunity to pull onto the road. I waved as she drove off and continued to busy myself until she was well out of sight. Only then did I go around to the front of my car where Fremont leaned against the fender.

"How do you do it?" I asked him.

"Do what?"

I gave a helpless shrug. "How do you always know where I am? How can you just appear without warning? Without even so much as a glimmer of light or a whisper of cold air? You're just…there."

"I told you, it takes a great deal of concentration."

"You were on my mind just now," I said accusingly. "Did I somehow summon you with my thoughts?"

He gave me a bone-chilling stare from behind those dark glasses. "Why does it matter?"

"Because I've never been able to ask before. You have no idea what this is like for me. Since I was a child, I've been surrounded by ghosts, but my father taught me to never acknowledge their presence. Like you, he called them leeches. Netherworld parasites to be dreaded and feared. Then you came along. You're not driven by hunger for warmth or the desire to exist in the living world. You're driven by the need to move on. You're still capable of emotion. You still have a conscience and you can converse with me. Is it any wonder I'm so curious about you?"

He took a moment to answer. "Your thoughts didn't

summon me," he said. "Not precisely. It's more like a shift of energy that pulls me to you."

"Has anyone else ever seen you?"

"I don't think so."

"How did you know about me?"

"We made eye contact on the Battery one day. I said hello and you heard me."

"And then what? You started following me?"

"Something like that."

I was silent for a moment. "I've been wondering what gave me away. I'm usually so careful around ghosts."

"But as you pointed out, I'm not like other ghosts."

"No, you aren't. And now I have to wonder if there are others like you. How many times have I been fooled? How many more are out there masquerading as human?"

"Masquerading?"

"You know what I mean."

I could feel his stare behind those glasses. "If there were others like me around, you would know it."

"How?"

"Because they wouldn't leave you alone until you gave them what they needed."

"Are you saying they would haunt me?"

"Our resources are limited," he said. "We use what we have."

I thought of that message scrawled over and over in the frost on my windows. I thought of Shani's plea and her determination that I should come find her. She, Robert Fremont and that unknown specter all needed my help because I was the only one who could see them. I was the only one who could hear them.

The weight of my burden pressed down heavily at that moment. Was this the true significance of Papa's warnings? I wondered. Was this what he had meant when he said that to concede their presence was to invite them into my world forever?

But it wasn't just a matter of being haunted. It wasn't just a matter of having my warmth and energy leeched. According to Fremont, I would be relentlessly pursued by those restless spirits needing my help, hounded by desperate entities until I did whatever was needed. If I helped Fremont and Shani…what else would be expected of me? How many other ghosts were out there searching for someone like me?

I turned away from Fremont and lifted my face to the sky as my heart thundered inside my chest. I'd been flirting with the notion of a noble calling, perhaps subconsciously ever since my first sighting. I wanted to believe in a higher purpose for my gift in order to justify my loneliness. In order to accept my true nature. A part of me had actually begun to think of it as liberation. No more pretending. No more hiding in my sanctuary. Acknowledge the dead and help them move on.

But there would be no moving on for me. I saw that clearly now. The shackles that bound me to the ghosts would only grow stronger as more and more of them sought me out.

My gaze dropped to the horizon, and I drew a long breath. All that was left of the sunset was a pinkish glow peeking over the treetops. It was that tremulous moment before twilight, before the in-between, when shadows lengthened and shifted, giving refuge to those dark silhouettes that crept out of the forest. Did they want something from me, too?

"I've said something to upset you," Fremont said.

"No, it's not that. I've learned some things and I'm just wondering where to start. Did you recognize the woman who just left here?"

"She looked familiar."

"Her name is Regina Sparks. She's the Charleston County coroner. I assumed you knew her from your time as a cop. Anyway, she may be able to help me get a copy of your autopsy report. I don't know why, but I have this really strong urge to see it. I could barely find anything online about your shooting. The investigation was kept very hush-hush, so I'm hoping there may be something in the records that will help us. I know it's a long shot, but at least it's a start."

"No, that's a good idea," he said, seemingly impressed. "I'd like to know what's in those records, too."

"Can't you just manifest inside the Beaufort County coroner's office and take a look at your file?"

"It would seem that I can't."

"Why not?"

"I don't know. That's why I need your help. Apparently, I have limitations."

"Along with amnesia?"

He let that one pass. "What else have you learned?"

"I went to see Rupert Shaw yesterday. I wanted to ask him about gray dust."

"Did I not warn you to be careful?"

"You did, but I trust Dr. Shaw. He told me that gray dust comes from Africa. It's important to certain religious rituals and so powerful that even the shamans use it sparingly. But the interesting thing about that visit wasn't so much what he told me about gray dust or even rootwork. I overheard a conversation between him and Tom Gerrity that was very disturbing. And I know that's a name you'll recognize because you pretended to be Gerrity when you first approached me last spring."

"Yes, I know Tom Gerrity."

"I saw a picture of the three of you—you and Devlin

and Gerrity—in his office once. That's when I realized that you had only been pretending to be a private detective and that you were, in fact, dead. But that's not at all to the point."

"What is the point?" he said with an edge of impatience.

"Gerrity is obviously blackmailing Dr. Shaw. Do you have any idea what he might have on him?"

"It could have something to do with Shaw's wife," he said.

"But she's been dead for years."

"There was talk within our community about a visit Shaw made to a root doctor once, a man known to sell powders and elixirs for nefarious purposes. Shaw was interested in acquiring an extract made from white baneberry. Every part of that plant is poisonous, but the berries are particularly lethal. They contain a carcinogenic toxin that sedates the cardiac muscles. It's highly desirable as a poison because there's no nausea or vomiting that might arouse suspicion, and the berries are sweet-tasting. Death would come quickly, especially in someone whose heart was already weakened. Shortly after the rumors surfaced, Shaw's wife died."

I stared at the ghost in shock. "You can't possibly think he poisoned her. She was ill for a very long time. Her death was hardly sudden or unexpected."

"We may never know. It's unlikely an autopsy would have been performed on a terminal patient that suffered heart failure," he said. "And if she was cremated, there's no chance of an exhumation."

"I still can't believe it. From everything I've heard, Dr. Shaw was completely devoted to his wife right up until the very end."

"Maybe he thought death would be a kindness to her. To both of them."

"You're talking about euthanasia. Mercy killing," I said.

"Yes. But in the eyes of the law, it would have been murder."

His blunt words sent a chill through me and I stood there shivering as dusk crept upon us. In my mind, I kept seeing Dr. Shaw's face when he returned to his office after his confrontation with Gerrity. He looked as if he'd seen a ghost and he'd called out a woman's name. Sylvia.

Was his guilt conjuring strange visions of his dead wife?

At least no one can accuse me of murder, Gerrity had said to him.

My pulse quickened as the damning puzzle pieces fell into place. I didn't want to believe it, of course. I was very fond of Rupert Shaw. I admired and respected his work. But I couldn't ignore what seemed to be staring me in the face.

Was it really going to be that easy to uncover Fremont's killer? Somehow, I doubted it.

"If Gerrity knew that Shaw had obtained the extract, he certainly had ammunition for blackmail," Fremont said.

"Yes, but how do *you* figure into all this? That's the question. Even if Dr. Shaw poisoned his wife, what motive would he have for killing you? You've obviously done some research into this plant. Did you confront him with your suspicions?"

"I don't remember any such confrontation."

"Think hard. You have all these memories of Dr. Shaw and Gerrity and even Regina Sparks. The rest is still there. You just have to somehow tap into it. Is it possible Dr. Shaw followed you to the cemetery that night?"

"Anything is possible. I'm standing here talking to you, aren't I?"

"Yes, that's a good point." I glanced down at my phone, idly checking the time. "I can't even imagine Dr. Shaw poisoning his sick wife out of mercy, let alone shooting a cop in the back."

"Maybe you just don't want to imagine it. He is a friend of yours, after all."

"That could be part of it," I conceded.

"You'd be surprised what a man is capable of when he's cornered."

"So, how do we find out the truth? From what I saw yesterday, Dr. Shaw is in precarious health, both mentally and physically. I don't want to be the one to push him over the edge. Especially when I'm not convinced he's guilty of anything more than eccentricity."

"Talk to Gerrity. If you catch him by surprise, he may give something away."

"The last time I caught Tom Gerrity by surprise, he pulled a gun on me," I said with a shiver. "I'm willing to help you move on, but I'd rather not go with you."

"You need to talk to Gerrity," he insisted. "I feel very strongly about it."

"Will you be there?"

"If I'm needed."

That wasn't much comfort.

"There's something else I want to talk to you about," I said. "This is even more of a long shot than the autopsy report, but it's been bothering me. I can't seem to let it go. You told me one of the last things you remember was meeting a woman. Her perfume was still on you when you died. Even now you can smell it on your clothing."

Maybe it was my imagination, but I sensed a sudden tension in him. "What about it?"

"Can you describe the scent? Is it flowery? Musky? Woodsy?"

"It smells like darkness," he said.

That wasn't much help. "Does the name Isabel Perilloux ring a bell?"

I had expected him to dismiss the name immediately. After all, there was nothing but my jealousy connecting Devlin's brunette to Fremont's murder. But to my surprise, he grew very pensive, and I could have sworn I felt a cold breath down my neck.

"Do you know her?" I pressed.

"I can't recall her face, but I see her hands."

His words unnerved me and I caught my breath. "You *see* as in a premonition? Are you having a vision? Or maybe it's a memory. She's a palmist. Maybe you went to her for a reading."

He was silent for another long moment. "She has blood on her hands."

My heart was pounding very hard as I gazed at his silent form. "Literally or figuratively?"

"Keep your distance from this woman," warned the ghost Prophet.

He lifted his head, pinning me with his shuttered eyes. "She has killed or will kill in the very near future."

Twenty-Four

Keep your distance from this woman. She has killed or will kill in the very near future.

All the way home, those two sentences kept running through my brain, but could I trust Fremont's premonition? After all, if he could see blood on Isabel Perilloux's hands, why couldn't he see his own killer?

Then again, maybe he had.

Maybe Isabel *was* the killer. Maybe it was her cloying perfume that still clung to his clothing.

I'd been gone all day, so Angus was eager to go out. But rather than wait for him in the backyard as I normally did, I left him to wander about on his own while I went to my office and opened my laptop. Ten minutes later, I'd learned little more about white baneberry than Fremont had already told me. The plant was common throughout the eastern part of the country, the berries resembled old porcelain doll's eyes (hence the nickname doll's eye plant) and the roots were sometimes ground up to make a tea. It was also used in mojo bags and banishing spells.

More food for thought. Maybe Dr. Shaw's interest in the extract was strictly from a necromantic perspective. Maybe he hadn't wanted to poison his wife but to drive off evil spirits.

Strange how I grasped at the flimsiest straw to clear Dr. Shaw even as the evidence against him mounted, but I was more than willing to indict Isabel on a ghost's premonition. And even worse, on the scent of her perfume.

Checking the time, I reluctantly shut down my computer and went to lure Angus inside with the rattle of his food bowl. While he ate, I showered, dried my hair and then dressed in jeans and a new sweater for my dinner with Ethan and Temple.

A little while later, I parked near the wharf and drew on my jacket as I walked up East Bay to Queen Street. Ethan was already at the restaurant when I arrived. He'd snagged a window table and sat gazing out at the evening traffic, seemingly lost in thought.

"Hello there."

He looked up with a start. "Amelia! I'm glad you could make it." He motioned for the waitress as he rose to greet me warmly. I placed an order for a glass of white wine, and we settled in to wait for Temple.

"So, how was your first day back at Oak Grove?" he asked.

"You know about that?"

"Father told me he planned to ask you back, and Temple mentioned earlier that the two of you spent the day there."

"Well, to answer your question, everything went fine. We had to chase away a gawker first thing, but other than that, the day passed without incident." Unless one counted my discussion with a ghost about the possibility of Ethan's mother having been poisoned by his father, but that conversation was best left between Fremont and me.

"I can't say that I'm sorry to have seen the last of that place," Ethan said as he picked up his drink.

"Regina Sparks said the same thing."

"She and I spent a lot of time in that cemetery over the summer. But now that the last of the remains have been identified, we can put that chapter behind us." His sympathetic gaze fell upon me. "All of us except you, that is. How long do you think the restoration will take?"

"A few months, at least. There's a lot of work to be done and I'd barely gotten started last spring when the police closed it off."

"Will you hire help?"

"When I need it, but I like to do most of the work myself. I'm picky about my restorations."

"Yes, I remember that about you. That's why Father has always been so impressed with your work. The devil is in the details, as they say. I take it you were able to see him yesterday?"

"We had a nice, long chat. I also met his new assistant."

"Layla."

"She seems..." I trailed off, searching for the right description.

He grinned. "Intense?"

"That's a good word for her. How long has she been at the Institute?"

"A couple of months. I tend to lose track of Father's assistants. They come and go so quickly."

I took a sip of my wine, wondering how I could broach the subject of his father's health. I decided the direct approach was probably the best way. "Ethan...

there's something I'd like to talk to you about. I hope you won't think I'm overstepping my bounds."

He set down his drink. "This sounds serious."

"I hope not. Actually, I'm hoping you can put my mind at ease. While I was at the Institute yesterday, your father had some sort of episode. He spaced out right in the middle of our conversation. And then when he stood to get a book, he had a dizzy spell. He asked me not to say anything, but I'm worried about him. He seemed very fragile. I just thought you should know."

Ethan frowned. "He was fine when I saw him yesterday. As I said, we had a nice visit. But I'll give him a call when I get home, make sure he's okay. I'll even try to get him in for a checkup, but that won't be easy. He never likes to admit he has a weakness."

"None of us do." I paused. "There is one other thing I feel I should mention. I forgot a book that he'd loaned me, so I went back for it. He was out in the garden with someone. I got the impression they were arguing. When Dr. Shaw came back into the office, he looked pale and shaken. I don't think I've ever seen him so distraught."

"Who was he with? Layla?"

"No. It was the man in the blue Buick. The car was parked in front of the Institute when I first arrived. You saw it, too."

Something unpleasant darted behind his eyes. "Yes, I saw it."

"You said you didn't know the driver."

"I'm afraid I lied to you. That car belongs to Tom Gerrity. He's a private detective Father once hired. He comes back now and then when he's down on his luck." Ethan leaned in, his expression tense. "Please don't say anything about this to anyone else. You said yourself

Father was very upset by Gerrity's visit. I would appreciate it if you'd let me handle this."

"Of course."

We both fell silent, and I could tell the conversation had distressed him. I wondered if I should have said anything. Despite my worry over Dr. Shaw's health, maybe it would have been best to observe his wishes.

I glanced around uncomfortably, wishing Temple would arrive. It was a weekday, so the restaurant was quiet, which made me even more aware of the awkwardness at our table. A candle flickered between us, and I could see the reflection dancing in Ethan's brooding eyes. He was an attractive man, and I'd always enjoyed his company. But now all I could think about when I looked at him was Fremont's assertion that he'd been in love with Mariama.

"What's wrong?" he asked. "You were staring at me pretty intently just now."

"Was I? Sorry. I was thinking about another conversation we had once. It was in Oak Grove at the beginning of the investigation. You told me about the circumstances surrounding Mariama and Shani's accident. Do you remember?"

"Yes, I remember. I knew you and John were getting close and I didn't want to see you hurt. I thought you had a right to know about his past. About the guilt that he still carries with him."

"Didn't you say you'd all been together on the day of the accident? And that John and Mariama had a terrible fight?"

"I'll never forget the things they said to each other. I'm sure John has relived that argument a million times over." Ethan stared down for the longest moment into his drink.

"He stormed out of the house," I prompted. "And he was still angry when you met up with him later."

"Angry, distraught and at the end of his rope. The marriage was in trouble. They both knew it, but there was Shani to be considered."

"The marriage was in trouble, yet Mariama still called to say goodbye when she knew she was trapped in a sinking car. That is what you said, isn't it?"

He looked very sad all of a sudden, and I berated myself for bringing up such a painful topic. But I wanted to hear his account of the events again now that I knew about his feelings for Mariama.

"She must have known help would never arrive in time so she called John to allow him the chance to say goodbye. But he didn't answer." Ethan polished off his drink and motioned for the waitress. "Yet another thing he has to live with. I'm sure he still wonders what might have happened if he'd taken that call."

"Nothing would have changed. What could he have done? There was no way he could have reached them in time."

"Rationally, I'm sure he knows that, but emotionally…put yourself in his place."

"I know." I watched his expression. "When did you find out about the accident?"

"Not until later when Father called in the middle of the night to say that John had left the Institute in a state and we needed to go look for him. I told you about that, too, right?"

"Yes, but you never mentioned whether or not you found him."

"Eventually."

"Where was he?"

He paused as the waitress brought over a fresh drink.

After she left, he swirled around the ice cubes for a moment before glancing up. "I can't help wondering why you're asking me all these questions. Why are you dredging all this up now? Are you and John together again?"

"No. But I guess I'm still trying to understand what makes him tick."

"John will never get over that night." Ethan looked very pale in the candlelight. Glum and self-pitying. "Maybe it's best just to accept it and move on. At any rate, I've told you all I know."

"Not quite all," I said. "I know about the alibi you gave to the police."

His hand froze in midair. Then slowly he set the drink on the table and slid it aside. "He told you about that?"

I smoothly evaded his question. "You don't have to talk about it if you don't want to."

"There isn't much left to say. A cop was murdered that night. He and John had exchanged heated words a day or two before, and the police naturally wanted to question him. But he was in no condition to deal with an interrogation, so I covered for him."

"You lied to the police. Some might say that's going above and beyond the call of friendship."

A frown flitted between his brows. "It was a bad time for all of us. We needed to stick together. John wasn't the only one suffering, you know."

"I'm sorry. I'd forgotten that Shani was your godchild. You must have been devastated when you heard about the accident."

"To say the least."

"And Mariama lived with you and Dr. Shaw when she first came to Charleston. The two of you must have been close, as well."

He turned to stare out the window. "Mariama was a very special woman."

"Anyone who crossed her path fell in love with her," I murmured.

He turned with a jerk. "What?"

"I heard someone say that about her once."

"John?" His eyes flared. "That doesn't sound like something he'd say. Toward the end, I think he'd almost grown to hate her."

"Hate is a very strong word," I said.

"Mariama elicited strong emotions. The one thing she couldn't abide was indifference."

"That day at Oak Grove you told me that John left town after the accident. He took a leave of absence from his job and just disappeared."

"Rumor had it he checked himself into a private sanitarium somewhere in the country, but who knows if there was any truth to it? I've never asked him about it. All I know is that he came back a changed man. I can't imagine what he must have gone through, but I've always believed he was dealing with more than grief. If I didn't know better..." He trailed away, his gaze still riveted on the traffic outside the window.

"What?"

He seemed to shake himself. "It doesn't matter. It was a long time ago and digging up all those old memories is painful for everyone involved."

"As I said, I'm just trying to understand him."

"There is no understanding John Devlin. I'm surprised you haven't figured that out by now." His voice sounded strained as he put his hand on mine, peering intently into my eyes. His skin was very cold and it was all I could do not to draw away with a shudder.

* * *

The conversation shifted when Temple arrived, which was a good thing. My questions had put Ethan in a funk. Even Temple's recounting of Ona Pearl Handy's attempt to thwart the cemetery relocation brought only a halfhearted smile from him. Finally, she gave up and ordered another glass of wine.

"What is going on with you two?" she demanded as our salads arrived. "Seriously, I've had more fun at a funeral."

"I'm just tired," I said. "It was harder going back to Oak Grove than I thought it would be."

"I knew it. You've been sitting there brooding this whole time, haven't you?"

"I'll get used to it."

"I hope you didn't let Father coerce you into going back," Ethan said. "He can be as stubborn as a mule when he gets something in his head."

"All he did was ask. The decision was mine."

"Speaking of Rupert," Temple said.

I shot her a warning look, but she ignored me. "How is he these days?"

"Amelia and I were just talking about him earlier," Ethan said. "Apparently, he had some sort of episode during her visit yesterday."

"You don't say? Any idea what it could be?"

"None," Ethan said. "But he is getting on in years. I suppose I should make more of an effort to check up on him these days."

Thankfully, the discussion moved on to other topics, and I found myself tuning in and out all through the meal. I was still preoccupied with everything Fremont and I had talked about. His revelation about Dr. Shaw, not to mention his premonition about Isabel, had thrown me for a loop. I was anxious for the evening to end so that I could go home and mull over these new developments.

Everyone must have felt the same way because we didn't linger over coffee. Temple and I said goodbye to Ethan at the restaurant and then walked back to our cars together. The night had grown chilly, and I was glad for my jacket. I pulled it around me as the breeze off the river swept back my hair.

"Brrr," Temple said. "Winter's just around the corner."

"I don't want to think about that. Cold weather depresses me."

"Speaking of depressing, what was up with Ethan? He seemed positively morose and he's usually so upbeat."

"I'm afraid that's my fault. We were talking about Mariama and Shani before you arrived."

"That is a depressing subject," she said. "Ethan was very close to them."

I nodded. "I'm glad you didn't mention your theory about Dr. Shaw's dizzy spells."

"I'm not quite that callous," she said. "But I stand by what I said. I've known Rupert for a long time, and from the way you described his behavior, I'm willing to bet he thinks he's been hexed."

"Did you know his wife?"

"Sylvia? I never met her, but it was common knowledge around school that she was terribly ill and had been for years."

"Her death wasn't unexpected, then."

"Not unexpected, but it was still devastating. Especially for poor Ethan. He took it very hard."

"This was before Mariama came to live with them, right?"

"I would think so."

"Do you remember that dinner last spring when Ethan first told us about Mariama? He had this faraway look in his eyes and his voice softened every time he mentioned her name. I've always wondered if he had feelings for her. Other than friendship, I mean."

"They lived under the same roof for a time, so I wouldn't be surprised," Temple said. "How could he not?"

"Even after she and Devlin married?"

Temple shrugged. "You can't turn your emotions on and off like a faucet. I know Ethan pretty well, though. He would never have acted on his feelings. Of course, he wasn't Mariama's type, anyway. I don't think he could have handled a woman like her."

"I seem to recall you saying almost the same thing about me. You thought Devlin was out of my league."

She gave me a sidelong scrutiny. "Maybe I was wrong. I don't know what it is exactly, but you seem different. Like you've been through something and it's changed you. If Mariama was still alive, I think you just might be able to give her a run for her money. But I guess that's something we'll never know, will we?"

The notion of tangling with Mariama, dead or alive, made me shiver.

We parted at the corner of East Bay and Queen, and alone, I picked up the pace. I walked with my head bowed, hands in my pockets, and maybe I was just a little too preoccupied because the man was almost upon me before I noticed him. There were other people about, so I wasn't overly concerned even when I saw that he was staring at me. It was only when I recognized him as the lurker from the cemetery that my internal alarm went off. I was certain he and the man I'd spotted on

King Street were one and the same. He was obviously following me.

My hand closed around the mace in my pocket as he approached. He was smiling, but I didn't get the sleazy vibe I'd picked up on that morning. Now there was something very cold and calculating about that smile. About his eyes.

"Good evening," he said.

I nodded, still hoping he'd pass on by. Out of the corner of my eye, I searched for other pedestrians. It seemed as though the streets had cleared all of a sudden. Where was the couple that had been strolling along in front of me? The family that had been behind me since Queen Street?

By this time, I had the top off the mace and my finger positioned on the nozzle. The man was still a few feet away, but as I surreptitiously scouted my surroundings, I spotted another silhouette lounging in the shadowy doorway of a building. He was tall and thin and I could feel the power of his gaze in the darkness.

He lifted his hand to his mouth and blew something into the night. Mesmerized, I watched the shimmering particles hang in the air for a moment until the breeze swept them toward me.

From high in the treetop, a nightingale started to sing. Strangely, it was that lyrical trill that frightened me more than anything. Because it couldn't be real. Was I dreaming?

I tried to remove the mace from my pocket, but my arms and legs felt boneless. I couldn't move, couldn't cry out for help. I could do nothing but stand there helplessly as the nightingale serenaded me and those tiny blue stars rained down upon me.

Twenty-Five

I awakened to the murmur of voices.

Awakened was perhaps the wrong word. I was conscious, but I seemed to be floating in some sort of dream state. Everything appeared very hazy and surreal, but that might have been due to the bad lighting, I decided as I gazed up at the bare lightbulb swaying above me.

I was seated in a parlor that was totally unfamiliar, and yet, I knew exactly where I was—in the blue Victorian on America Street. The room was furnished with shabby antiques and faded rugs, and the only illumination seemed to be from that low wattage bulb overhead and dozens of candles. The flickering flames cast giant shadows on the water-stained wallpaper, and I felt almost hypnotized by the movement. It was only with some effort that I shook off the lethargy and continued my survey.

A large archway led into the foyer, and I could see the front door just beyond. It stood open to the night, and an endless stream of people drifted in and out.

On the other side of the room, another opening led

into the dining room. A man with dreadlocks was seated at the table eating something from an earthenware bowl. Layla stood over his shoulder sipping a glass of red wine. Only, she didn't look so much like Layla anymore. Gone was the tailored, sophisticated attire of Dr. Shaw's assistant, and in its place, she'd donned a purple caftan with intricate embroidery at the neck and around the hem. She was barefoot, and her hair was unbound, spilling over her shoulders in a cascade of tight, wiry curls. She and the man were laughing, and even though I willed their gazes, neither of them paid me the slightest attention.

The man from King Street sauntered into the room then, followed a moment later by Tom Gerrity who seemed to be on some urgent business. A metal box was tucked underneath one arm, and his eyes, even in the candlelight, looked overly bright. Both men disappeared into the dining room, and I didn't see them again.

More people strolled in while others left, not one glancing in my direction. I observed the endless parade for several minutes before it came to me that I could get up and drift out with them. I wasn't bound in any way and no one had even noticed me. I could just float on out the front door and be on my merry way.

When I tried to move, though, I experienced a curious boneless effect, and I realized that I was very much a prisoner even though no ropes or shackles constrained me. Why this didn't cause me great panic, I had no idea. I seemed to be disturbingly accepting of the situation.

I turned my gaze back to the candles, watching the flickering light for the longest time. I could smell eucalyptus and camphor and a tinge of something that might have been sulfur. I didn't find the scent unpleasant, nor did it distress me.

After a time, a hush fell over the room. All eyes turned toward the foyer where a newcomer had just come through the door. He stopped to chat with a woman in tight-fitting jeans, and as his voice drifted in through the arch, I felt a shudder go through me. The sound was deep and melodic. Utterly captivating.

A moment later, he strode into the parlor, and I was taken aback by his appearance. He was very tall, six feet five, at least, with skin the color of polished mahogany. Despite the cooler weather, he wore linen slacks and that same loose shirt I'd seen before, but now I noticed the silver embellishment. The neck was open, and a medallion gleamed at his throat. I thought him unnaturally handsome. Godlike, I would almost say.

He spoke to a few more people, and then the room seemed to clear as he came over and drew up a chair facing me. He sat leaning forward, elbows on knees, chin on folded hands, as he peered directly into my eyes. The effect was oddly calming.

"You're the one they call The Graveyard Queen." His voice reminded me of the nightingale song, lyrical and infinitely mysterious.

I nodded.

"Do you know who I am?"

"Darius Goodwine."

"So you've heard of me."

"You came to visit me last night."

He merely smiled.

I glanced around the candlelit room. "Why am I here?"

"I thought it time we had a proper introduction."

"Why?"

"I understand you have an interest in something I possess." He sat back in the chair, seemingly relaxed, but his gaze was very intense. His eyes were an odd shade of gold, I noticed. Almost like glowing topazes. The color was very striking against his dark skin.

He glanced away as someone moved through the room, and for the first time, I noticed a deep scar beneath the jaw line where a crude blade had just missed his jugular. How I knew this, I had no idea. There was another scar on the back of his right hand, and I searched for more wounds because those marks made him seem a little less godlike to me.

"What do you know about gray dust?" he asked me.

"It stops the heart and people die."

His smile turned numinous, like that of a witch. "It does more than that," he said softly.

"It allows you to enter the spirit world without the crutch of hallucinations."

"Aw." The topazes glittered. "Dr. Shaw has informed you well. Now I need to know who else you've talked to about this."

"No one else. Only Robert Fremont."

His brows soared. "The dead cop?"

"Yes." I had no idea why I mentioned Fremont's name. That wasn't at all like me. I never talked about the ghosts. But I seemed incapable of subterfuge at that moment, and I had to admit, I took a certain amount of satisfaction in the surprise that flashed in those golden eyes.

"Do you mean you go out to the cemetery and talk to his corpse?"

"No. I talk to his ghost."

"You can cross over?"

"I don't have to. He's here. In the living world."

I could have sworn I saw a flicker of fear in his eyes

before he leaned forward once again, trapping me with his gaze. "What does he want?"

"He wants to know who killed him. He means to have justice before he moves on and I'm going to help him get it."

That seemed to amuse him. "You're not what I expected."

"Did you think I would be frightened of you? That I would cower in your presence?"

He waved a hand toward the mingling throng. "These people do."

"I'm not like them."

He took my chin in his hand and tilted my face to the light. "Then what are you? How is it that you're able to converse so freely with the dead?"

"I'm a caulbearer."

The eyes gleamed now, and I felt an electrical jolt pass from his body into mine. I wanted to shove his hand away, but I still couldn't move. "You were born behind the veil. That makes you special. And very powerful."

What an odd thing to say to someone who couldn't move her arms or legs.

He waved a hand toward the group in the hallway. "You possess effortlessly what most people here seek artificially. I think I shall enjoy getting to know you."

"What if I don't want to get to know you?"

He laughed. "You won't have a choice. I'll come to you in your dreams. There isn't a root or a charm or a mojo bag that can stop me. Neither can John Devlin, though I have no doubt he'll try."

Twenty-Six

Somewhere behind me, I heard the screech of tires and the roar of a powerful engine. I was still staring up into the trees, searching for the nightingale that had now gone silent. Not until a hand fell upon my shoulder did I break free from whatever spell had bound me.

"Amelia?"

I turned at the sound of Devlin's voice, my breath catching at the sight of him. He was dressed all in black as usual, and I could see the glow of the streetlamp in his hair and in his eyes. He seemed so much a part of the night that I could scarcely picture him in sunlight. I wanted to lift my hand to his chest, feel the beat of his heart beneath my palm to assure myself he was real, but the effort was still too great. I had no will to do anything more strenuous than to stand there listening for that phantom songbird.

"What are you doing here?" I asked nonchalantly.

The breeze ruffled his hair as he stared down at me. "You called me."

"I did?" My gaze dropped to the phone I clutched in my hand. "When?"

"A few minutes ago. I got here as quickly as I could." He scanned the street, eyes alert for trouble. "Are you all right? What happened?"

"I don't know," I said, still in that airy, detached voice. "I don't even remember calling you."

He put his hands on my shoulders, turning me so that he could search my face in the lamplight. I stared up into his eyes, and my pulse quickened. He seemed very mystical to me at that moment. As dark and hazy as a dream.

"You're shivering," he said. "Let's get you home."

He took my arm and tried to guide me to his car, but those few steps to the curb were too much for me. I was still caught in the boneless stupor that had held me prisoner in the blue Victorian house.

Come to think of it, how had I gotten back here?

"What's the matter?" Devlin asked.

"I feel very strange and my legs don't seem to work."

Another sweep of my face and then he scooped me up and carried me to his car, depositing me on the front seat as though I weighed no more than a bundle of twigs. Romantic visions danced in my head. I clung to his jacket, drinking in the scent of him, the feel of him. His nearness was like a drug, but perhaps I was still swimming in the backwash of that glittering blue powder.

He fastened my seat belt, then went around and slid behind the wheel.

The interior of his car smelled like leather and the barest hint of his cologne. I drew a long breath, shivering again, though not from the cold. My head dropped back against the seat, and I turned to him with a languid sigh. "It's warm in here."

"Good." He adjusted the vents so that the heated air cocooned me.

I couldn't stop staring at him. His face was in shadows, but I had no trouble tracing the masculine contours of his profile. I had the strongest desire to reach out and take his hand, lift it to my cold cheek, but I had no way of knowing whether he had been afflicted by the same starry-eyed spell. Best not to make a fool of myself, especially when I was already feeling so off-kilter.

"What about my car?" I asked. "I'm parked in the lot at the wharf."

"Give me your keys. I'll have someone pick it up later."

I fished around in my pocket until I produced them. "I'll need the door key. Although there's a spare underneath a paving stone in the garden."

"I'll remember that if I ever need to break in."

"You won't find it unless you dig up my whole yard."

I turned to gaze out the window. Now that the lethargy was waning, my stomach felt a little queasy. The motion of the car didn't help.

"Can you tell me what happened?" he asked as he turned onto Queen Street. "You seem disoriented."

"I don't know. I was there one moment, someplace else the next, then back again. It's all very confusing."

"Are you sure you're okay?" I heard worry in his voice.

"I think so. Except...I don't feel very well at the moment. Your car is so nice. I hope I'm not sick in it."

"Is that a possibility?"

I swallowed hard. "A distinct one, I'm afraid."

"Should I pull over?"

"Can you just lower the window a little? Some fresh air might help."

He cracked the window, and I turned my face into the chilly wind. The cold revived me, and I thought the nausea had passed, but the moment he slowed and pulled into my driveway, another wave washed over me.

I all but fell out of the car in my haste and stumbled up the porch steps, breaking into a cold sweat as I waited for Devlin to unlock the front door. Angus met us in the hallway, but I brushed him aside as I rushed to the bathroom, both dog and man at my heels. Somehow I managed to pull myself together long enough to wave them away.

"What can I do?" Devlin asked solicitously. "You want a cold cloth for your head?"

"No, just get out! Please," I added weakly.

I held back for as long as I could, even somehow managing to turn on the water in the sink to drown out the sound of my retching. Then I was sick for a very long time. I remembered reading online that the plants consumed in certain African initiation ceremonies caused extreme nausea, purging the body of negativity so that it could more readily accept the hallucinations.

Had I been drugged? I wondered. How else to explain the sickness? How else to explain my visit with Darius Goodwine?

After it was over, I washed out my mouth and brushed my teeth. Then I took a quick shower and pulled on my fluffy robe, which was not at all sexy but warm and snuggly. Just what I needed at that moment. Then I padded out into the hallway and went in search of Devlin.

I found him in my office reading the book Dr. Shaw had loaned me. Angus was stretched out at his feet, and I thought that despite everything that had happened, despite the ghosts that undoubtedly lurked in my garden, this was a very homey scene. Devlin with my dog. Me in my cozy bathrobe. But I refused to indulge in any more romantic fantasies. That awful nausea had brought me back to earth with an unpleasant jolt.

Devlin laid aside the book and stood when I came in. “Arc you fccling better?”

“Yes, much better. Thank you.”

“I made tea,” he said. “I thought it might help settle your stomach.”

He passed through thc doorway, and I turned to watch him move about my kitchen. When he handed me a cup, I clung with both hands, sipping slowly so that the warmth could seep down into my bones.

We went back into my office, and I sat down at my desk while he took his place on the chaise. He picked up the book, idly thumbing through it, then set it aside again.

“I’m still puzzled by tonight,” he said. “And I’m still very worried about you.”

“I’m fine now. The tea helped.”

“I could tell the moment I heard your voice on the phone that something was wrong,” he said. “You sounded so strange. I wasn’t even sure it was you.”

“But you came, anyway, in spite of the fact that you told me not to contact you. You’re not angry?”

“I’m not angry.” He gave me a look, direct and intense. “And of course I came.”

I took another sip of my tea, buying a moment or two until I could breathe evenly again. “What did I say?”

“You told me where you were and asked if I would come get you.” He studied me for a moment longer, his eyes unblinking, and I set the cup down with a rattle. I’d forgotten how forceful his gaze could be, how that singular focus could unnerve me as no other. "You're not going to tell me it wasn't you on the phone," he said.

"The phone was in my hand. I just don't remember making the call."

"Did you have too much to drink tonight?"

"Did I seem drunk to you?"

"Since I've never seen you inebriated, I can't speak to that with any authority," he said. "But no, you didn't seem drunk. If anything, I'd say you were drugged."

"That's what I think, too. I just don't know when it could have happened. I met Temple and Ethan for dinner, and as I walked back to my car from the restaurant, I saw two men on the sidewalk. I'm pretty sure one of them had followed me before. He came to the cemetery this morning pretending to be a reporter. I think the other man was Darius Goodwine."

Everything seemed to go deathly still inside my office. Devlin's expression, bemused a second ago, was now stone cold. "How do you know Darius Goodwine?"

"I don't. But I've heard his name. Dr. Shaw must have mentioned it."

Devlin sat there scowling while I talked. He didn't move or interrupt, but I could tell that he was listening intently. He leaned forward, almost crouching, like a panther ready to spring. I'd thought of him that way before, but tonight his power and grace caught me newly by surprise. I felt an uptick in my pulse and took a deep breath to steady myself.

"He blew something into the air," I said. "Some sort of powder, I think. Maybe I absorbed it through my skin and it knocked me out. The next thing I remember is waking up in a strange room. I'd never been there before, but I knew that I was in a house on America Street. An old blue Victorian. There were a lot of people inside, including Dr. Shaw's assistant, Layla, and Tom Gerrity."

Devlin's gaze had moved to the back window, but now his head whipped around. "Gerrity? What was he doing there?"

"I don't know, but I followed him to that same house yesterday after I left the Institute."

"Why on earth would you follow Tom Gerrity?"

The explanation was a little tricky, considering my arrangement with Robert Fremont's ghost. "It's a long story and it has to do with Dr. Shaw. Gerrity and I happened to be leaving the Institute at the same time and I found myself behind him. So I followed him. It was an impulse."

Devlin stared at me as if I'd sprouted a second head. Clearly, he couldn't fathom such an action from me. "Do you have these impulses often?"

"I seem to lately. Anyway, Gerrity parked and went inside the house. While I waited for him to come out, I saw a man on the third-story balcony staring down at me. He was very tall, very thin. I'd never seen him before, but I somehow knew he was Darius Goodwine. I never got a good look at him until I found myself in that house tonight. He was the only one who talked to me. The others didn't even seem to notice me."

Devlin's voice held a peculiar edge that I couldn't interpret. "What did he say to you?"

"He asked what I knew about gray dust."

"What do you know about gray dust?"

Was that suspicion I heard now?

"Only what Dr. Shaw told me."

Another flicker of doubt. "Go on."

"Darius and I talked for a few minutes and then the

next thing I remember is being back on the street, looking up into the trees. And then you were there."

"You must have been dreaming or hallucinating," Devlin said. "You couldn't have been in a house on America Street."

"Why not, if they drugged me? They could have taken me there and brought me back."

"That's impossible. There wasn't enough time. It took me less than five minutes to get to you after you called."

He must have driven like the wind, I thought, and the notion of his urgency was exhilarating. "But if it was just a dream or a hallucination, how could I remember details like the bare lightbulb swaying overhead or the purple caftan Layla wore or the smell of camphor and eucalyptus and all those candles? How would I know that Darius Goodwine has a scar on his throat and another on the back of his hand? He wears an amulet around his neck and his eyes are the color of topaz."

Devlin got up abruptly and paced to the window, head bowed in thought. "You said you saw him the day you followed Tom Gerrity."

"From a distance. I never spoke to him. Not until tonight."

"He was there on the street with you. He made you think you were somewhere else, but it was all just an illusion. I've seen him do it before."

"Are you talking about hypnosis?"

"Drugs, hypnosis. I don't know how he does it. But I once saw him convince a woman she had snakes crawling inside her body. I thought she would claw her skin off before we could subdue her. Darius just laughed and called it a parlor trick."

"Why would he do such a thing?"

"He enjoys having power over people."

"And gray dust gives him power?"

"So he would have you think." Devlin turned to face me. "What else did he say to you?"

"That he would come to me in my dreams and no amulet or spell or mojo bag could stop him. Nor could you."

"We'll see about that," Devlin said with clenched fists.

I got up and went over to him. "What are you going to do?"

"Something that should have been done years ago." I could sense that restless tension in him again, and it scared me.

"What does that mean?" When he didn't answer, I placed a hand on his sleeve. "Why do you have so much animosity for Darius Goodwine? It isn't just about the gray dust, is it? Your quarrel with him is personal. Does it have something to do with Mariama?"

He turned and caught my arms, his dark eyes glittering coldly. "I don't give a damn about Mariama."

Twenty-Seven

I actually gasped, my gaze going at once to the back garden where I was sure Mariama must lurk. The way he said her name so coldly, so contemptuously, seemed almost like blasphemy. She had once broken a window in my office out of anger. She'd shoved me down in Clementine's garden and knocked her own portrait off the wall in Devlin's house. What manner of vengeance she would seek for this desecration of her memory, I could only wonder and dread.

Devlin was still holding my arms. His face was a dark, impassive mask except for those glittering eyes. Slowly, he brought me to him, one hand sliding up into my hair as he lowered his mouth to mine.

"You're the one I care about," he murmured against my lips.

For one insecure moment, I thought he might be trying to convince himself as much as me. Then I wasn't sure I even cared. Not while he stood so close. Not with that dark promise shimmering in his eyes.

His lips moved to my ear and nipped at the lobe.

"You're the one I want," he drawled, and I was lost. Utterly and completely and perhaps stupidly lost.

It was then that I realized Devlin had magic of his own because somehow I found myself backed up against the wall, and I had no memory of how I'd gotten there. He stood in front of me, blocking me from the garden as if he could sense Mariama's presence and wanted to protect me. I could see little beyond the windows, but I had no doubt she was out there, seething with rage.

If I hadn't already been in a precarious state, maybe I would have found the strength to push him away. We were asking for trouble, and Mariama would surely see that we got it.

But the drug still held me enthralled. I was trapped in the haze of that blue powder and had no will of my own.

The ties of my bathrobe had loosened and Devlin shoved it aside to trail kisses along my bare shoulder. I wrapped my arms around his neck, bringing his mouth to mine as his hands slid inside the robe. And all the while, he continued to kiss me. Even when my knees weakened, even when I shivered uncontrollably, he kept right on kissing me and didn't stop for a very long time.

At some point we relocated to the chaise. I lay curled in Devlin's arms, my head nestled beneath his chin as I rested a hand on his chest, basking in the afterglow of all that kissing. He was very good at it. I knew from our past that he was good at other things, too, but I wouldn't think about that. Best not to rush. Our passion had once opened a terrible door, and I had no doubt the Others would yet again be drawn to our heat. We were safe in my sanctuary, at least for now, and I told myself I should be content to live only in the moment.

But I could already feel the exchange of energy, the stealthy siphoning of my warmth as Devlin unwittingly replenished his life force with mine. One of the ironies of falling for a haunted man. My haven protected me from his ghosts, but hallowed ground couldn't shield me from him.

We hadn't spoken or moved for a very long time, but now I felt him stir restlessly. His lips skimmed my hair, and I closed my eyes on a shiver.

"Tell me about Asher Falls," he said.

The low rumble of his drawl vibrated against my cheek. I wanted to press myself even more closely to his heart, but instead, I pulled away. "I don't like to talk about that place. I'm never going back, so why does it matter?" Although at the very mention, I felt a pang of loneliness for some of the people I'd left behind. Not just Thane Asher, but Tilly and Sidra. The two women—one old, one young—had had a profound effect on me. But, no matter, I wouldn't be returning to Asher Falls. It was too dangerous.

"Did you meet someone there?" Devlin's voice was carefully devoid of inflection.

"Why would you ask me that?"

"Because there's a new wariness about you. A guardedness that won't let me in. You seem stronger and yet more vulnerable at the same time."

"I don't think I was guarded at all a few minutes ago."

"You know what I mean. There's a reason you don't want to talk about Asher Falls. What happened there?"

I gave a deep sigh and relented. "There was a man," I said reluctantly.

"Were you in love with him? *Are* you in love with him?"

I answered quickly. "No. I might have been if I'd met him first. Now there will never be anyone else for me."

His arms tightened around me. "Such a romantic," he murmured.

"Actually, I'm a pragmatist. I just know myself really well."

A frown fleeted across his face. "But you don't know me."

"You are a mystery," I agreed. "There's something I've always wondered about. You were so quick to warn me about Dr. Shaw and the Institute when we first met. You had such utter disdain for his work. And yet, I found out from Ethan that you were once Dr. Shaw's protégé. A paranormal investigator, of all things. I find that so hard to believe."

"It was a long time ago," he said, his fingers idly sifting through my hair. "I was looking for any possible means to annoy my grandfather, and that seemed as good a way as any."

"It's an odd way to rebel. Drinking, partying…that I understand. But the occult?"

"Ethan was my best friend, don't forget. I was exposed to a lot of strange things through his father."

"Including Mariama?"

His fingers paused in my hair for a fraction. "She was the ultimate rebellion."

"Because of her race? Because of where she came from?"

"All of that. She was exotic and mysterious and she had an uncanny way of knowing when and how to push buttons. She was scandalous in my grandfather's circles, and I enjoyed that for a while."

I wasn't sure I wanted to hear any more, and yet, a part of me listened eagerly. Despite what Devlin claimed about me, he was the guarded one. He didn't like to share anything of himself, and so I knew these glimpses into his past, into the man, even into his relationship with Mariama, were moments to be cherished.

"Was it love at first sight?" I asked cautiously.

He grew pensive. "I'm not sure it was ever love. But whatever we had…it was powerful. All-consuming at first. And then Shani came along and everything changed. With my daughter, it was most definitely was love at first sight." His voice softened, and I heard a catch when he said Shani's given name.

He fell silent, and I knew that he'd revealed all he intended to for one night. He'd told me a lot, actually, and now I had to get something off my chest.

"I need to tell you something," I said after a moment.

"I'm not sure I like your ominous tone."

"It's a confession."

He paused as if to brace himself. "Let's hear it."

"I didn't learn about gray dust from Dr. Shaw. We did have a conversation, but I already knew what it was. I went to the Institute specifically to ask him some questions about it."

"I thought as much. How did you learn about it?"

"I overheard you and Ethan talking about it the other night at your house. It was the night I came to see you. I'd parked down the street, remember?"

"Because you were afraid you wouldn't have the nerve to knock on my door."

"I made it all the way to the steps and then I heard voices. I didn't want you to find me there so I hid in the bushes beside the veranda. Another of my impulses," I said ironically. "After that it was too embarrassing to reveal myself. You have no idea how mortified I am admitting this to you even now."

"How much of that conversation did you hear?"

"All of it."

I could tell he was thinking back.

"I'm sorry. I should never have eavesdropped. It was very wrong of me, but then you were both so tense when you talked about gray dust and Darius Goodwine, and I'll admit, I became curious."

"So you went to see Rupert Shaw."

"Yes, and he had a similar reaction. He told me I shouldn't repeat anything of what was said in his office."

"At least he had the presence of mind to warn you," Devlin said.

"Why did I need to be warned? What is gray dust, really? I know it's a plant derivative that supposedly stops the heart and allows the user to cross over to the spirit world. I can understand why someone might be tempted to take it if they've lost a loved one, but otherwise..." I shivered. "If Darius Goodwine isn't in it for the money, what does he get out of bringing it here?"

"You can't be a god without true believers," Devlin said.

"Does he really have that kind of power?"

"He has tricks and illusions. Some people don't know the difference."

"Are you sure that's all he has?"

"You don't still think you were somehow magically transported to that house on America Street tonight, do you?"

"It just seemed so real."

"That's why gray dust is so insidious and why Darius Goodwine is so dangerous. If he can make someone like you believe, think of the influence he has over people who are weaker and more gullible."

Someone like you. If he only knew.

"He has to be stopped," Devlin said.

"Why do I still get the feeling you're not speaking as a cop?"

"My motivation is immaterial. People die when he's around. That's reason enough."

"Did you go see Darius the night after Mariama and Shani's accident?"

"So you heard that, too." He stared up at the ceiling. I couldn't tell a thing from his expression. "I don't know what happened that night. When I think back, all I have are bits and pieces of memories that don't make a lot of sense."

"Do you remember seeing Robert Fremont?"

He gave me a frowning glance. "Why would you ask that?"

"Because when the police wanted to question you, Ethan gave you an alibi. There must have been a reason why he thought you needed one."

"Maybe you should ask Ethan why he felt so compelled." Devlin's eyes flashed, but his expression remained passive. "I didn't kill Fremont, if that's what you're implying."

"I never thought for a moment that you did."

"I didn't kill him," Devlin said darkly. "But I had a motive. The oldest one in the book. He was having an affair with my wife."

Twenty-Eight

A little while later, I let Angus out into the back garden, but I didn't stay out there with him as I should have. My confrontation with Darius Goodwine—whether imagined or real—and my time with Devlin had left me shaken, and the last thing I wanted was a face-to-face with Mariama's ghost. I had no idea what kind of power she possessed from the grave, but I had a feeling what she'd shown me so far was merely the tip of the iceberg.

I wandered aimlessly down the hallway, a premonition of impending doom dogging my every step. It was strange to think that for so many years, my fear of ghosts had stemmed almost solely from their parasitic nature. The ravenous craving of human warmth and energy that sustained their presence in the living world. Now I knew it was possible for ghosts to cause physical harm, perhaps even death. I couldn't help but shudder when I thought of how far Mariama might go to keep Devlin and me apart. Not even Papa's rules could protect me from the wrath of a vengeful specter.

In the bathroom, I splashed cold water on my face,

then glanced in the mirror where a pale, gaunt woman stared back at me. The dark circles under my eyes were even more pronounced tonight, and my pupils seemed abnormally dilated. I wondered if that was a side effect from the blue powder. Or had one of Darius Goodwine's minions managed to slip something in my drink at dinner?

Why he would order such a thing, I could only imagine. Maybe he really did want to get to Devlin through me, but after tonight, I had a feeling his motivation had shifted. He'd been very interested in my communication with Robert Fremont and my legacy as a caulbearer. *That makes you special and very powerful,* he'd said. But I didn't feel so powerful at the moment. Mostly, I felt confused and out of my depth.

All of this was assuming my conversation with him had even been real. Devlin seemed convinced I'd been the victim of a trick or an illusion, and I wanted to believe that, as well. Darius Goodwine's claim that he could come to me in my dreams was a whole new threat, one that took away the safety net of hallowed ground. In dreams, there would be no boundaries or safe havens. My only defense against him would be insomnia.

Maybe he really was nothing more than a hypnotist or a clever illusionist who preyed on the weak and the susceptible. But I was a woman who saw ghosts, a woman who had been hounded by evil. I knew firsthand there were things that couldn't be explained by any living world rationale, so, unlike Devlin, I couldn't discount the possibility of a man who had tapped into the power of the spirit world. A man who could traverse both sides of the veil and visit me in my dreams.

Pushing all that aside for the moment, I tried to focus on something more productive—like solving Robert

Fremont's murder. But those were hardly soothing thoughts, either. The possibility that a man I respected and admired could be guilty of poisoning his wife was deeply troubling. The only thing more distressing was the revelation of Devlin's motive. *The oldest one in the book.*

Why had Fremont not told me about the affair? His selective amnesia was beginning to seem just a little too convenient.

Why did I suddenly have a feeling that I was being played, not only by Robert Fremont and Darius Goodwine, but by other forces in the universe?

The text message from Devlin—or whomever—had been sent to bring me back from Asher Falls. The nightingale on that first night was meant to lure me into Clementine's garden so that I would see Devlin and Isabel Perilloux. So that I would once again be pulled into his orbit. Everything was connected, but the links were too random. All the clues were there, I was certain, but I couldn't yet see the whole picture.

Could Mariama have been the woman who'd been with Fremont before he died? Although I'd never associated a scent with her, maybe it was her perfume that clung to him. On some level, I'd entertained those suspicions all along, but my jealousy of Isabel Perilloux had made me too quick to point the finger at her. But didn't everything always come back to Mariama?

Her betrayal must have been a terrible blow to Devlin. Even if the love had waned by that time, something had remained. An emotion so powerful it had brought Mariama back from the dead and kept her here, draining Devlin of his warmth and energy. I had a terrible feeling she would still be at his side long after I was gone.

Pacing back to my office, I allowed Angus a little

extra time to explore while I glanced through Dr. Shaw's book. Then I went to the back door to call him in. When he didn't come at once, I stepped outside. I hadn't bothered with slippers, so I went no farther than the terrace. I called again and was just starting to get a little uneasy when he loped out of the shadows, fur bristled in agitation.

Quickly, I scanned the garden, probing all the dark corners. The breeze had risen, and the tinkle of the wind chimes set my nerves on edge. Nothing moved in the garden except for the rustling palmettos. But something was out there. Something wasn't right about that wind. It didn't come from any weather front. It came from the other side.

As if to confirm my suspicion, a gust tore at my hair and whipped at my robe. I shivered but held my ground even as Angus growled beside me. I reached down to give him a tense pat, my gaze moving across the yard to where the swing swayed in the breeze. A cloud moved over the moon, throwing the garden into darkness, and I could feel a perverted chill creeping through the shadows toward me. Not Shani or Mariama, I was almost certain, but some unknown spirit that had made its way to me. Some restless phantom seeking my help along with my warmth and energy.

I could see nothing in the darkness. No glowing eyes or aura. No humanlike form floating through the bushes. But I sensed a presence. I could feel it watching me. That dead gaze was like a spider-crawl up my spine.

Was this a test? I wondered. A trial run to see if I had the mettle for a higher calling.

Should I put out a hand? Should I try to make contact?

All of this raced through my mind in the space of

a heartbeat. So paralyzed was I by indecision, I didn't notice at first that the wind had died away. The garden had gone very still as if the night waited in breathless anticipation for my answer.

I didn't move or utter a sound. Neither did I pretend indifference. I stood there with quivering legs and pounding heart, almost daring the ghost to manifest.

In the split second before the moon popped back out, I could have sworn I saw a revealing shimmer. A fusty odor drifted across the garden, mingling with the datura, and I could almost hear the whisper of Papa's voice in my ear. *Go inside, Amelia. Hurry! Do not tempt fate, child. Do not acknowledge another ghost's presence. You are already in far deeper than you know.*

The pavers were cold beneath my bare feet, and the sting of an ant bite had me scurrying back inside.

So much for a higher purpose and a noble calling.

I locked the door and peered out into the darkness, remaining at my vigil for several minutes until Angus whined and brushed up against me for attention. I knelt to pet him before busying myself in the kitchen, rinsing out cups and putting away the tea tin.

As I picked up his bowl to replenish his water before bedtime, I noticed what appeared to be blood smears across the floor, as if he'd nicked a paw on something sharp. Dropping down beside him, I examined each pad, but I couldn't find a wound or any blood. I dampened a paper towel to clean up the floor, and as I turned from the sink, I saw more crimson spots. The blood was coming from me, not Angus.

I danced about, examining first one foot and then the other. As I cleaned away the blood, I saw the glitter of ground glass embedded in my skin. The particles were so fine as to be little more than powder, but the skin had been irritated in several places. Odd, because as far as I knew, nothing had shattered in the garden.

Hobbling to the bathroom, I washed the soles of my feet with antibacterial soap, picked out the glass and then doused the abrasions with peroxide and antiseptic. *There,* I thought as I cleaned up the mess. Surely no germs could survive those precautions.

The chore had given me something concrete to focus on, and now, strangely, I felt much calmer. I crawled into bed, preparing myself for another long night as I stared up at the ceiling, wishing Devlin had stayed.

I fell asleep almost instantly only to awaken sometime later to a powerful thirst. I got up and padded into the kitchen for a glass of water. Angus heard me stir and came out of my office to check his food bowl.

"Sorry. It's not time for breakfast yet."

Those limpid eyes appealed to the pushover in me, and I went to the cupboard to get him a treat. As I turned, I caught a glimpse of the windows in my office. Someone stood gazing in at me.

I didn't turn but kept the silhouette in my periphery. The face had the pale translucence of a ghost, but that could have been an illusion cast by moonlight. I wondered why Angus hadn't growled a warning. Whether human or ghost, he must have sensed another presence. But he merely stood there gobbling his treats with unabashed delight. He never lifted his head, even when another shadow appeared at the backdoor, even when the knob rattled as the intruder tried to force his way in.

I looked around for the phone and couldn't find it. I looked around for a weapon and couldn't find one. It was then that I realized I must be trapped in a dream.

How else to explain Angus's apathy? How else to explain my own strange paralysis?

As I stood there watching helplessly, the dead bolt clicked, and the door flew back with a bang, allowing that wind from the other side to sweep in. My hair blew across my face and, as I peeled it away, I saw Darius Goodwine on the threshold. He looked the same as he had earlier, only now he wore several necklaces, including one that looked like a string of human teeth. In his right hand, he carried a wooden bowl and, in the left, an old leather pouch which he shook to produce a rattle.

Into the bowl, he poured the contents of the pouch—bones, shells, pebbles, nuts and a few coins. Then he knelt and threw these items onto the floor. They formed a pattern which seemed to amuse him greatly.

He looked up, topaz eyes gleaming. "Prepare yourself," he said.

"For what?"

"A long journey."

"Where am I going?"

He turned to stare out into the darkness, and I looked past him to where the dead had assembled in my garden. Their faces were painted a stark white, their bellies open and distended. Drawn by the light, black beetles with large, snapping pincers crawled from the autopsy gashes and scurried into the house. I spotted one scuttling into the cupboard where I kept Angus's treats, and another dashed beneath the stove.

Suddenly, his food bowl teemed with the insects, and he looked up at me with a piteous whimper. The beetles were crawling up his legs and moving down through his fur, attempting to burrow under his skin. He howled in pain, and I dropped to his side, picking them off one by one and flinging them toward the door.

But dozens turned into hundreds. The floor blackened, and I could feel them on me now. They ran up my arms, into my hair and down the collar of my pajamas.

I was still flailing when I woke up. Chest heaving, I flung the covers aside and leaped to my feet as I reached for the light. The bed was clear. My hair was clear. It had just been a dream.

Or a visit from Darius Goodwine.

I resolved myself to staying awake for the rest of the night. I even went back to my office and fetched Dr. Shaw's book.

But my eyes soon grew heavy, and I kept nodding off despite my best efforts. The last thing I remembered hearing was a tree limb scrape against the house. In my drowsy state, it sounded like someone running across the roof.

Twenty-Nine

"Zombie powder," Temple said the next morning as she helped me unload my tools from the back of the SUV. Sometime after Devlin had left my house, he'd arranged to have the car delivered and then texted to let me know where I could find the key. I had to wonder if our conversation had precipitated the dream. In the light of day, it seemed impossible that Darius Goodwine had been able to invade my sleep.

"Ground glass is a common component, along with datura," Temple was saying. "The glass irritates the skin so that the poison is more quickly absorbed into the bloodstream."

"Zombies in Charleston?" I glanced at her in mock horror as I locked my car and deposited the key in my pocket. "Isn't that more of a New Orleans thing?"

"By way of Africa and Haiti. Traditionally, all we have to worry about around here are hags, haints and plat-eyes," she said naming the holy trinity of Lowcountry legends.

"Papa used to tell stories about plat-eyes that would

curl your hair," I said. "Boo hags, too. It got so I was afraid to close my eyes at night for fear one would slip into my room and steal my skin while I slept." But for all my shivering under the covers back then, I'd never really believed in the mythical plat-eye creatures that supposedly gobbled up willful children, nor the hags that shed their own skin at night to inhabit another's. But haint was a colloquialism for ghost, and I'd learned all too soon that they were real.

"I can go you one better," Temple said as we struck out through the weeds toward the cemetery gates. "I once dated a guy from Louisiana whose grandmother practiced voodoo. She claimed when she was a young woman that her brother had been turned into a zombie by a powerful priestess. He was pronounced dead by the local coroner and a funeral and burial ensued. Years later, the sister saw him in New Orleans with that same priestess. The woman had dug him up and kept him as a slave the whole time his family had thought him dead."

"What happened to him?"

"The last the sister knew, he was still with the priestess."

"Why didn't she call the police?"

"Nothing the authorities could do. Nothing she could do, either, because the priestess was too powerful."

"But you don't believe that, do you? Not you, Miss Skeptic."

"Of course I don't believe it. The point is, *she* believed it. And the brother, too, apparently. As far as I'm concerned, voodoo, rootwork, conjure…all different names for the same con, and the stock-in-trade is mystery and persuasion. People want to believe they can obtain the seemingly unattainable, be it love or wealth or protection from their enemies by virtue of a few spells and incantations. That's why they'll spend their last dime on come-to-me potions and go-away-evil candles." She paused while I unlocked the gates. "This man you told me about, this Darius Goodwine. It sounds to me like he's trying to mess with your head. A sliver of doubt is all it takes for a particularly clever con artist to worm his way in."

"But if he possesses no real power, how can he influence me?"

"Mind over matter. Just like all those mishaps we had with Ona Pearl Handy. She created a little doubt and we did the rest to ourselves. Call it the power of suggestion or a self-fulfilling prophecy. The mind has the ability to influence the body on a subconscious level. You know that."

"The ground glass wasn't just in my head, though. I saw the blood."

"Yes, that it is disturbing," she agreed. "Do you normally go outside barefoot? Enough so that it's somewhat of a habit?"

"I don't know about habit, but it's not unusual."

"He'd know that if he's had someone watching you. For whatever reason, this man obviously views you as a threat. And now he's looking to gain the upper hand."

"What should I do?"

"If he's a true believer, you could go to a root doctor and buy some protection. Mind over matter works both ways. But if he's just a snake oil salesman, then the only thing you can do is be on guard. Keep your eyes and ears open. And for God's sake, don't walk around barefoot. If he does anything truly threatening, call the cops. Or Devlin. I have a feeling he'd be only too happy to take care of this guy for you."

Yes, and that was perhaps my biggest fear of all. What Devlin had in store for Darius Goodwine.

I spent the rest of the day cleaning headstones, a tedious project that required hours upon hours of squatting and kneeling so my leg muscles had become quite developed over the years. This was not a job I ever recommended to amateurs because even the gentlest scrubbing could cause damage, particularly to older stones. With every cleaning, a portion of the surface was lost, so one needed to approach the project with conservation rather than restoration as the end goal.

Even in cemeteries where a water supply was readily available, I used non-ionic detergents only rarely, preferring instead the low-tech method of soft bristle brushes, sponges, scrapers and plenty of patience. I always started at the bottom and back of the stone to prevent streaking, and normally, once I became absorbed in the task, time would pass quickly. Today, I kept hauling out my phone to check the clock. Earlier, I'd placed a call to Tom Gerrity's office and left a message. When he returned my call a few minutes later, I pretended to be a potential client in need of his services. If he recognized my name from our previous meeting, he didn't let on. He would be out for most of the day, he said, but would return to the office late in the afternoon and suggested I drop by around six.

I had no idea what could be accomplished by such a visit or even what I would say to him once I got there. I couldn't ask him outright what he had on Dr. Shaw, nor could I pretend to be a friend of the Fremont family looking to hire a private detective. Gerrity had seen me in his office last spring, so even if he hadn't recognized my name, chances were he'd place me the moment I walked through the door. Then he'd remember my connection to Devlin, and given the animosity between the two—not to mention his possible association with Darius Goodwine—I couldn't imagine he'd be all that cooperative.

Moving to the face of the stone, I wet it with the pump sprayer I'd lugged from the car and scraped at the lichen as I ran through a dozen possible scenarios in my head, none of them particularly appealing. Maybe I just needed to trust in the universe, I decided. Have a little faith that Fremont had a reason for sending me to see Gerrity. He had once been called the Prophet, after all, and apparently, some of his soothsayer abilities had been retained after death. The blood he'd foretold on Isabel Perilloux's hands came to mind, but this wasn't about her. This was about Tom Gerrity. What was the worst that could happen if I went to see him? He'd throw me out? Hadn't he basically done that the last time I'd gone to this office?

On and on my thoughts rambled as I continued to work. By the end of the day, I had been rewarded with several lovely inscriptions. As I rinsed away the grime from the final headstone, an anchor appeared, a symbol as old as the catacombs. In its straightforward interpretation, an anchor symbolized hope and steadfastness on the graves of sailors, but in olden times, it had often been used as a disguised cross to guide the devoted and the persecuted to secret meeting places. On this day, I found new significance in the symbol because it reminded me that something as innocuous as an anchor—or a songbird—could have hidden meaning.

At four o'clock, I gathered up my tools and supplies, leaving the heavy water jugs behind so that I wouldn't have to cart them back and forth. Temple had finished her survey of the exhumed graves and left midafternoon. Her job was done. From here on out, I'd be working in the cemetery alone. Maybe it was a blessing I had so many things occupying my thoughts these days. I had little time to brood about the past or worry about the perpetual pall that hung over Oak Grove Cemetery.

Still, as I locked the gates and turned my back on the graveyard, I felt a little chill go through me. I didn't glance over my shoulder but instead ran my gaze along the edge of the woods, searching for movement in the deep shade at the tree line. The sun hung low, but there was still plenty of daylight left. No reason in the world to be frightened, I told myself. And yet…I was.

I tried to shake off the disquiet as I started down the overgrown path to the road. My imagination really was doing a number on me because at one point I could have sworn I heard footsteps behind me. Nothing was there, of course. It was too early for ghosts. Too early even for the shadow beings that stirred just before dusk.

Storing my tools in the back of the SUV, I climbed behind the wheel and turned the ignition. Nothing happened except for a faint, ominous click. The battery was dead, which made no sense since it was fairly new.

I popped the hood and checked the cables, then used one of my wooden scrapers to clear away the chalky corrosion around the posts. Sliding back in, I tried the ignition once more. The engine kicked over immediately, and with a sigh of relief, I hopped out to lower the hood. As I moved back around to the door, I saw that a beetle had climbed onto my shoe, and I bent down to examine it. Unlike the beetles from my dream, which were rounded and huge, this insect had a flattened body and a pale yellow platelike cover near the head.

Goose bumps rose on my arms and at my nape as

I shook it off. Until my dream the previous night, I wouldn't have been disturbed by such a sight. Since childhood, I'd suffered from a mild case of arachnophobia, but insects never worried me, even the giant cockroaches—palmetto bugs—so prevalent along the southeastern coast. Now I had to wonder if the beetle was a warning or a sign. A creepy-crawly with a hidden meaning.

I climbed back into the car and locked the doors as I scanned my surroundings. I told myself I was being ridiculous. Because of a nightmare, I now had a thing about beetles?

But no rationale could convince me that the one crawling on my shoe had been an accident. I no longer believed in the randomness of the universe or the happenstance of everyday occurrences. Everything happened for a reason, and I was very much afraid this current synchronicity would be the death of me.

Thirty

I drove straight home and took Angus for a quick walk, then showered, dressed and headed out again. In a way, it was a relief to have a mission, because it kept me from stewing about that blasted beetle or, worse, worrying how Devlin intended to stop Darius Goodwine.

He'd been adamant that his quarrel with Darius had nothing to do with Mariama, but I was hard-pressed to believe it. Darius and Mariama had been raised together as siblings by their grandmother, Essie, so they must have been close. According to Robert Fremont, there had been many in the community who considered Devlin taboo because of his race and background, and I wouldn't have been surprised to learn that Darius was one of his detractors.

Despite his impressive résumé in academia, he obviously identified closely with the magic and mystique of his heritage, going beyond Essie's teachings as a local root doctor to study and practice with an African shaman in Gabon. By bringing gray dust back to Charleston, he'd placed himself on the wrong side of the law. As a cop's wife, Mariama might have felt she had to make a choice.

Of course, all of that was based on nothing more than wild conjecture, exhaustion and my overstimulated imagination. I reminded myself that time would be better spent on how to approach Tom Gerrity. As I fought my way through the rush hour traffic on Calhoun, I once again tried to decide what I would say to him. I needed a goal for this meeting, something a little more concrete than Fremont's assertion that he felt very strongly about it.

And speaking of Robert Fremont, where was he? He'd told me he would be around if I needed him, so why hadn't he materialized to help me devise a plan? He was the one with the expertise in this partnership, and yet, he'd offered very little in the way of guidance or advice.

I'd never tried to summon a ghost—far from it—but now I focused my thoughts on Fremont, hoping the energy shift would pull him to me. I even said his name aloud three times but to no avail. Either he was unable to come through the veil or he was patently ignoring me, which made no sense because this whole investigation was his idea. He was the one who needed to move on.

By the time I reached Gerrity's street, I was thoroughly annoyed, although some of my irritation might have been due to nerves and lack of sleep. I drew a few calming breaths as I looked for a parking space.

The shabby neighborhood had once been a quaint, residential haven, but developers had ruthlessly crushed many of the lovely old homes. Now squatty monstrosities of progress resided alongside the fading grace of Victorian-style houses with sagging verandas and long-neglected gardens.

Gerrity's office was located in an old, two-story clapboard that hadn't seen a paint job in decades. I couldn't find a space near the building, so I parked one block over and checked the clock. I was nearly half an hour early and decided I'd prefer to pass the time in my locked car rather than loiter in the dingy hallway outside his office.

I settled in to wait, feeling a little drowsy in the sunshine streaming in through the windshield. I'd brought Dr. Shaw's book with me and opened it to the bookmarked page. My eyes soon grew heavy, and I found myself reading the same passage over and over: *Among the early root workers that lived in the Sea Islands and along the Georgia-Carolina coast, divination was a highly prized skill, along with dream interpretation and the ability to recognize omens in nature. With the onslaught of urbanization, omen-reading became a lost art, but foretelling remained strong, among the favored methods, reading tea leaves and "throwing the bones." Candles were almost always used in divination rituals and sometimes a glass of water for scrying.*

I must have drifted off for a few minutes because my eyes flew open with a start. The book had fallen from my hands, and as I leaned over to pick it up, I checked the time. I'd only been asleep for ten minutes or so, but I decided to go ahead and walk over to Gerrity's office. The nap had revived me, and I now felt calmer about the meeting.

The neighborhood was run-down, but despite recent events, I wasn't overly concerned to be out alone. It was still daylight and traffic was heavy. Even so, I walked with my hands in the pockets of my jacket, fingers curled around phone and mace. I nodded to a few passersby on the street, but none of them seemed to notice me. That was a good thing, I decided. Blending in made me less vulnerable.

As I rounded the corner to Gerrity's street, I saw a car double-parked in front of his building. It pulled away as I approached, and the back window lowered. For a moment, I could have sworn I saw the gleam of topaz eyes in the gloom. Startled, I turned to track the car. It made the corner and disappeared.

A tiny kernel of my earlier trepidation returned. I hadn't actually seen anything, but my momentary panic proved just how on edge I was these days. I tried to shake off those lingering jitters as I entered the house.

The once elegant foyer was much as I remembered it from my visit a few months ago. A couple of plastic lawn chairs had been added to the decor, and, if possible, the rug looked even grimier, the Venetian blinds droopier. I didn't think a mop or dust cloth had touched the place in months. It had the musty odor of an attic, and as I climbed the stairs, I couldn't help noticing how eerily silent the building seemed. I suspected most of the tiny offices stood vacant these days, and those businesses that remained had probably closed their doors at five.

On the second floor, I headed all the way to the end of the hallway where Gerrity's office was located. His door was closed, too, but it was just a few minutes before six, so it was possible he was already inside. I tapped on the door and waited for an answer. I heard what I thought was someone moving about, so I knocked a little harder, waited another minute or two and then tried the knob. It turned in my hand, and I opened the door, hovering on the threshold as I warily scanned the dim interior.

A lone candle burned on the floor, the flame flickering wildly from a chilly breeze that blew in through an open window. Not open, I realized almost at once.

Smashed. I could see the glitter of glass fragments on the floor and something else…something that moved among the slivers, although I told myself it was merely reflected candlelight.

My gaze flashed to the desk where papers fluttered like bird wings beneath an upside-down tumbler.

Something obviously wasn't right. I knew I should back away and run out of the building as fast as I could. Darius Goodwine's fingerprints were all over that office. How else to explain the candle? The broken window? The smell of sulfur that lingered?

How else to explain the lethargy that suddenly gripped me?

I thought of those eyes gleaming from the backseat of the car, and suddenly I knew that I had been brought here for a reason. Not by Robert Fremont's ghost but by a man capable of invading my dreams. From the very first, Darius Goodwine had been guiding everything. For what purpose, I didn't yet know, but it had something to do with Devlin. And now with me.

My every instinct warned me to leave, but instead I took a tentative step inside the office. I even called out Gerrity's name, though the space was so small, I didn't see how he could be hidden from me.

I moved toward the desk, my movements almost dreamlike. A beetle had been trapped beneath the tumbler. As if sensing my presence, the frantic insect began to scurry about, trying to climb the glass walls of its prison only to crash back down upon the papers. It fell on its back, legs flailing helplessly, and I had a notion that, like the beetle on my shoe, here was yet another omen—perhaps even a warning—if only I knew how to read it.

I reached for the glass, intent on setting the insect

free, and that was when I saw Tom Gerrity on the floor behind his desk.

At least…I thought it was Gerrity. The man's face was obscured by a moving blackness.

I could see no blood or wound, but the beetles were there for a reason. They'd been attracted by death, and I watched in horror as they crawled in and out of the corpse's eyes and mouth, feeding on the unthinkable.

A scream rose in my throat, but I couldn't utter a sound. Neither could I make my fingers work to call 911. Instead, I stood frozen, something intangible paralyzing me as my gaze remained riveted on that teeming mass. Then I realized what held me immobile. A scent lingered in the air, so weak it might only have been my imagination. Not the sulfuric remnant of a struck match or even the sickly sweet odor of death, but something dark and musky.

I tried to place it, but already the breeze from the broken window had swept the fragrance away, and I was left with nothing more than a creeping dread that someone I knew had been in that office only moments before me.

Out in the hallway, a floorboard creaked beneath stealthy footsteps. I whirled, certain that at any moment Gerrity's killer would open the door and find me standing over his body. That the murderer had probably long since fled the building didn't occur to me. I'd plunged too far down the rabbit hole of panic to think rationally.

I needed to hide, but where? There were no closets, no bathroom. Only one door, only one way in and out except for that smashed window. Glass crunched beneath my feet as I glanced out. A ledge ran the length of the house, but from there it was a two-story drop to concrete.

Whirling, I scanned the office. The only possible place of concealment was beneath the desk, but that meant crawling over the body.

The footsteps were getting closer. I could hear the floor popping right outside the door.

Shuddering, I dropped on all fours and scrambled through the narrow opening, pressing myself up against the back of the desk. One of Gerrity's arms was flung toward me, and it was all I could do to scrunch myself into a small enough ball to avoid touching it.

Hugging my knees, I tried to suppress the sound of my breathing as the door opened.

All was silent for a moment, and then I heard the crinkle of plastic, followed by footsteps rounding the desk. I could see nothing of the assailant, but Gerrity's body shifted, and I realized he was being moved. The arm flopped up against me, dislodging a beetle that crawled up my leg, drawing an uncontrollable shiver.

As the hand moved away from me, I saw the gleam of a silver chain wrapped around the dead man's fingers. A medallion dangled from the end, and I recognized it at once, my mind flashing back to the last time I'd seen it nestled against Devlin's bare chest.

I blinked away the image as I put a finger on the medallion, pressing it to the floor, so that it remained behind as Gerrity's killer dragged him onto the plastic.

Thirty-One

After the killer left with the body, I called Devlin from beneath Gerrity's desk. Never mind that he'd warned me not to contact him. Never mind that I'd found his medallion clinging to a dead man's fingers. He was the only one I wanted to see, the only one who could calm the hysteria bubbling inside me. The idea of his strong arms around me at that moment was irresistible.

When he didn't answer, I left a mostly incoherent voice mail and hung up. It was cowardly of me, but I couldn't bring myself to leave my hiding place. The paralysis turned out to be a very good thing because the killer—or someone—returned to Gerrity's office. Not once, but twice.

I huddled beneath the desk, quaking in fear and shuddering in horror as another beetle crept up my arm, inching ever closer to my face. Finally, I could stand it no longer and flicked it away. I heard the click as the shell hit the floor, and then, I could have sworn, the scurry of those tiny feet.

As the killer moved about the office, I tracked other

sounds. The shuffle of papers. The metallic clang of file drawers being opened and closed. The occasional rasp of an impatient breath. And then the echo of retreating footsteps for the final time.

Still, I waited. I didn't know how many minutes passed before I worked up enough courage to crawl from my hiding place. The body was gone, the beetles were gone and the candle had been snuffed. Nothing remained of the violence that had been done there, and for a moment I questioned whether I might have been dreaming. But the cramps in my legs and back felt very real.

Breathing deeply to quiet my nerves, I slipped across the room and listened at the door for footsteps or any sound at all that would alert me to danger. I wasn't sure what terrified me the most—the idea of remaining hidden in that room or venturing out into the hallway, into the open.

I had no idea if Devlin had even gotten my message, and I flirted briefly with the notion of calling 911. But that little matter of the medallion plagued me. Devlin's wasn't unique. Anyone who belonged to the Order of the Coffin and the Claw would own a similar talisman. And yet…I somehow knew the one clutched in my hand belonged to Devlin. I just didn't know—and was afraid to speculate—how it had come to be entwined around Tom Gerrity's cold, lifeless fingers, as though he'd yanked it from Devlin's neck before he died.

But I refused to entertain even a moment's doubt. I knew Devlin's character well enough by now. He had his secrets and, God knew, a dark enough past, but he was not a murderer. On that I would stake my life.

I eased into the hall and made my way to the stairs,

pausing once again to listen. Was that a footfall? The soft thud of a door closing?

A floorboard creaked somewhere in the building. I couldn't tell if the sound came from behind or in front of me, nor did I stop to find out. Adrenaline and panic drove me headlong down the stairs, and then I drew up short as a silhouette emerged from the gloom in the foyer. I wavered on the stairs, not knowing whether to go up or down or to try and make a dash for the door.

Then as the shadow came forward, I saw that it was Devlin. He stood at the bottom of the steps, dressed darkly as always, staring up at me. *"Amelia?"*

I flung myself at him, and he caught me awkwardly with one arm, letting me savor his warmth for a moment before holding me gently away from him. I didn't want to go, and so I clung shamelessly to the lapel of his jacket. I wanted to stay nestled against that hard chest forever, drinking in the essence of him, that dark blend of mystery and magnetism that belonged only to him.

With an effort I pulled myself together. "Thank God you got my message," I said on a breath.

His gaze shot past me up the stairs, and even in the dim light that managed to penetrate the grimy windows, I saw a telling puzzlement in his eyes as he searched the shadows above us.

I turned to follow his gaze with a shiver. "We should go."

My urgency didn't seem to penetrate because he took his time scouring first the landing and then my face before he drew me back into the shadowy corner from which he had materialized. His grasp was firm and comforting, but I wanted to be back in his arms, encased so tightly that our heartbeats sounded as one. Never had his presence affected me so strongly. Never had I needed him more than I did at that moment, but something wasn't right about his demeanor. Outwardly, he seemed in perfect control, as stoic and elegant as ever, but I could sense his tension and a carefully suppressed agitation that made me think of the silver medallion stuffed in my pocket. Why I didn't haul it out and present it to him then and there, I wasn't quite certain.

He lowered his voice, but the echo of it vibrated through the murk, giving my pulse an extra kick of adrenaline. "Are you all right?"

"Yes, but…we have to get out of here." My own voice was little more than a quivering rasp.

His hands slid up to grasp my forearms. "Tell me what happened. Quickly."

"But he could still be up there," I whispered frantically. "We have to *go*."

He held me firmly in place. "Calm down and tell what happened."

"Tom Gerrity's dead," I blurted.

His fingers dug into my flesh, and when I winced, he eased up at once. "How do you know?"

"I found the body a little while ago in his office. At least…I think it was Tom Gerrity. His face was covered with beetles."

"Beetles? What are you talking about?"

"Insects. I know it sounds strange but I saw them."

His gaze narrowed. "Are you sure you weren't dreaming or hallucinating?"

"I was wide awake and perfectly lucid. And I'm telling you his body was covered in them." A shudder went through me. "One was trapped beneath a glass, and I think it was left as a message or a warning. And I think Darius meant for me to find that body."

"*Darius?* He was here?" The emotion that flashed across Devlin's face made my blood run cold.

I said hesitantly, "I didn't see him, but I dreamed about beetles last night and I saw one today on my shoe. And now this—" I broke off, glancing wildly around the foyer as though Darius might be lurking in the shadows. "It has to be a sign, doesn't it?"

"A sign of what?"

"I don't know. My own death maybe."

Devlin gave me a little shake. "Don't do that. You're letting him get to you."

"I know, but it was just so terrifying."

Devlin still held me, but I could tell his mind had gone elsewhere. He was looking past me again as if trying to picture the scene I'd just described to him.

When he started toward the stairs, I grabbed his arm. "Where are you going?"

"I need to have a look around."

"You won't find Gerrity. The body's been moved. He was wrapped in plastic and dragged away."

"How long were you up there?" Devlin's voice held an edge of something I couldn't quite name.

"Fifteen, twenty minutes. Maybe a little longer. I lost track of time." It had still been daylight when I arrived, but now sunset had come and gone. We were on the cusp of twilight and any moment now, Devlin's ghosts would come through. I searched behind him for that dreaded glimmer.

For the first time, a chink appeared in his armor. "Why did you come here in the first place?" he asked sharply.

I blinked at his tone. "Does that matter right now? I think we should just get out of here."

"Yes, it matters. A man's dead, according to you. The police will want to know what you were doing here."

"But you are the police."

"For now," he muttered.

"What does that mean?"

"Just tell me why you're here. The truth. It's important."

"I came to talk to Gerrity."

"What about?"

I sighed. "It's a long story. It has to do with blackmail—"

He looked down at me incredulously. "How in God's name do you know about the blackmail?"

I drew back in shock, my gaze searching his face. "I overheard a conversation between Gerrity and Dr. Shaw. I'll tell you everything I know about it, but...can we get out of here first?" I glanced around nervously. "If he's not here now, he could come back at any time."

"Are you sure the killer was male?"

"No, but whoever it was didn't seem to have much trouble moving the body."

Devlin's hands came back up to tighten around my arms. "Did you see anything? The killer's shoes? Clothing? Anything at all?"

"I couldn't see anything. I was hidden underneath the desk."

"Thank God," he said, still in that strange tone. "Where are you parked?"

I gave a vague wave. "A block over."

"Go there now," he said. "Get in your car, lock the doors and drive straight home. Don't talk to anyone about this."

"What are you going to do?"

His gaze moved back to the stairs. "I have things to take care of here."

"Aren't you going to call for backup?" I asked naively.

He hesitated. "If I need it."

A minute ago I had been all but pleading with him to leave. Now I heard myself say plaintively, "Why can't I stay here with you?"

"Because you said yourself it's not safe."

"But I'm a witness. *You* said the police would want to talk to me."

"Not if I can help it."

His tone alarmed me, and I felt the iciest chill slide down my spine, tapping the fear that had been niggling at me since I'd seen him at the bottom of the stairs. "Did you already know about Gerrity?"

He scowled down at me. "Why would you ask that?"

I bit my lip, trying to suppress a suspicion I didn't want to blossom. "You got here so quickly and you seemed surprised to see me. And now you're so anxious to send me away." I clutched his arm. "You never got my message, did you? That's not why you're here."

"Go home, Amelia."

"What aren't you telling me?" I whispered.

"Go home and wait for me. I'll be there as soon as I can."

He took a step back from me, and my hand fell away. "If that's what you want."

"It is." His dark gaze burned into mine. "I need you away from here. I need you safe."

That would have been the perfect time to show him the medallion I'd found in Gerrity's office, but I said nothing. I was too afraid of my own suspicions.

As I watched him disappear up the stairs, I had to battle the impulse to follow, but the last thing I wanted was to cause him any trouble, so for now I would do as he asked. I would go home and wait on pins and needles to hear from him.

Halfway back to my car, I realized the hand that had clutched his arm was smeared with blood.

I was still staring at that blood a few minutes later when I climbed into the SUV.

Was that Devlin's blood on my hand? It had to be. I hadn't seen any in Gerrity's office, and I wasn't hurt. Although it was certainly possible I'd come into contact with it without even realizing it.

But what about Devlin's odd behavior and the fact that he'd arrived at Gerrity's office so quickly? If my frantic plea for help hadn't brought him there, what had?

Too many questions swirled in my head. I felt overwhelmed and weighed down by my suspicions. I kept telling myself I could do nothing but go home and wait for Devlin. I had to trust that my questions would be answered and my doubts laid to rest all in good time.

Safely sequestered inside my car, I dug through the console for the pack of wet-naps I kept stored there. As I scrubbed the blood from my hand, I detected a stealthy movement in my periphery. Under normal circumstances, I would have shown no outward reaction. All my years of living with ghosts had steadied my nerves. But it wasn't every day one found a dead body covered in beetles, so I was a little off my game and I whirled with a start.

A woman with matted blond hair shuffled up to the car, and my finger went automatically to the lock button even though the mechanism had engaged when I closed the door. I saw no weapon, and from her tattered clothing, I took her for one of the homeless that gathered in nearby Marion Square. She was probably just looking for a handout, but my every instinct sounded a warning as she peered into my window.

Her unblinking stare chilled me. The irises of her eyes were colorless and frosted as though afflicted with cataracts, but she was a young woman. Her skin was unlined, her complexion pale and translucent. My heart went out to her. She was so painfully scrawny I wondered how long she'd been on the street.

I remembered something Devlin had said about some of the unfortunate souls who made their way back from a gray dust trip. His description fit this woman perfectly—glazed eyes, a shuffling walk as though she'd dragged something back from hell with her.

She wasn't a ghost. I was almost certain of that, unless she had the same ability as Robert Fremont to present herself as human.

"Will you help me?" Her voice through the glass sounded flat and defeated, and I had the unwise urge to take her home and feed her a decent meal.

Digging in my bag, I found some bills and lowered the window just enough to shove them through. "Please, take them," I said. "That's all I have on me."

The money fluttered to the ground unnoticed. "Will you help me?" she repeated in that same, strange monotone. Her voice, those eyes…everything about her deeply troubled me. If not money, what did she want?

Anxiously, I scanned the street behind her as I reached for my phone. "Are you hurt?" I asked through the window. "Should I call somebody?"

"Will you help me?"

"I'm calling 911—"

"Will *you* help me?" The inflection was barely perceptible, but it stopped me cold.

I clutched my phone. "What do you want me to do?"

"Make it go away."

I swallowed in dread. "I don't know what you mean."

She was still muttering as she turned to shuffle away, back bowed like that of an old woman.

It was only after she reached the shadow of a nearby building that I saw the fragile, glimmering outline of the ghost that clung to her.

Thirty-Two

As soon as I got home, I went straight to the bathroom, stripped and took a shower. I'd scrubbed all the blood away earlier, but I could still feel those beetles crawling over me. I stayed under the hot water for only a few minutes, though, because I was afraid of missing Devlin's call. Dressing warmly in jeans, boots and a thick sweater, I took Angus out for a quick walk around the block, but I could hardly enjoy our time together. My mind kept bouncing from Gerrity's murder to Devlin's medallion to that poor girl on the street who had wanted my help.

How had she known to come to me? Was this yet another door that I'd inadvertently opened?

I longed for the time when Papa's rules had kept me safe, but those days were long gone. My life was changing in ways that I could hardly imagine—didn't *want* to imagine—but there was no going back. Papa had warned me about the dangers of falling for a haunted man, but even now, I couldn't bring myself to wish

Devlin from my life. He was too important to me. He was everything to me.

My fingers curled around the medallion in my pocket, and I rubbed my thumb over the cool texture as though the talisman could somehow connect us. Where was he? I wondered desperately. Why hadn't he called?

The breeze blowing through the trees sounded like whispers, and I found myself huddling in my sweater as I hurried Angus along. I remembered thinking how close the spirit world had seemed on that night I'd gone to Devlin's house. The nip in the wind had been unusual, a sudden gust tainted by the frost of death. I felt that same chill now, and my skin rippled as I sensed the stealthy creep of a ghost.

I kept my head lowered and accelerated my pace. Angus growled a warning and dropped back beside me, my constant protector. I murmured to him in a soothing tone as we sped down the darkened street toward home, the unknown phantom at our heels.

They were coming out of the woodwork now, seeking me out as though I emitted a ghostly signal. I wouldn't be able to ignore them for much longer because, like Robert Fremont and Shani, like that poor girl on the street, the spirits came to me for a reason. And they wouldn't go away until I found a way to give them what they wanted.

A little while later, I sat down at my desk and opened my laptop. Now that the shock of finding Gerrity's body had subsided, I could think about that whole scene a little more rationally, and I decided to do some research on those beetles. Scrolling through insect photographs, I quickly identified the one that had crawled onto my shoe at the graveyard. The name was hardly a comfort. *Necrophila americana.* A carrion beetle.

No doubt the beetles on Gerrity's body had been carrion, as well, but their arrival to a carcass was usually preceded by blowflies. I'd seen no other insects or any other evidence of decomposition except for a very slight scent that may or may not have been the odor of death.

I'd talked to Gerrity only that morning when he informed me he would be out for most of the day. Assuming he'd only returned to the office at five or so, he couldn't have been dead for more than an hour when I arrived. Much too early for an insect infestation, I would think.

Plus, the killer had still been in the building. Or at least, *someone* had dragged off the body and then returned to go through the files. If that someone hadn't been the murderer, why take the time to wrap and dispose of the corpse? Why light a candle and trap one of the beetles underneath that glass if not to send a message or a warning?

The beetles from my dream were a little harder to identify, which wasn't surprising. My imagination had undoubtedly created a hybrid. The closest I could come was a cross between a scarab and an African Goliath.

The longer I read, the more intrigued I became with insect folklore and mythology. That I was seeing beetles all of a sudden meant something. They played an important role in divination and were considered both the bringers of good luck and ill fortune and, in some cases, the harbingers of death.

The sound of the doorbell startled me from my research, and I hurried down the hallway to peer through the side window only to draw back in surprise. My visitor wasn't Devlin as I had hoped, but Clementine

Perilloux. I hesitated to open the door because I didn't want company when Devlin arrived. And truth be told, Fremont's premonition of blood on Isabel's hands had made me a little wary of both Perilloux sisters. But my car was in the drive, and I was fairly certain she'd spotted me at the window.

I opened the door to greet her and she smiled nervously. "I'm so sorry to drop in on you like this. I know I must look a fright," she said, tucking back an unruly strand of hair.

I would never describe her appearance as frightful, but she was a bit unkempt. She'd tossed on an old baggy sweater over leggings, and messy tendrils crept loose from her ponytail, giving her the disheveled air of someone who had left home in a great hurry.

"It's fine," I said. "But how did you know where I lived?"

"John sent me."

My breath caught and I moved back from the door. "Come in."

"No, I can't stay. In fact…" She paused to glance over her shoulder, and I began to grow uneasy. The drama of this night seemed unending. "I'm here to collect you," she said.

"I beg your pardon?"

"I'm to take you to Isabel's house."

An alarm sounded inside my head. "Why?"

"John is waiting for you there."

"Why is he at Isabel's house?" My tone was much too sharp, and I saw Clementine wince. "Sorry. I didn't mean to snap at you. You caught me by surprise."

"I know. And I'm sorry for that."

"Why is he there?" I said in a more even tone. She had no idea what that detachment cost me.

"He didn't think it a good idea to come here, and he couldn't go to the emergency room."

"Emergency room?" Her words frightened me, and my heart started to pound as I thought instantly of that blood on my hand. "He's hurt? How bad?" Even as I bombarded her with questions, I reached for my jacket.

"He'll be fine," Clementine assured me. "Isabel fixed him up. She's had some medical training. Anyway, all I know is that I'm to bring you to him."

"Just let me call the dog inside." I left her hovering in the doorway while I went to summon Angus. He came eagerly, no doubt hoping for some attention. I checked his water bowl and then hurried back to Clementine.

"I'll follow you over there," I said as we went down the porch steps.

"No, you're to ride with me," she said. "He was very clear about that."

"Did he say why?"

"Your car shouldn't be seen there."

"This is all very cloak-and-dagger," I said shakily.

"Yes, and quite nerve-racking," she agreed. "I don't handle this type of excitement all that well, I'm afraid. Isabel is the rock."

"Would you like me to drive?"

"It's only a few blocks. I'll be fine," she said as we climbed into her car.

I had hoped she would take me up on the offer because being behind the wheel would have given me a measure of control. It was a little reckless to place my trust in a woman I barely knew, and I berated myself for not having taken the time to call Devlin's cell phone. It was too late now. We were off, and my fate was already in her hands.

As I watched her grip the wheel, I thought again of

Robert Fremont's vision about Isabel. *She has killed or will kill in the very near future.*

And yet, there I was, hurrying off into the night with her sister.

Clementine shot me a glance as we sped along the street. "I had no idea you even knew John Devlin. Why didn't you say so that morning in my garden?"

"I don't know. It was awkward. I wasn't sure how to bring it up."

"Are you two—"

"It's complicated."

"Meaning you don't want to talk about?"

"No, it really is complicated," I murmured. She had no idea. "Are you sure he's okay?"

"Don't worry. He's in good hands."

I turned to watch the passing scenery without comment.

"I knew something would happen today," Clementine said as she slowed for a traffic light.

"How so?"

"My grandmother saw something in her tea leaves this morning. She's rarely ever wrong. But then, you don't put much stock in that sort of thing, do you?"

"I never said. I just don't like to have my fortune told. The future is a little scary to me."

"Why?"

I watched the light with a frown. "A lot of strange things have been happening to me lately and I had a very disturbing dream last night. I think it means something."

"What was the dream?" she asked curiously. "That is, if you don't mind telling me."

"I dreamed about beetles and now I'm seeing them everywhere."

She glanced at me in alarm. "You haven't stepped on any, have you?"

"Not to my knowledge."

"That would be very bad," Clementine said. "Especially if you find one in your house. But beetles in a dream…that's interesting."

I turned to study her profile. "Interesting good or interesting bad?"

"Beetles are signs. If you dream about one, it means you have a destructive force at work in your life and a lot of negative energy surrounding you."

Her words struck a chord. "What should I do about this destructive force?"

"My grandmother would tell you to pay attention to your nocturnal activities to see if you can pick up on any more signs. Be wary of unexpected journeys and be especially mindful of synchronicities."

I pulled my jacket more tightly around me. "Synchronicities?"

"According to Grandmother, when you experience a series of what she calls meaningful coincidences, it's because they've been arranged by your spirit guide and should never be ignored."

"This all sounds vaguely new-agey," I said. "I'm not even sure I know what a spirit guide is."

"Some people call them angels, others think of them as energy. To some they may appear as the ghost of an ancestor." She gave me another curious scrutiny. "I'm very surprised that someone like you isn't more in tune with your guide."

"Someone like me?"

"You have a quality about you," she said. "An aura. It's like a warm light. Almost a beacon, I would say. I find it very soothing."

My mind drifted back to Rosehill Cemetery and to the first ghost I'd ever encountered. I hadn't given much thought to the old white-haired man since my return from Asher Falls where I'd seen him for the second time, but now there he was in my head. For what purpose, I had no idea. Papa had been afraid of him, and so I was afraid of him, too. But maybe he had appeared to me that day for a reason. Maybe, like Shani, he was trying to tell me something.

Maybe every ghost that had ever crossed my path had tried to tell me something, but Papa's rules had kept me from listening.

It was an unsettling thought.

Clementine murmured something, and I turned back to her. "I'm sorry?"

"You said you were seeing beetles everywhere."

"Yes. Earlier, I saw one on my shoe at the cemetery." And then later, all over a dead man's face.

"On your shoe?" she asked anxiously.

"Yes, why? Does that mean something?"

"A beetle crawling across your shoe is considered a death omen."

Thirty-Three

Clementine pulled to the curb in front of Isabel's house, and my gaze went immediately across the street to the Charleston Institute for Parapsychology Studies. The lights were still on, and I wondered if Dr. Shaw was there alone or if Layla might still be around.

I hadn't thought much about her since my conversation with Temple, but the fact that I'd seen the woman in the blue Victorian house on America Street had to mean something. I didn't trust her nor the circumstances of her employment at the Institute, particularly if she had close ties to Goodwine. I still couldn't forget that Dr. Shaw's first episode had occurred right after she'd brought him the tea.

Clementine turned off the engine. "Is something wrong?"

"No, sorry. I was just lost in thought for a minute."

We went through the front garden and up the porch steps together. Clementine let us in, then led me down a dim hallway toward the back of the house. The door to the bathroom stood open, and I caught a glimpse of

Isabel at the sink washing her hands. She looked up as we walked by, and my heart gave a little jerk as our gazes met briefly in the mirror. Then she reached over and closed the door. The eye contact lasted no more than a split second, but I felt unnerved by her stare.

At the end of the hallway, Clementine opened a door through which a soft light spilled. The blinds had been drawn to shut out the night and a lamp glowed from one corner. Candles had been lit, too, which struck me as an odd touch for this occasion.

Clementine stepped aside for me to enter, and I saw that Devlin waited for me in the room. He turned when he heard the door, and I caught my breath. He was shirtless, and the play of candlelight over skin and lean muscle ignited an unwise impulse. I couldn't tear my gaze from him.

He reached for his shirt and I noticed then the bandage on his left forearm. Isabel's handiwork, I thought, and wondered briefly if the blood that Fremont had envisioned on her hands had, in fact, been Devlin's. I didn't want to resent her. She'd patched him up, according to Clementine, and I knew I should be grateful, but her first aid was yet another intimacy between them.

Clementine backed out of the room and closed the door softly behind her. I went straight to Devlin. "Are you all right?"

"It's just a cut. Nothing serious."

A dot of blood had already seeped through the bandage. "Are you sure you don't need to see a doctor?"

"Isabel went to medical school. She knows what she's doing."

"And now she's a palmist."

He gave a careless shrug. "That makes her no less skilled."

"No, of course not." I wondered if he felt camaraderie with her because of the choice she'd made. He'd gone to law school but instead of joining his family's prestigious firm, he'd enrolled in the police academy. In that respect, the two of them had far more in common than he and I ever would.

Then I reminded myself sternly that this wasn't a competition. Whatever his history with Isabel, he'd sent for me. He'd wanted me here, and that was the only thing that should matter.

He struggled into his shirt, but as he reached for the buttons, I made a choice. Putting my hand on his chest, I said, "No, leave it."

Heat flared in his eyes, and he pulled me to him roughly, kissing me deeply. I clung to him for the longest time, shiver after shiver rocking me. His hand moved to my breast, his lips to my ear. A flick of his tongue, a dark whisper. My head dropped back as I savored the slow, perfect seduction.

Finally we broke apart and he cupped my face, dark eyes burning into mine. "Do you have any idea how much I want you?" he said on a ragged breath. "I can't stop thinking about that night at my house. I can't stop thinking about you."

His confession both thrilled and terrified me. He wasn't yet free of his ghosts, might never be free of them, so where did that leave us? With a life half lived before twilight?

I sighed. "I think about you, too."

He pulled back. "Even when you were in Asher Falls?"

"Especially when I was in Asher Falls."

"Good," he said, and kissed me again.

Now it was I who drew away, searching for his

ghosts. Had the candles kept them at bay? Or that faint scent of sage and incense? Where were they? I didn't trust their absence.

"What are you looking for?" he asked.

He still held me loosely as I glanced over his shoulder. "Nothing. I was just wondering about all these candles."

"Isabel lit them."

I didn't like the way he said her name. It reminded me of the way he said *my* name, and I wanted to believe he reserved that aristocratic drawl just for me.

"Isn't it lucky that she was here to take care of you?" I said coolly, not at all proud of my jealousy.

"She's always been good in a crisis."

"I can imagine."

"She reminds me of you in that respect."

I sent him a frown. "I don't think we're at all alike."

"But you've only met her once." His eyes glinted as if my annoyance amused him. "You don't know anything about her."

"I know she's very beautiful." Then I added meaningfully, "And apparently good with her hands."

"Hardly an undesirable trait," he said.

I was glad that he could find humor in the situation, because I saw none. "How did you cut your arm?"

He sobered instantly. "I got careless."

He was still staring down at me, and despite my momentary irritation, I knew those eyes might yet be my undoing.

And just like that, I found myself once again swimming in very dangerous waters, craving desperately what could never be mine.

"The kind of carelessness that comes from breaking the glass in a second-story window?" I asked.

He lifted a brow in surprise. "How did you know?"

I pulled out the silver medallion and placed it in his palm.

His fingers curled around the chain, as he said in disbelief, "You've had it the whole time?"

"I found it in Gerrity's office. Is that why you were in the building? Did you return to look for the medallion?"

An emotion flashed in his eyes.

"Yes."

"So you really didn't get my message." I glanced away, rattled by his confession. "Why did you break into Gerrity's office?"

"He had something of mine and I wanted it back."

"You don't mean the necklace, I take it."

"No. Something far more dangerous."

My pulse accelerated at the hard glitter in his eyes. He was usually so stoic, but now I sensed a recklessness in him that wasn't altogether unappealing. "So you broke in. Just like that."

"I had no choice. I'd already searched his house."

I shook my head. Reckless, indeed.

"Now I have a question for you," he said. "Why didn't you tell me earlier that you'd found my medallion?"

"I was afraid to."

"Because you thought I killed Gerrity?"

"It crossed my mind," I admitted. "But only for a moment. All of your vague warnings about keeping our distance and remaining silent should you disappear and now this clandestine meeting at Isabel's house…" I spread my hands helplessly. "You must understand how confusing all this is to me."

He turned to glance restlessly around the room. "I

didn't want to get you involved. I wanted to keep you safe."

"It's too late for that, I think. I burned that bridge when I didn't report Gerrity's murder."

"But you did report it. You told me. So your hands are clean."

"I'm not even worried about that," I said with my own careless abandon. "I just want to know that you're all right. Please tell me I shouldn't worry."

He seemed to consider the pros and cons of a confession, and then said tensely, "We should sit."

We moved to a small sofa positioned in front of the windows and he drew me down beside him. He put an arm around my shoulders, pulling me close, and I settled in against him. Even after everything he'd been through that night, he still smelled so good. I closed my eyes and took a depth breath, committing that scent to memory so that I could savor it later in my dreams.

"You asked if I'd gone to see Darius after the accident," he said.

"And you said that you didn't remember anything about that night. Just vague memories that didn't make sense."

"That is what I said," he agreed. "But the truth is, I did go see him."

I pulled back so that I could study his face. "For gray dust?"

"Yes."

"You must have been very desperate." I mentally kicked myself. What a stupid observation. He'd lost his wife and daughter only hours earlier. Of course he'd been desperate. Desperate enough to demand that Dr. Shaw help him contact their ghosts. Desperate enough to take a drug that stopped his heart in the hopes of entering the spirit world to find them. This was a side of Devlin that I'd only ever glimpsed before, but it made me think that perhaps we had more in common than I knew.

"What happened?"

"I woke up sometime later in Chedathy Cemetery," he said, watching the flicker of the candles with a brooding frown.

I wanted to ask him about his gray dust journey, but instead, I said, "And Robert Fremont. Did you see him as well that night?"

"Not alive. He was already dead when I came to. He'd been shot in the back."

"But you didn't report it. The papers said the body was found the next day."

"No, I didn't report it." He glanced at me. "I'm not trying to excuse my actions. I did a lot of things back then that I'm not proud of. But I was still under the influence of the drug, operating in a dream state. None of what I saw or did seemed real."

"Did you see...ghosts?"

He ran a hand over his eyes. "I'm not sure what I saw. It was all very disjointed. Surreal. Even so, some part of me must have had the presence of mind to realize that after a public argument with Robert Fremont, I shouldn't be found in the cemetery with his dead body."

"So you just left?"

"I don't remember leaving. I don't even remember driving home. But I woke up the next evening in my own bed, and my car was parked in the driveway. The previous twelve hours were completely lost to me. Ethan told me later that the police had been by that afternoon. They already knew about the argument with Robert. Someone had overheard me threaten him."

"*Did* you threaten him?"

He stared grimly into the candle flame. "Mariama let it slip one day that she might be going away. Since I knew about the affair, it wasn't hard to put two and two together. She mostly said it to goad me, but I lost my temper, which I'm sure was her intent. I told her, and later Robert, that I didn't give a damn what they did, but if they ever tried to take Shani away from me, I would kill them both."

"Oh, John."

He didn't try to excuse or soften. He merely shrugged. "You can see why the Beaufort County detectives were interested in me."

It was a sordid tale, and I really didn't want to hear any more. It was like peeking through the keyhole of Devlin's past, and I didn't feel right about picking apart his most painful and private memories. But I also couldn't help him if I didn't know the complete truth.

"They had no proof against you. And Ethan gave you an alibi."

"Actually, there was proof. A smoking gun," Devlin said. "They just weren't able to find it."

"What do you mean?"

"The ballistics report revealed that Robert had been shot with a .38. My service weapon was a 9mm Glock. But I also had a .38 registered in my father's name. I kept the gun locked in a drawer in my office at home. After I heard about the report, I went to check. The gun was missing from the case."

"You think it was the one used in the shooting?"

"I'm almost certain of it."

"Who had access? Or even knew about it?"

"My grandfather knew about it. And Mariama."

"But she died before Robert was murdered," I said.

"And, anyway, if she planned to go away with him, why would she kill him?"

"She could have told someone else about the gun."

"Like who?"

"Darius."

Another shiver crawled up my spine. "Why would she tell him?"

"They were very close. Like brother and sister. He hated me for taking her away from what he considered her rightful place. He wanted her to go back to Africa with him, but instead she chose to stay in Charleston with me. It was the only time she ever went against him. She was the most headstrong woman I ever knew, but Darius held some kind of power over her. If he wanted the gun, she would have given it to him."

"Even if she knew he meant to murder an innocent man?"

"Yes."

His blunt answer shocked me. How could he have stayed with such a woman for so long? What kind of hold did she have on him?

"Robert and I both knew that Darius was bringing in gray dust," Devlin said. "It was hard to go after him because no one wanted to admit such a drug existed. And because he was—*is*—well connected. But people were dying from that stuff, and we were both determined to shut him down."

"And yet, you, yourself, took the very drug that you knew to be potentially lethal."

"Yes."

I put a hand to my forehead, trying my best to process his story.

"I did warn you," he said softly. "You don't know me. You have no idea about my past."

I was painfully aware of that.

"Should I go on?" he asked.

I nodded.

"It was only a matter of time before we collected enough evidence to make an arrest. Darius must have felt the heat, so he came up with a plan to kill Robert and have me take the fall. I was the perfect patsy. I had means, motive and opportunity. And that night, I played right into his hands."

"But I don't understand. How could he have known that you would come to see him? Or that Robert would be in Chedathy Cemetery at just the right time? That's all too convenient."

"Not if Darius arranged to meet Robert in the cemetery after he'd seen me."

"Did Darius already know about Shani and Mariama?"

"Yes. Otherwise, he would have suspected a trap. He would never have given me the drug."

"So, you were supposed to be found in the cemetery with Robert's dead body and your bloodstream full of an illegal substance that may or may not be anything more than a powerful hallucinogen."

"That's what I think, yes."

"But the .38 wasn't found in the cemetery. If Darius was trying to set you up, why didn't he leave the weapon?"

"That's just it. I'm sure he did leave it. Someone else must have come into the cemetery and taken it."

"Who?"

"I don't know for certain, but I've always suspected Tom Gerrity."

I felt my eyes widen in shock. *"Gerrity?"*

"He came to me after the shooting. He said he had

proof that I was in the cemetery that night, and he could make things very difficult for me if I didn't pay up."

"Did he have the gun?"

"He didn't come right out and say so, but in the two years since that night, no one else has made contact."

"Did you pay him off?"

"I called his bluff. Gerrity had been on the take for most of his career. With very little effort, I could have dug up enough dirt to make things just as uncomfortable for him. He knew that. It became a standoff until Darius returned to Charleston."

"And you decided to go after him again."

Devlin was still gazing into the candle flame. "You said you followed Gerrity to a house on America Street. He was probably hoping to make a deal with Darius."

"No wonder you were so desperate to find that gun. That is what you were looking for tonight, I assume."

"Yes. But I was too late."

"So, who do you think killed Gerrity?"

"Darius, of course. Probably with the gun he bought from Gerrity. There's an irony for you."

"But you didn't see the body. How do you know he was shot?"

"An educated guess."

I glanced at him fearfully. "If that gun turns up now, it can be traced back to Robert's murder. If the police find out that you were in the cemetery the night he was shot and that you broke into Gerrity's office on the day he was murdered…"

"Means, motive and opportunity," Devlin said grimly.

"What are you going to do?"

"I have to find that gun before the body turns up."

"That won't be easy if Darius has it. Ethan said he has devotees all over Charleston."

"I'm not without my own connections in this city," Devlin said, rubbing his thumb over the silver medallion.

"So, this is why you didn't want to go to the hospital," I said slowly.

"There's a broken window in a dead man's office. Not a good time for me to be treated for a cut arm," he said.

"And it's why you said we should keep our distance."

He put his hand on my knee. "I didn't want Darius coming after you to get to me."

"He already knows about me. And there's no way to stop him because he can come to me in my dreams."

"That's ridiculous," Devlin said. "The only power he has is the power you give him. Don't let him get to you. Don't let him in."

"I think it's too late," I whispered as a draft blew out of nowhere to snuff out the candles.

Thirty-Four

"It's just a draft," Devlin said. "Someone probably opened the front door."

I sat there shivering in the lamplight. It wasn't just a draft. I could feel a death chill seeping down into my bones. Darius was coming. Or was it Mariama?

"Can't you feel it?" I whispered.

"Feel what?"

"The cold. It's like an icy breath."

"I don't feel anything."

He was lying. I could see it in his eyes. He knew something was in that room with us. He just didn't want to admit it.

I watched a large beetle crawl down the wall and disappear into a crack in the plaster.

"There are things in this world that can't be explained," I said. "You must know that. Why else would you have taken gray dust?"

He glanced away. "I already told you. I was desperate that night. Out of my mind with grief."

"I think you've tried to convince yourself of that

for a very long time. But when you lost Shani, you retreated back into your belief in the supernatural. You never would have gone to see Dr. Shaw or Darius unless there was some part of you that still believed you could contact the other side."

He looked shattered for a moment, but the mask slipped quickly back into place. "Why are you doing this?"

"I have to make you open your eyes."

"To what?"

I took the medallion from his hand. "You can't fight Darius with this. The Order can't help you. You have to accept what he's capable of so you can be on guard. So you can find a way to protect yourself."

"And just what do you think he's capable of?"

"I have no idea," I said with a shudder. "But I have a feeling we're about to find out."

Isabel drove me home a little while later. Clementine had already left, and Devlin was still of the mind that it would be best if we weren't seen together. I could only shake my head at his stubbornness. Darius already knew about me. He'd come to me in a dream. He'd trapped that beetle in Gerrity's office so that I would find it, and he'd been there tonight at Isabel's. He would come to me again. Of that I was certain. I just didn't know when or how. Or what he ultimately wanted.

So I had accepted Isabel's offer of a ride because it seemed easier to acquiesce than to come up with a suitable excuse.

We rode in silence for a few minutes until I finally got up enough nerve to broach the subject of Devlin.

"How long have you known John?"

She gave me an enigmatic glance. "We go back a long way."

"Really?" I wished that I could relax in her company, but she was so much more reserved than Clementine. I wondered if her cordial facade masked some resentment toward me, but she was probably a far better person than I. "He's lucky he could come to you for help tonight."

"I'm just glad all those years of med school could be put to some use."

"Why did you leave medicine?"

She shrugged. "I like helping people, but being a doctor wasn't for me. It may sound strange, but I found it limiting. So I decided to follow my grandmother into chiromancy."

"That's quite a leap."

"It was the right decision for me. I would have been miserable otherwise, and I'm good at what I do."

She turned back to the road, and I covertly studied her profile. She was a gorgeous woman, but hers was a cool, remote beauty whereas Mariama's had been fiery and exotic. Comparatively speaking, I felt a bit of a mouse. I had always thought of myself as a quiet pretty. A blue-eyed blonde with a clear complexion and a nice smile. Thin and fit from my years of working in cemeteries, but there was nothing extraordinary about me at all. Except that I saw ghosts.

"How did you meet?" I asked.

She took a moment to answer. "I killed someone. John was assigned the case."

I stared at her in astonishment, my mind conjuring an image. Her hands, covered in blood, clutching a dripping knife. I felt my own fingers curl around the armrest. "That's…quite a meeting."

"Hardly the stuff of fantasies," she agreed. "It was

a very difficult time for my family. John was a saint. I hate to think what would have happened if another detective had shown up at our house that night."

"What did happen? Or should I not ask?"

"I don't mind you knowing. I would be curious, too, if I were in your place."

My place?

"The victim—if one could call him that—was Clementine's husband. It was a matter of me killing him before he killed her."

"He was abusive?"

"We didn't know for a long time. She hid it well. She married young against all our wishes and when things got bad, she was ashamed to come to us. It finally escalated to the point where she had to leave him. But he wouldn't let her go. They never do. At first it was phone calls and emails. Then he started showing up at her work and at home, leaving little notes for her to find, all scented with her perfume."

"That's why she doesn't wear it anymore," I said.

"Despite all the precautions we took, he was able to get inside the house, into her bedroom. The police were useless because he was very careful about not getting caught. He knew our habits, our schedules, how to deactivate the alarm system. The love notes turned into threats. We were all terrified that it would end badly. And, of course, it did."

I was thinking about something else Clementine had said. She hated to think that anyone could come back from the dead. No wonder the notion of ghosts terrified her.

"We were both living with Grandmother at the time," Isabel said. "I came home one night to find him in the house. He'd cornered my sister with a knife, still insisting that he loved her, that he would do anything to win her back. All he wanted was another chance. On and on like that. When I saw how helpless she was—how helpless she'd been during that whole relationship—something snapped. I could have called 911 or even a neighbor for help. But I knew that, even if we managed to stop him that time, he would be back. He would keep coming back until one or both of them ended up dead. So I got my grandfather's gun and I shot him."

"But surely that would be considered justifiable homicide," I said.

"I wasn't the only one who shot him, you see."

"What do you mean?"

"Clementine took the gun from my hand and emptied the chamber in him. I believe the term is overkill," Isabel murmured.

I couldn't quite reconcile that harsh description with the soft loveliness of Clementine Perilloux. "I thought you said you killed him."

"I guess that depends on whether or not he died from the first bullet," she said.

I was still gripping the armrest. "Why are you telling me this?"

"Because there's a bond between John and my family…between John and me that is never going away."

"I…see."

Her glance, I thought, was defiant. "He took care of us. He made everything go away, and my sister was able to get the help she needed. It took years of therapy and confinement, but she's finally ready to move on with her life."

"Confinement?"

"In a psychiatric hospital."

"I see." I remembered my breakfast with Clementine—the trembling hands, those odd hesitations, her determination to stand on her own two feet. It all made sense now. "How did John make everything go away?"

"The D.A. never brought charges even though he was under considerable pressure to do so. That was John's doing."

I was shivering a little because I didn't like where this conversation had been or where it was likely headed.

"It's important for you to understand how close we are," she said, and I wondered if there might not be a hint of madness in *her* eyes. "I would do anything for him. If anyone ever tried to hurt him, I don't know what I would do."

I said nothing, lest I set her off.

She sent me another bold look, and then her expression softened unexpectedly. "But it is just friendship. Nothing more. And that's what I wanted you to know."

I wasn't sure I believed her entirely, but I also thought it best to let sleeping dogs lie. "Did you know Mariama?"

She inhaled sharply. "She was a very powerful, very beautiful woman, but she was evil through and through."

"Evil is a strong word."

"I don't use it lightly. She could be utterly charming when she wanted or needed to be, but she wasn't above using a young woman's mental frailty to her advantage."

"What do you mean?"

"She drew Clementine into her mind games. My sister was very vulnerable as you can imagine and she adored Shani. She had no idea she was being used. I don't want to go into detail, but suffice to say, Mariama made John's life a living hell."

"Because of her affair with Robert Fremont?"

She turned in surprise. "You know about that?"

"John told me."

She shrugged. "By then, I don't think he even cared. He would have been well rid of her. What he did care about was his daughter. He lived in fear that Mariama would run off to Africa with her again and disappear for good. Or worse."

"Worse?"

"Why do you think he didn't leave her?" Isabel's hands tightened on the steering wheel. "He was afraid she would take her revenge out on Shani."

I stared incredulously. "Her own daughter?"

"No one was sacred to Mariama."

But her own child. I could hardly comprehend it.

I thought about that night at Devlin's house when Shani had appeared at my side. The moment Mariama put out her arms, the little ghost had vanished, as if she was afraid of her mother's spirit.

"John cares about you," Isabel said. "I think he may be falling in love with you. If Mariama was still around, I'd be worried for your safety. So I'm glad she's gone. I'm glad she can't hurt you or anyone else from the grave."

If only that were true. But I had a terrible feeling that Mariama was more dangerous to me dead than she ever would have been alive.

The moment I walked into my house, I felt the cold. The bone-frost of an otherworldly visitor.

I walked slowly down the hall, calling to Angus. He came at once, and when I reached down to give him a pat, I noticed that his fur was icy and bristled.

I'd left the kitchen light on, and it spilled into my office where the chill seemed to be concentrated. I moved to the door, hovering there for the longest time before I gathered the courage to enter.

Shani sat cross-legged on the floor inside my office—*inside my sanctuary*—surrounded by a shimmering aura that cast her in the palest glow.

As I stepped into the room, she looked up, dark eyes shining in that strange light.

"Will you help me?"

She spoke aloud this time. I was certain of it. Or maybe I could no longer distinguish between reality and the world that existed only in my head.

My teeth chattered from the cold. I pulled my jacket tightly around me as I stared down at her. "Yes, I'll help you."

She held out her hand, and I saw the glitter of a tiny garnet ring on her finger. It was the same ring she'd once left in my backyard. I'd taken it to her grave because Papa had told me I should get rid of it. It was the only way to get rid of *her*.

Obviously, Papa had been wrong.

I knelt in front of her. "What should I do?"

Already, she was starting to fade. "Come find me," she said, her words echoing as though spoken from the bottom of a very deep well. "Come find me, Amelia."

I put out a hand to her. She slipped off the ring and placed it gently in my palm. And then she vanished.

Thirty-Five

I headed south the next day into Beaufort County, the garnet ring glittering on the tip of my pinkie. Even after a few hours of sleep and a morning spent clearing brush in Oak Grove Cemetery, I was still reeling from the knowledge that Shani had found a way into my home. The heart on my bathroom mirror had been her first attempt, I supposed. And now if she could get in, others could, too.

Since childhood, hallowed ground had been my one foolproof protection. My only escape. That was gone now. Shani's manifestation had punched a hole in my illusion of a safe haven, and now, without Papa's rules, without a sanctuary, I had nothing standing between me and the ghosts.

My only hope was to help her move on before she led more spirits to me. And my only clue of how to find her was the garnet ring. She had brought it from her grave and placed it in my hand, so the logical place to start my search was in Chedathy Cemetery.

But I had other business to attend to in Beaufort

County before I drove out to the graveyard. Shani wasn't the only ghost to whom I'd promised my assistance. Robert Fremont was still out there somewhere. He was keeping his distance for whatever reason, but I had no doubt he would materialize one morning on the Battery or next to my car at Oak Grove Cemetery expecting answers.

I wondered if he even knew about Tom Gerrity's murder. Was that the reason he'd sent me to the private detective's office? He'd felt very strongly that I should go there. Maybe he'd had a vision or a premonition. Like his memory, his prophecies seemed to come and go, but then he was dead, after all. I supposed I should cut him some slack.

My first stop was the Beaufort County Coroner's office. I hadn't yet figured out how to finesse my way into Garland Finch's good graces, but I had the card from Regina Sparks in my pocket. I was fully prepared to pull it out if need be, along with a spiel about South Carolina's open records law. But as it turned out, I needed to do nothing more than introduce myself.

"Amelia Gray," the woman behind the front desk mused as she scratched her head with a pencil. Her beehive was a thing of beauty. I might have thought it a cutting-edge fashion statement if I didn't have the feeling she'd worn that same style since the sixties. "I have a note about you around here somewhere." She scavenged through the papers on her messy desk to produce a manila envelope with a pink Post-it note attached. "Ah, here we are. You're picking up some records for Regina Sparks. Garland said to give you whatever you needed."

"Thank you. I appreciate that." I perked up. This was going to be so much easier than I'd anticipated.

The woman gave me a reproachful look over her

glasses. "You didn't need to make a special trip down here, you know. I could have emailed the reports to the Charleston County Coroner's office."

"I had business in the area, anyway."

"Well, here you go, then." She handed me the envelope.

I took it reluctantly. "What's this?"

She lifted an overplucked brow. "The reports? That is what you're here for, isn't it? Check and make sure everything is in there before you leave. Be a shame if something is missing after you came all this way."

"But how did you know what I needed?"

"Garland told me." She eyed me curiously. "Is something wrong?"

"No, I just...no."

I opened the flap and glanced through the pages, stopping cold when I saw the names. Now I understood. Regina had assumed the friend I'd referred to was Devlin. The autopsy reports she'd requested were for Shani and Mariama.

"There seems to be one missing," I said. "Didn't Regina also request the report of a man named Robert Fremont?" I held my breath, hoping I hadn't set off an alarm for her.

"Garland didn't mention him, but I guess it could have slipped his mind. He's no spring chicken, although he's not about to admit it." She tapped a few keys on her computer. "Robert Fremont, you say? Why do I know that name?"

"He was a Charleston cop who was killed down here a couple of years ago."

"I don't remember the particulars, but that name sure rings a bell. Has something new turned up on his case?"

"I don't know. Regina didn't discuss it with me. I'm just supposed to collect the postmortems."

She studied the computer screen. "You may as well take a seat. We're slow as molasses today. Now, is that F-r-e-e-m-o-n-t?"

"One *e*."

"All right, hold your horses."

I was afraid she would have to check with the coroner before she released the records or, worse, verify with Regina. But instead, I heard the whir of a printer, and a moment later, she handed me a single sheet of paper.

"This is just the summary," she said. "If Regina wants the full report, she'll have to submit a formal request. But she knows that."

"I'm sure this will be fine," I said, as I stuffed the page in with the others. "Thanks again for your help."

"No problem. Y'all take care."

I hurried out of the building and climbed into my car before anyone had a chance to stop me. Pulling out the reports, I scanned all three, then read back through them more carefully. Something niggled but I didn't know why. Everything seemed to be in order. Nothing leaped out at me, so I put them back in the envelope and set it aside for the time being.

Chedathy Cemetery—and Shani's ghost—waited for me.

On my way to the cemetery, I stopped at the bridge where Mariama's car had gone over the guardrail. I'd been there once before when Shani had first appeared in my garden because I thought I might find answers in the place where she'd drawn her last breath. Back then the heart on my window and the garnet ring had been our only communication. Now I knew that she wanted me to come find her and I dreaded what that might entail.

I had no idea why I'd come back to the bridge, but the compulsion had been too strong to resist. Something or someone was trying to direct my actions, be it my instincts, the universe or my spirit guide. These impulses didn't happen out of the blue, and according to Clementine, I needed to pay particular attention to whatever meaningful coincidences might be headed my way.

Parking on the side of the road, I got out and walked up the incline to stand at the railing, gazing down at the water. It was a still day and the sun warmed my face. I could smell brine from the marshes and pine from the forest. The leaves of the hardwoods had already turned, painting the landscape in brilliant shades of russet, crimson and gold.

It was very peaceful here. I'd noticed that on my previous trip. I wouldn't have been surprised to sense some disturbance remaining from the accident. If a house could harbor the emotions of previous residents, then surely a place could capture a scream.

I heard nothing.

In that quiet setting, I thought of my conversation with Isabel. Devlin had remained with Mariama because he'd been afraid for Shani. It must have been a horrible situation, one I could hardly imagine.

With his money and clout, he could have taken Mariama to court and sued for full custody. And if granted, he could have taken every precaution, installed the best security system, hired a full-time guard. But nothing would have kept Mariama away if she'd been bent on revenge. Nothing could keep her away now.

I took out my phone to check for messages in case

Devlin had tried to call, but I couldn't get a strong enough signal to connect with my voice mail. As I stood there contemplating the water, a patrol car from the Beaufort County Sheriff's office eased alongside me.

My first thought was those autopsy reports in the front seat of my car. The woman at the coroner's office must have caught on to my deception. But then I remembered that, technically, autopsy reports were a matter of public record. Surely I'd done nothing to warrant an arrest.

"Everything okay here?" he asked through his open window.

"I'm just enjoying the scenery," I tried to say casually.

"Thought you might be having car trouble." He nodded to the phone in my hand. "You won't get a signal out here. Have to drive up the road a piece."

I turned to stare out over the bridge. "What about on the water?"

"Nah. I ran out of gas not too long ago and had to wait all morning before anyone came along to give me a tow. Not enough towers in the area," he said. "You're out in the boonies."

"Well, thank you for stopping to check on me."

"I wouldn't hang out here for too long," he cautioned. "These swamps are full of meth heads. They'd knock their own mama in the head for a buck."

Suppressing a shiver, I nodded. "I'll remember that."

He drove off slowly, and I tried the phone from both ends of the bridge before climbing back into my car. I sat there for a moment, staring at the guardrail as I dredged up Ethan's account of the accident.

According to him, Mariama had contacted 911 and

then Devlin from her sinking car. How had she managed one call, let alone two, without a signal?

A little while later, I pulled around to the back of Chedathy Cemetery where I'd parked on my last visit. It was early afternoon, but the eerie tremolo of a loon tapped an icy tattoo down my spine as I jumped the ditch of brackish water and set out through the cemetery.

In the Gullah tradition, personal mementoes decorated the graves, along with seashells and broken pottery. Every now and then the sun shone down through the heavy canopy to catch a mirror just right, and the flash of light simulated a spirit in flight. I loved these old seacoast cemeteries. Everything that had been left upon the mounds—lamps, clocks, bits of porcelain and glass bottles—was an acknowledgement that life did not end with death.

I knelt beside Shani's resting place and cleaned away leaves until I uncovered the seashell heart. The antique doll that I'd seen Devlin place on the grave last May had been taken away, probably having been ruined by inclement weather. I slipped the garnet ring from my finger and placed it inside the heart just as I had done before. Then I covered it back over with leaves to wait for Shani.

It was only three-thirty, too early for her ghost to appear, so I decided to take a walk by Essie's house. I wouldn't call on her unannounced, but if she happened to be sitting on her front porch, I could stop by and say hello. Maybe even work the conversation around to Darius. He was her grandson, though, so I'd have to be very careful not to offend her with my questions.

The sun was still warm on my shoulders as I walked

down the gravel road toward the small community of clapboard houses. Birds sang from the treetops, and I could hear the distant laughter of children. It was all very tranquil until my gaze was drawn to one of the houses where several men stood around a hole that had been cut in the siding. As I stopped to watch, a draped stretcher was passed through the opening into their waiting hands. That the sheet covered a body, I was certain. A hearse was parked in the dirt drive, and I could hear weeping from inside the house.

As I gazed upon the bizarre scene, a girl of about sixteen ambled down the road toward me. She carried a baby in her arms while she shepherded a small child on a tricycle. Like me, she stopped to watch the house, and I turned to nod an acknowledgement. She was tall and gangly with high cheekbones and dark, luminous eyes. I thought her vaguely familiar, but I couldn't place her.

Resting the baby on her hip, she eyed me with open curiosity. "Did you know old Mr. Fremont?"

Fremont. My scalp bristled as every instinct warned me to pay close attention. Here was yet another of those meaningful coincidences. "Mr. Fremont?"

She nodded toward the house. "He died this morning. They're carrying him down to the funeral home now to get him ready."

"I never met him," I said. "But I did know another Fremont from this area. His name was Robert."

"That cop? He was Mr. Fremont's grandson." Despite the time of year and cooling weather, she wore flip-flops with her jeans. I could see a flash of hot pink toenail beneath the tattered hems. "How did you know Robert?"

"We met in Charleston."

"He was a friend of yours?"

"Yes, I guess you could say that. Such a tragedy what happened to him. His death must have been a blow to the community."

"Mama said the old man never got over it."

We stood watching the strange proceedings in silence for a moment. "Why didn't they bring the body through the door?" I asked. "What's the significance of the hole in the wall?"

"In case he comes back," she said with a shiver. "Once that hole is closed, his spirit won't be able to find its way into the house."

"I see."

She shifted the baby to her other arm. All three stared at me with those dark, shimmering eyes. "You have folks around here?" she asked doubtfully.

"No. I was just visiting Chedathy Cemetery." And just like that, it came back to me where I'd seen her before. "I know you," I said. "Your name is Tay-Tay."

She glowered. "No one calls me that anymore. I'm Tamira. These are my brothers." She bounced the fretting baby to quiet him. "This one here is James and that's Marcus."

I said hello to all of them. "I'm Amelia."

"How do you know me?" she demanded.

"I walked past your house once with Essie and Rhapsody Goodwine. We saw you on the porch."

Her eyes widened, and I could have sworn I saw a flicker of fear. She called down the street to another girl chatting with a group of friends. She looked only a year or two younger than Tamira. "Timberly, you get your butt over here *right now!*"

The girl rolled her eyes and said something to one of her companions, then sauntered over to Tamira. "What do you want?" she asked sullenly, bending to scratch behind her knee.

"I need you to carry the baby home and give him a bottle. Take Marcus with you."

"Why can't you do it?"

"Because I can't," Tamira snapped imperiously. "Now you do as I say or I'll tell Mama you been sneaking out at night to meet up with that old Peazant boy."

"You wouldn't!"

"Oh, yes, I would," Tamira threatened. "And don't give me no more lip about it, either."

The girl took the baby and plopped him none too gently on her scrawny hip. "I'm *never* having kids. They ruin *everything*."

She trudged off with Marcus in tow, and Tamira turned back to me. "You come to see Miss Essie?"

"No, I told you. I'm visiting the cemetery."

"You got people buried there?"

"I'm a cemetery restorer. I take care of graveyards," I said vaguely. "Chedathy is one of my favorites."

"That old place?" She turned to stare down the road toward the cemetery. "I reckon that's where they'll plant Mr. Fremont even though they wouldn't bury his grandson there."

"Why not?"

Despite that earlier flash of fear, she looked to be enjoying herself now. Her eyes gleamed with self-importance. "Because of the *wudu*."

"*Wudu?* You mean magic?" I asked.

"*Black* magic." She leaned in. "She was very powerful, they say. Powerful enough to come back from the dead. His people were afraid she wouldn't let him rest in peace and they didn't want *him* coming back. So they buried him someplace else."

"Who wouldn't let him rest?"

"Mariama Goodwine."

I felt the chill of a ghostly breath down my collar even though it was hours until twilight. "Did you know her?"

"I used to see her in the bone-yard sometimes. She went there to meet him."

"Robert?"

She nodded.

"You saw them together?"

"Lots of times. You want me to show you something?"

"I…sure."

She led me back to the cemetery, pausing outside the lichgate to make the sign of the cross over her heart. Then we walked deep into Chedathy where the thick canopy all but blocked the sun.

"See this?" She pointed to a carving in a tree trunk. "This is where they used to meet. They cut these initials in the bark when they was just kids."

"What does that symbol mean?"

"Love everlasting."

I thought about Robert and Mariama's history. They'd been together as teenagers. He'd both loved and hated her, and then he'd moved to Charleston and discovered there was a world beyond her. And yet, he'd allowed her back into his life.

"When was the last time you saw them here?" I asked.

"The day he got himself shot. I stood right over there behind that tree and listened to every word they said."

I knew I should stop her, but I was spellbound and morbidly fascinated. "What did you hear?"

Her eyes rounded, and she waved her arms theatrically. It was almost as powerful as having been there. "She kept grabbing his shirt, like this." Tamira demonstrated with her own T-shirt. "She clung with both fists, begging him to run off with her. She said he was the only man she'd ever loved and she didn't want to live without him. He just laughed at her, and said she'd never really loved anyone but herself, and the only reason she'd come back to him was to taunt her husband. It had been a mistake to start things up with her again and even if he had been in love with her, his job was too dangerous to take on a family. He had no room in his life for a wife, much less one with a *kid*." She finished with a dramatic flourish, shivering a bit as if overcome by the memory of all those emotions.

"You remember all that?" I asked in awe.

"I never forget a thing. Just ask Timberly."

"I believe you."

"You want to know the scary part?" She leaned in with a conspiratorial whisper. "I think Mariama comes to me in my sleep sometimes and tries to mess with me. I'm the only one that knows the truth about her and she don't like it."

"What truth?"

Tamira made a production of glancing over her shoulder. "She told Robert he would be sorry if he left her and the very next day I saw his body *right here* in the exact same spot where they'd stood talking. It was like she put a root on him or something."

"You found him?" I asked in surprise.

She nodded proudly.

"But Robert was shot. Mariama couldn't have done it because she was already dead."

"If she came back as *bakulu*, she could have made

somebody do it for her. That's what they do. They make slaves of the living."

"Tamira, listen to me. Were you in the cemetery the night Robert was murdered? Did you see what happened?"

Her eyes bulged suddenly, and her hands flew to her throat. She opened her mouth, but no sound came out. I thought at first this was just more of her theatrics, but then I followed her gaze.

Rhapsody Goodwine stood between two graves, the resemblance to her father, Darius, so uncanny in that eerie setting as to raise goose bumps on my arms. She lifted her hand and pointed to Tamira.

"Tie your mouth, Tay-Tay!"

Beside me, the girl began to choke.

Thirty-Six

Tamira fell back against the tree in a fit of gagging and coughing. I stared at her in alarm. "Are you okay?"

As quickly as the spell came on, the choking subsided. Gasping for breath, she looked beyond me to Rhapsody. "Stay away! You hear? *Stay away from me!*"

I shot a glance at Rhapsody. She stood there between those two graves looking almost angelic in a pale yellow dress and lace-up boots, her wild mane of hair framing her lovely face.

Tamira backed away, hands still clutching her throat. Once she'd cleared the trees, she whirled and took off running through the cemetery, sandals flapping.

Rhapsody laughed. "Look at her go!"

"What did you do to her?" I hadn't meant to sound so accusing, but I couldn't help it. I was a little freaked out.

"Nothing." Her shrug was completely innocent. "She did it to herself."

"What do you mean?"

"You were here. I never laid a hand on her, did I?"

Power of suggestion, Temple had said.

I remembered how intimidated Tamira had seemed that day on her front porch as Essie, Rhapsody and I had walked past. Whether it was mind over matter or something else, the poor girl was obviously scared to death of Rhapsody.

"Do you remember me?" I asked.

"You're Amelia," she answered promptly. "Granny's been waiting for you."

"How did she know I was here?"

"She sent for you," Rhapsody said.

"Sent for me? How?"

She didn't answer but instead took my hand, and we walked back through the graveyard together. Her skin was warm and smooth, and she smelled of line-dried linens and rosemary. She'd inherited her father's bone structure and numinous smile, but her eyes were green rather than topaz. She was striking, nonetheless, with those flowing dark curls and a kind of airy grace that almost made one wonder if she floated rather than walked. She clutched my hand as if to keep herself grounded, and I found myself unaccountably troubled by the contact. Was I keeping her grounded or was she holding me prisoner?

A silly thought. She was just a charming girl with a fair dash of drama and mischief.

She'd blossomed since I'd seen her last, and already she'd had a coquettish quality that, along with her beauty, did not bode well for her great-grandmother's future peace of mind.

As we strolled along, she chatted nonstop, the episode with Tamira already a memory. But I hadn't forgotten. Whether or not the coughing spell had been of the girl's own doing, it had effectively stopped her from talking about the night Robert Fremont was murdered.

Out on the road, we passed by the elder Fremont's house, and I noticed that the hole had already been patched, blocking the old man's spirit. Rhapsody paused to watch the hearse pull away from the curb.

"Did you know Mr. Fremont?" I asked carefully.

"He used to sit out on his front porch smoking a pipe," she said. "Sometimes I came over and sat with him. I liked the smell of his tobacco. It reminded me of High John the Conqueror."

"I've heard of that before. It's a root, isn't it?"

She reached in her pocket and pulled out a dark, woody tuber, which she placed in my hand. Tentatively, I lifted it to my nose. It did smell a little like cherry-scented pipe tobacco with a touch of nutmeg and cinnamon. "What's it for?"

"It's very powerful," she said. "Put it in your pocket and it'll bring you luck and give you mastery over tricksters."

"Thank you. That should come in handy."

Speaking of tricksters…

"The last time I was here, you told me that your father was in Africa," I said. "Has he come back?"

She gave me a sidelong look through her thick lashes. "Why do you want to know?"

"I'm just curious. You told me how much you missed your home in Atlanta and all your friends."

"I have friends here now," she said. "And I have Granny."

I wondered if the girl even had a clue her father was in Charleston.

The breeze picked up as we neared the cottage. I could hear the flap of sheets on the clothesline and the tinkle of garden bells at the side of the house. Just like before, Essie sat on the front porch hunched over her quilt blocks, a crocheted shawl tossed over her shoulders. She'd propped her feet on a little wooden bench and I could see the toes of her sneakers peeking from beneath the hem of her long skirt.

"Here she is, Granny," Rhapsody announced as we moved up the steps. "I brought her to you just like you asked."

Essie looked me up and down, her mouth a thin line of disapproval. "Sit, gal, 'fo dat wind snatch you right off dis porch. Lawd, if you ain't nuthin' but skin and bones."

I dropped down on the top step, remembering my previous visit. I'd fainted on this very porch, my last conscious thought of the haint blue ceiling that had seemed to press down on me. Later when I'd come to, Essie had told me that Devlin would someday have to make a choice between the living and the dead and that Shani wouldn't be able to rest until he found the strength to let her go.

"Should I go make some tea?" Rhapsody asked her grandmother. "And bring out some cookies like last time?"

"Please don't trouble yourself on my account," I said quickly. "I can't stay long."

"Then can I go back out and play, Granny? Please? I've done all my homework."

Essie searched the sky. "You be back yuh 'fo daa'k," she said sternly. "Don' mek me come look fo you agin."

"I won't." Rhapsody gave me a sweet, beaming smile, which I didn't fully trust. "Maybe you can stay for the Ring Shout."

"Shoo!" Essie waved her away and Rhapsody scampered off.

I turned to Essie. "She said you sent for me. How did you know I was here?"

"Dat gal say a lot of t'ings," she grumbled, ignoring my question.

"Do you know why I drove down here from Charleston?"

She kept right on sewing.

"I'm here because of Shani."

"She the one sent fo you, I spec."

"In a way, yes."

"I bin dreamin' 'bout dat baby muhself," Essie said. "She git mo' restless ever night. She can't stay yuh and she can't move on. She don' know weh she b'long. She needs help."

"That's why I'm here. I want to help her, but I don't know how."

Essie looked up, her faded eyes solemn and beseeching. "Tell'um."

I drew a breath. "You mean John."

"He can't hold huh yuh no longer. Time he let huh go."

"What if I tell him and he doesn't believe me?"

"Din you mek him believe, cuz it has to be *now,*" she said.

Her urgency mirrored Robert Fremont's, and I found myself leaning forward anxiously. "Why now?"

"Da signs say so, dat's why." She picked up her scissors and clipped a thread. I waited for her to continue, but then I realized that as far as Essie was concerned, the conversation was over. I wanted to ask about Darius, but what did I expect her to say? That her grandson was evil? I suspected that like Rhapsody, she was oblivious of his return.

I sat there watching her stitch, the rhythm and shimmer of her needle and thimble almost entrancing. After a while, I realized that I should probably get back to the cemetery.

She looked up as I stirred. “You spy dat Rhapsody, you send huh home.”

“I will.”

Then she said something very strange to me. “The root be both light and daa’k. Tek care who you trus’. Watch the signs, gal. And mind the time.”

Thirty-Seven

Watch the signs, gal. And mind the time.

I pondered Essie's cryptic message all the way back to the cemetery. The signs could be interpreted as the synchronicities and meaningful coincidences that had been plaguing me since that first night in Clementine's garden. But had I missed other signs? And how was I to mind the time?

The root be both light and daa'k. Tek care who you trus'.

Maybe she did know that Darius was back. Maybe that vague caution was her way of warning me about him.

My head swirled, and I could feel the onslaught of a headache. All those obscure warnings and signs and dreams crowded to the forefront of my brain, making me long for a time when I'd had nothing more pressing than the avoidance of ghosts. Those days were gone forever, I feared. Papa's rules had been shattered and my sanctuary invaded, but I couldn't afford to dwell on any of that at the moment. If there was any hope for my future peace of mind, it lay in finding Shani's ghost and helping her move on.

Once again, I passed through the lichgate and made my way to her grave, where I sat on the ground to await dusk. I did this with no small measure of trepidation. Not all graveyards were haunted, as evidenced by the lack of spirits in Oak Grove. But I felt certain that, despite the elaborate precautions taken before and after burials in this little community, come twilight, Chedathy would be rife with entities.

It was very quiet there beside Shani's grave. So silent, in fact, that I could hear the distant murmur of voices. As the sun slipped beneath the treetops, a group of men with shovels left the cemetery. I assumed they'd been there to dig Mr. Fremont's grave, and that made me think of Robert's final resting place forty miles north of Charleston in Coffeeville Cemetery.

According to Tamira, he'd been buried there so that his spirit would be free of Mariama. But even with miles between them, he hadn't been able to rest. What was distance and time behind the veil? Besides, it wasn't Mariama who disturbed Robert's sleep. He couldn't rest until his killer was found and brought to justice.

At sunset, the temperature dropped, and I started to shiver. I sat with my legs drawn up, chin resting on knees as the day came to a quiet end and dusk crept in from the marshes. The glow on the horizon began to fade, and in the rising wind, the dead leaves sounded like tiny clappers. There was a strange rhythm to the sound. A stirring of energy that made my heart quicken.

A chant came to me then, the singsong of a child's nursery rhyme. I lifted my head to listen.

"Little Dicky Dilver
Had a wife of silver.
He took a stick and broke her back,
And sold her to a miller.
The Miller wouldn't have her,
So he threw her in the river."

I got up to follow the chant through the cemetery. It wasn't Shani who summoned me, though. The voice was older and more earthly, without the metallic echo from the other side. But hearing the nursery rhyme in Chedathy Cemetery, of all places, most definitely meant something. One of those signs both Clementine and Essie had told me to watch out for.

As I neared the spot where Tamira had taken me earlier, I moved cautiously, easing myself behind the same tree from which she'd spied on Robert and Mariama. I listened to the disturbing little song for a moment longer before chancing a peek around the trunk.

Rhapsody sat on the ground poking through an old tin box as she sang. On the ground around her was an assortment of bagged roots and tiny jars of powders and herbs. Slipping one of the vials into her jacket pocket, she returned everything else and closed the lid. Then she stood and shoved the box into a hole in the tree as far as her arm could reach.

She scurried off then but not toward home. Instead, she headed toward the back of the cemetery where I'd parked my car. I was torn between following her and investigating the contents of that tin box. I wasn't particularly proud of myself for spying on a child, but the fact that she had been singing the nursery rhyme Shani had used to lure me into Clementine's garden surely meant something. It was a clue. Perhaps even a message from the ghost child.

I hurried to the tree and thrust my arm into the hole as far as I could reach until I felt the cool metal against my fingers. Then, box in hand, I knelt on the ground and opened the lid, gasping in shock at the contents. I was no expert in weapons, but I felt certain that I'd located Devlin's .38. How it had come to be in Rhapsody's possession, I couldn't imagine. Surely she hadn't somehow been involved in his murder. She was just a girl. Daunted by my findings, I closed the lid and returned the container to the tree hole. Then I went in search of Rhapsody.

Twilight had deepened, but the moon had not yet risen. I could spot her slight silhouette now and then weaving in and out of the trees. In the distance came an eerie chanting and the seductive rhythm of a drum.

Leaving Chedathy, Rhapsody jumped the ditch and crossed the road to disappear into the woods. I waited a moment, then followed.

The forest was very dark. I could no longer catch even a glimpse of the girl. Instead, I followed those drumbeats through thick curtains of ivy and Spanish moss. The ground softened as I neared the marshes, and the air thickened with brine, smoke and a scent I couldn't identify.

The singing grew louder as the trees gave way to a clearing. A crowd had gathered, pounding the ground with sticks and poles to create a frantic tempo. Inside the clearing, dancers moved counterclockwise around the circle, stomping and clapping to the beat, sometimes shouting when the spirit moved them.

It was a joyous celebration, and I shouldn't have felt in the least threatened, but I did. Not by the ritual or the pounding of the sticks or the dancers, but by something else that lurked in those woods. I could feel the decadent chill of approaching spirits. I had no idea if they were being drawn by the ritual or by me. A little of both, I suspected, because the synergy generated by the ceremony was astounding.

Maybe that relentless rhythm had somehow hypnotized me. Maybe that was why I didn't see the tall shadow until he was almost upon me.

I heard the nightingale a split second before a fine, shimmering dust settled over me. I tried to hold my breath, but already I could feel the powder tingling on my skin, and when I finally gasped for air, I tasted the bitterness of an alkaloid on my tongue.

My heartbeat slowed as my movements became sluggish. I felt no pain or fear. Instead, I was cocooned in a dreamy tranquility that reached all the way down to my core. My ears buzzed with a myriad of noises. If I listened closely, I could separate them from the pounding and singing. Up in the tree, the trill of the nightingale. Farther away, the sound of deep laughter. I even heard Essie calling for Rhapsody.

The sounds were real and not imagined. I wasn't hallucinating or tripping. I must have entered some altered state because, as I floated upward, I saw my body on the ground.

Thirty-Eight

I found myself at the edge of the crowd, swaying to that hypnotic beat. At first, I worried that I might be asked to leave, but no one paid me the slightest attention. The ceremony continued, the drumming and dancing becoming more frenzied as the night wore on.

As I looked around that circle, I spotted some familiar faces. Rhapsody had joined the dancers, her bare feet thumping the ground as her body writhed and shimmied, her arms extended toward the sky. Across the clearing, I saw Layla swaying to the music. Her presence made me think that Darius must be nearby, but I wasn't particularly concerned by this notion. I felt no fear at all, just a quivering excitement that brushed along every nerve ending.

Away from the main clearing, a fire had been built, and as people grew exhausted, they left the circle to gather around the blaze. As I stared into the flames, the image of an embracing couple formed. They were naked and entwined, their bodies pulsating to the beat. I could see the sway of Mariama's hair against her bare back, the gleam of her skin in the firelight. She splayed her fingers over Devlin's heart, and he put his hand over hers, whether to shove her away or pull her to him, I couldn't tell.

She turned to stare at me as she always did in my dreams. But this time there was no seductive smile or taunting invitation. In that moment, I saw nothing but rage in her face, and it frightened me in a way that it never had before because I wasn't just worried for myself. I was terrified for Devlin.

Robert Fremont appeared at my side. He, too, stared into the flames.

"You see them, too," I said.

"Yes, I see them."

"She'll never let him go, will she?"

"Not unless you find a way to stop her."

"How?"

Flames danced in his dark glasses as he turned to me. "Tell Devlin what she's done."

"What do you mean?"

"You know."

Yes, I did know. The evidence had been there all along. I just hadn't wanted to see it. I hadn't wanted to believe that anyone could be capable of such an abomination, of such an unspeakable act of cruelty. "You met Mariama the day before you were shot in Chedathy Cemetery. It was her perfume you smelled on your clothes when you died," I said numbly.

"Yes."

"You argued. You told her that you had no room in your life for a wife, much less one with a child. And when she left you, she purposefully drove her car through that guardrail. Ethan Shaw told me that she called for help from the sinking vehicle. But she couldn't have because there is no signal on the bridge or in the water. She must have placed those calls from the cemetery. She already knew what she was going to do when she left you. But why has no one questioned any of this until now?"

"Why would anyone question a call for help? Everyone thought it was a tragic accident. Even John."

"But you knew better."

"I knew *her.*" His voice sounded very cold, very distant. "She wasn't the type to take her own life. She meant to swim ashore and leave Shani behind, but the seat belt trapped her. Mariama tried to rid herself of her only child, and now they are bound to each other forever."

"She took Devlin's daughter from him," I whispered. "The only thing that would have mattered to him."

"And now she feels threatened by you," Fremont said. "Shani is her tie to the living world and you're the only one that can set the child free."

"How?"

"By convincing John to let her go."

"I don't know if I can do that."

"No one, least of all Shani, will have peace until you do."

A tall figure came out of the shadows and walked toward me, topaz eyes gleaming in the firelight.

"Why are you here?" I asked.

"I came to see you."

"Am I dead?"

"You're not dead, not yet."

"But you blew gray dust in my face."

"That was merely a harmless charm," he said. "This is gray dust." He took a vial from his pocket and I saw the shimmer of a very fine powder as he handed it to me. "Take it," he urged. "You'll need this for your journey."

I wanted to ask what good the powder would do me in a dream, but instead I accepted the vial and put it in my pocket. "You've had me followed," I said. "Why?"

The topaz eyes glittered. "Because of who you are. Because of what you are. You have so much untapped power, and you have no idea how to use it. But you'll soon understand. I'll teach you everything."

"And if I refuse? Will you kill me the way you killed Tom Gerrity?"

"Do you think I killed him?" He sounded amused. "Why would I bother with someone so inconsequential?"

"To pin the murder on Devlin."

"I have no interest in John Devlin. Unless he gets in my way again."

"Again?"

"He once took something very valuable from me. And now at long last I've found a way to get it back." His gaze moved past me, and I whirled to see Shani at the edge of the woods. She held her hand out to me, but when I started toward her, she vanished.

Darius bent and put his lips to my ear. "You can't help her in a dream. You'll have to cross over. And I'll be waiting for you on the other side."

Thirty-Nine

I heard Devlin calling my name and turned dreamily toward the sound, blinking to bring him into focus. He was staring down at me, and I realized now that he was shaking me.

"Amelia! Can you hear me?"

"Yes, I can hear you. How did you know where to find me?"

"Essie sent me to look for you. She was worried about you."

"You drove all the way from Charleston to look for me?"

"I was already here," he said. "We just missed each other at Essie's house."

"Oh." I realized then that the pounding and dancing had stopped. The woods were completely silent as I lay on the ground peering up into the trees. "Did you hear it?" I asked Devlin.

"Hear what?"

"The nightingale. It always sings when Darius is around."

His voice hardened. "You've seen Darius?"

"He blew powder in my face and then he came to me in a dream. Do you think he brought the nightingale back from Africa?"

"It's just another of his tricks. Here, " Devlin said, taking my arm. "Can you sit up?"

I tried, but the trees started to spin, and I lay back down. "I need a moment."

"Can you at least tell me why you came down here?"

"I'm trying to find out who killed Robert Fremont."

"Why?"

"I…don't want you blamed for his murder."

"You let me worry about that."

"But I can help you," I said excitedly. "I've found your missing gun."

"What?"

"It's true. I saw Rhapsody remove a box from a tree hollow. There was a gun inside. I don't know much about weapons, but I'm certain it was yours."

He said in a strange voice, "Maybe you were still dreaming."

"No, that was before Darius came. I remember it clearly."

"And where is this tree hollow?"

"In the cemetery. I can take you there if you want."

He helped me to my feet. "Are you strong enough to walk?"

I took a wobbly step and he scooped me up into his arms. "Nevermind. I'll carry you."

I buried my face in his shoulder without protest. "You're very strong. Stronger than you look."

"You're very light," he said. "You've lost weight since last spring."

"That's because I'm haunted."

"What haunts you?" he asked softly.

"You do."

I heard the quick intake of his breath, but he said nothing else until we reached the road where my car was parked. Then he set me gently on my feet.

"Where to now?"

I pointed to the maze of headstones at the back of the cemetery. "Through there."

A breeze rippled the leaves as we moved silently along the pathway. Ghosts stirred, too. I sensed an icy presence behind us, but I didn't look back. I wasn't as frightened with Devlin beside me.

When we got to the tree, I stuck my arm down the hollow, grappling for the box with my fingers. I felt nothing.

"It was here a little while ago. Rhapsody must have moved it."

"I don't understand how she came to be in possession of my gun," Devlin said. "If it is my gun."

"I've thought about that. She must have been in the cemetery that night and stumbled upon the body. Maybe she suspected Darius was responsible and she took the gun to protect him."

"Are you sure she didn't know you were following her?"

"I don't think so."

"I'll need to talk to her," Devlin said. "But I'm taking you home first where you'll be safe."

"What if she gets rid of the gun while you're gone? Or gives it to Darius?"

"She probably already has," Devlin said.

"Still, you should talk to her. You don't have to take me home. I'm not afraid. Not when I'm with you."

"No matter," he said. "I'm afraid enough for the both of us."

But he didn't seem frightened at all to me.

We walked back to the car together and he held the door for me. Despite everything that had happened, I had the strongest urge to kiss him. To stake my claim in case Mariama lurked in the shadows. Which was foolish because I still had no idea what she could do to me. To us.

"What about your car?" I asked.

"I'll pick it up later. You can't drive home in your condition. Besides, I'm not leaving you alone until we know what Darius is up to."

He went around and climbed in on the other side. I turned my head on the seat so that I could stare at his profile.

"It's cold here," I said. "Do you feel it?"

"I'll turn on the heat."

"It won't help."

He scowled at the road. "Why do you say that?"

Because it's coming from her.

I glanced over the backseat. Shani's dark gaze met mine as she lifted a tiny finger to her lips.

I was still trembling when we got home even though Shani had already vanished. Devlin ran a hot bath for me and when he started to leave the room, I took his hand and drew him to me. Eyes dark and hooded, he undressed me and helped me into the water. Maybe it had something to so with all we'd been through or maybe I was still under the influence of Darius's drug, but I wasn't at all shy about my nakedness. I didn't even blush when Devlin knelt beside the tub to bathe me.

Afterward, we lay on the bed and I settled myself in the crook of his arm.

"Better?" he asked.

"Yes."

"But you're trembling."

"Not from the cold."

His arm tightened around me. "Are you going to run away from me this time?"

"I don't want to, but I may not have a choice." I gazed at him in the moonlight. "She'll do everything she can to keep us apart."

"Who?"

"Mariama."

He didn't move, but I already felt distance between us. "Mariama is dead."

"But she's still here. You know she is. You've felt the draft in your house. You've felt *her.* She hasn't moved on and neither has Shani."

His whole body tensed. "What are you talking about? They're dead. They can't come back. I know that better than anyone."

"But they're still here. I've seen them."

"You must have had a dream or a hallucination," he said harshly. "That's all it was."

"John—"

"Don't," he said and turned his head away.

I lay on my back and stared at the ceiling. I wanted more than anything to help Shani move on, but Devlin wasn't ready to hear the truth. He wasn't ready to let her go. Maybe he never would be.

The room was very dark when I awakened. Devlin was still stretched out on top of the covers, and I lay curled against him. I wanted to remain there beside him forever, but I could still taste the bitterness of Darius's drug, so I got up and went into the bathroom to brush my teeth. When I came back into the bedroom, I felt the cold at once. Moonlight spilled in through the windows, and I could see Devlin clearly in that pale light. A ghostly shimmer hovered over him. Just like Shani, Mariama had found a way to breach my sanctuary, even though she hadn't fully come through.

I must have made some involuntary sound because her gaze shot across the room and her rage at the sight of me gave her the burst of energy she needed to manifest.

She turned quickly back to Devlin and bent over him, pressing her cold lips to his.

So great was my terror, I stood frozen as she began to drain his life force. I had the notion that she also fed on my fear, so I took a deep breath, using every ounce of my willpower to suppress my emotions.

To my surprise, she instantly faded. Was it really that easy to be rid of her? Or had I only imagined her manifestation?

I went to Devlin then and pressed a hand to his chest, feeling the beat of his heart against my palm. He bolted upright in bed and grabbed me roughly, staring down at me with unseeing eyes. I wondered if he might still be in the throes of sleep. Or if Mariama might still be in his head.

"It's all right. It's me. Amelia."

He put his hand over mine, but I couldn't tell if he meant to shove me away or pull me to him.

"John?"

His unblinking focus chilled me as his eyes burned into mine. Slowly he entwined our fingers as he curled my arm behind my back. Then he slid his free hand over my breasts, down my stomach, between my thighs, and I drew a sharp breath. He held me lightly. I could easily have slipped from his grasp, but I didn't want to. If Mariama still lurked, a perverse part of me wanted her to see how much Devlin desired me.

When he stood to remove his clothing, I rose, too, slipping his shirt off his shoulders and unbuckling his belt. Where normally I would have felt unsure of myself, I was now emboldened, and something Darius had said in my dream came back to me. *You have so much untapped power and you have no idea how to use it.*

Devlin and I were both naked now, standing face to face in the moonlight. He touched my hair, letting the strands slide through his fingers before cupping my neck and drawing me to him. We kissed for a very long time. The build-up was unbearable. I trembled all over, and yet I had never felt more in control. My hand found him, claimed him, and he groaned into my mouth.

"Don't stop," he whispered.

I had no intention of stopping. In fact, I was just getting started. I wasn't exactly a novice in the bedroom, but neither was I an expert. And yet, I knew exactly how to pleasure him. The flick of my tongue, the whisper of my lips, and he was mine.

I could have sworn I felt the frost of Mariama's breath on my neck, the chill of her touch against my hand, guiding me, as I slid to my knees before him. But when I glanced over my shoulder, it wasn't her ghostly face I saw in the mirror. It was my own. Eyes gleaming, lips curled in a secret smile.

"Yes, look at yourself," Devlin murmured, his gaze meeting mine in the mirror. "Look at what you're doing to me."

I rose slowly, sliding up his body, draping my arms around his neck, pulling his mouth down to mine.

He drew back, searching my face. "You're different tonight."

"Am I?"

"You're glowing. It's like you've tapped into something that's been hidden inside you."

"Or maybe I'm just…"

"What?"

In love.

But I didn't have the courage to utter the words aloud. "Maybe I just want you," I said.

His eyes flared. "Come here, then."

The windows had fogged, cocooning us in hazy moonlight. If ghosts looked in on us, I didn't see them. My focus had narrowed to Devlin and to the quivering heat that welled inside me.

We lay down on the bed and I rose over him. He grasped my hips to bring us together, and we began to move slowly as we found our rhythm.

Rising and falling like the tide of an ocean, I leaned forward to kiss him. His tongue met mine eagerly as he sat up and wrapped my legs around him. The shift created a new friction, a new pressure and I gasped as the first ripple of release caught me by surprise.

And then a wave swept me up and over, and I heard Devlin drawl my name as I closed my eyes and clung to him.

I woke up in an empty bed and went in search of Devlin. He was sitting on the terrace in the moonlight, eyes fixated on the swing as it moved slowly back and forth. He almost seemed mesmerized by the movement. I watched, too, captivated by the sway of Shani's hair and the billow of her little blue dress as she pumped her legs.

Devlin didn't look at me when I sat down beside him. His eyes remained on that swing.

"How long have you been out here?" I asked.

He didn't answer.

"Are you okay?"

"There's no wind." He turned to me, then, and my heart quickened at the look on his face. "There's no wind."

"I know."

"Then tell me how," he said in a hushed voice.

I reached over and took his hand, almost expecting him to pull away, but instead he clung to me. His skin was very cold. He'd been out in the night air for a long time.

"You know how," I said softly. "You've felt those strange drafts in your house."

He frowned. "It's an old house."

"You've felt the cold spots. You've probably experienced electrical fluctuations. Inexplicable sounds and scents."

"It's not possible!" I understood his anger. I was forcing him to confront something he'd wanted desperately to keep buried.

"They're still here, John."

He closed his eyes on a shudder.

"Shani's in the swing. But you know that, don't you? She's wearing a little blue dress with a ribbon in her hair."

Devlin stared at me in horror. "She was buried in a blue dress. How could you possibly have known that?"

"I can see her. I can see ghosts. I inherited the ability from my papa. Since the first night I met you on the

Battery, Shani has been at your side. She's been trying to tell you something, but you can't hear her. You can't see her."

"God." He put his hands to his face.

I swallowed hard past the lump in my throat. "Your guilt and grief have kept her earthbound, but it's time for her to move on. You have to let her go." I saw the sparkle of Shani's ring in the grass, the same one I'd placed earlier on her grave. She must have left it there for me to find because she knew her father would need proof. I plucked it from the grass and placed it in his palm. "Is this not her ring?"

He stared down at the glittering garnet, then curled his fingers around it. "Where did you get this?"

"She brought it to me. It's her way of communicating with me."

He drew a ragged breath. "I gave her this ring for her birthday. It was on her finger when—"

"I know. But how else would I have come by it? Twice I've taken it to her grave and twice she's brought it back to me."

"It's impossible," he said again.

The motion of the swing stopped, and Shani was suddenly there at his side. She placed a ghostly hand on his cheek.

"You can feel her, can't you? Concentrate."

His eyes closed again and he lifted a hand to his face.

"Your fingers are touching her hand."

His stoicism cracked then, and I heard an awful sound in his throat. "Shani…"

"She's here, John. She's always been here."

Like a drowning man, he gulped in air. "I smell jasmine."

"Yes. That's her."

Shani knelt and laid her head on John's knee. His hand went automatically to his leg.

"What happened to her wasn't your fault," I said. "She wants you to know that." Now was not the time to tell him what Mariama had done. His moment with Shani was too precious.

"I should have protected her." The torment in his voice broke my heart. "I should have been there to save her."

"It's time to let go of the guilt. You have to let it go so that she can move on. But a part of her will always be here with you. She'll always have a special place in your heart. She needs to know that you'll be okay without her. She needs to know that it's okay for her to go."

He opened his hand, and Shani reached for the ring. The garnet sparked in the moonlight as she slipped it on her tiny finger. Devlin watched in wonder and amazement. He couldn't see her, of course. But he could see the ring float up from his palm.

"Shani," he whispered.

She took his hand and then reached for mine. I couldn't help shivering at her icy touch.

"I'm scared," she said.

"What are you afraid of?" I asked her.

"The bad man won't let me go. He won't let me leave the dark place. Will you help me?" she asked.

"Yes."

"Promise?"

"Yes, I promise."

I left Devlin on the terrace. He needed to be alone and I needed to figure out how to find Shani. Darius had said that in order to help her, I'd have to cross over.

But how did I know that wasn't another one of his tricks?

I went into the bathroom and searched through the pockets of my discarded jeans until I found the vial of gray dust. I had only dreamed about it, so Darius must have physically slipped it into my pocket at some point. I wasn't surprised to find it there. He'd given it to me for a reason, after all. And when I crossed over, he'd be waiting for me on the other side.

I carried the vial back out to the kitchen, and as I stared at the shimmering dust, Devlin's warning ran through my head. *It stops the heart and people die.*

But how else could I pass through the veil with even a glimmer of hope of coming back? How else could I get to Shani?

Sprinkling a bit on the back of my hand, I lifted it to my nose. There was a slight scent, but nothing unpleasant. Before I could change my mind, I inhaled the dust.

At first, I didn't think anything was happening. No slowing of the vitals, no lethargy. Thankfully I had the presence of mind to lower myself to the floor a split second before a brilliant white light exploded inside my brain.

I heard a whirring in my ears, felt a deep vibration in my chest and then I opened my eyes slowly as if swimming up from a very sound sleep. I didn't know where I was at first, but I experienced a strange familiarity as I gazed around. The air and sky were the color of twilight, and I could see the swirl of mist in the distance. Before me a lichgate opened into a great cemetery. I could see rows and rows of statues and monuments, but then I realized they weren't statues at all, but silhouettes of the dead. I was in the Gray, that nebulous space in between the Light and the Dark.

Darius Goodwine appeared at my side and waved an arm toward the cemetery. "To pass through the gate into the realm of the dead, you must have a guide," he said.

I didn't trust him to guide me anywhere. He wanted something from me, but at the moment, my main concern was finding Shani.

"You know why I'm here," I said. "Where is she?"

He started walking toward the cemetery. "In here," he said and disappeared through the gate.

I followed him into an even grayer world where legions of the dead watched me through frosted eyes. I saw many ghosts from my distant and recent past. A long line of Ashers. My birth mother, Freya. Papa's people were here, too. I wanted to converse with all of my dead ancestors, but Essie's warning rang in my ears. *Mind the time.*

As I neared the back of the cemetery, the gray darkened to midnight and a great forest loomed before me.

"You'll find her in there," Darius said.

"How do you know?"

"Listen."

We both fell silent and I heard the faint strains of a nursery rhyme. Shani was leading me to her.

I turned back to Darius. "Are you coming with me?"

"This is the end of our journey together," he said. "You'll need to go the rest of the way alone."

"Why?"

He merely smiled and faded back into the mist.

I started toward the forest, but a woman appeared on the path in front of me. She seemed familiar and I thought she must be another dead ancestor. She didn't look old, but her hair was as white as cotton and she had no eyes.

I stared into those gaping sockets and shuddered. "Who are you?"

"My name is Amelia Gray," she said.

I gasped. "That can't be. I'm Amelia Gray."

"What you are, I once was," she said. "What I am, you will someday become."

Her eerie prophecy left me trembling. "I need to find a child. Her name is Shani. Have you seen her? I think she may be hiding in these woods."

"Don't go into the Dark," she warned. "You'll never find your way out in time. That's what he wants."

"Who?"

"The tall man," she said. "He means you harm. He and the woman. She seeks to remain in the living world, and you are her vessel."

Dr. Shaw's description of gray dust came back to me then. *After a certain amount of time passes, the physical body can't be resuscitated. The shell withers and dies or, in some cases, is invaded by another spirit."*

Was that why I'd been lured through the veil? So that Mariama's ghost could invade my body?

"Go back," the woman warned.

"I can't. Not until I help the child move on—"

"Shush." She cocked her head. "Do you hear it?"

I turned my head to listen. Nothing came to me but a faint buzzing that sounded like a hive of bees.

"They're swarming," she said.

"Bees?"

"The ghosts," she said, and vanished.

Despite her warning, I left the Gray and moved into the woods. Into the Dark. From my periphery, I caught the dart of shadows as I walked along, the slither of some otherworldly creature in the underbrush. On and on I trudged until I was so deeply inside the forest I worried the sightless woman would be proven right. I might not find my way out in time. Already I could feel the tug of my physical body, but I ignored the pull and kept going. I could no longer hear the chanting, and I wondered if I'd been deliberately led away from Shani.

I called her name and suddenly I caught a glimpse of her through the trees,

"Come find me, Amelia!"

"I'm trying! Where are you?"

"Over here!"

I hurried toward the sound of her voice. She waited for me in a clearing, but she wasn't alone. A tall silhouette loomed over her. A black cloak hid the face, but the hand that snared Shani's wrist had the curved nails of a claw.

"Let her go," I said.

"It's too late," the thing taunted. "You're out of time."

He drew Shani into the trees, and I went after them, battling terror and the tug of my earthly body. We came to another clearing lit with torches. I somehow knew that this place was neither heaven nor hell. We were not in the Light or the Dark, but a realm of my own making. And if I had created this world, then I could control it.

"Come to me, Shani."

The creature clung to her and she whimpered.

I knelt and put out my hand to her. "I know what you've been trying to tell your father. I know what really happened that day, what your mother did to you, but she can't hurt you now. I won't let her. Please come with me."

She reached for me, and as our fingertips touched, the creature dissolved into black mist.

I picked her up and held her for the longest time.

"I'm taking you someplace safe," I murmured. "Someplace beautiful."

The scent of jasmine drifted to us as we emerged from the woods. The perfume led us to a garden where Robert Fremont waited for us.

"Why are you here?" I asked him. "You can't move on. We haven't yet found your killer."

He gazed down at Shani. "It doesn't matter. It never mattered."

And suddenly I understood. "Because that wasn't why you were earthbound. You were waiting for her."

"I didn't know," he said in wonder. "I never knew until now."

I thought of those autopsy reports in my car. The blood types that would have told me the truth if I had been paying attention to the signs. Shani was Robert Fremont's daughter.

Devlin, I thought. My poor Devlin. He would never know the truth from me. Mariama had taken Shani from him once. I would not be responsible for taking her from him again.

The sun rose over the garden wall. So dazzling I couldn't stand to look into the light. But Shani and Robert were already walking toward the garden gate. The child hesitated and glanced back. Robert had already disappeared, but she hovered just inside the gate, a fingertip to her lips.

I felt a presence and turned.

Devlin stood behind me.

I said in shock. "You can't be here. Unless you're..."

He looked at me sadly.

"But you can't be," I whispered. "I won't let you be."

"You have to go back," he said. "You're almost out of time."

"I don't want to go back. Not without you. Please come with me."

"I can't."

His gaze went past me to the gate where Shani still waited.

Forty

I felt a jolt, like a shot of pure adrenaline, and I opened my eyes on a gasp. I could have sworn I saw Mariama hovering over me, but she was too late. I was back inside my own body, lying on my own kitchen floor. Devlin was prone beside me. He looked very pale, very dead.

I tried to reach out to him, but I was so cold I could do nothing but lie there trembling in my misery.

A shadow moved and I looked across the room, expecting to find Darius Goodwine or Mariama's ghost, but I was shocked to see Ethan Shaw.

He gazed at me defiantly. "It would have been so much easier if you hadn't come back."

He slid down the wall and sat with his back against the door frame.

"What have you done?" I whispered.

"What I had to do. He was going to take her away from me."

"John?" I asked in confusion?

"Robert Fremont. I heard Mariama on the phone that day after John had stormed out of the house. She was making plans to run off to Africa with Fremont. I couldn't let that happen. I couldn't bear the thought of never seeing her again."

A gun dangled from his hand, and I wondered if it was the same one I'd found in the tree hole. Devlin's .38. Had Ethan followed me to Chedathy Cemetery?

I tried to inch my hand toward Devlin. If I could just touch him…

"You knew about the gun John kept in his desk, didn't you?"

"Mariama showed it to me once. She even hinted that, with John out of the picture, his money would be hers, and she would be free to spend it with someone who truly loved her. I thought that someone would be me."

His hands trembled, I noticed. I wondered if he could really muster the courage to shoot me in cold blood. But then, he'd killed Robert Fremont and probably Tom Gerrity. And now Devlin lay dead at my side.

"I'd been with John earlier that day," he explained. "I told you about that. He and Mariama fought viciously and he made plans to stay at a friend's place on Sullivan's Island until they both had time to cool off. I knew he would be alone out there with no alibi. So I went to her house, got the gun and then I called Robert and asked him to meet me at the cemetery. I told him I had information about Darius."

"And then you ambushed him. You shot him in the back with Devlin's gun. But Mariama was already dead."

"I didn't know she was gone until Father called. By then, it was too late."

I thought about Rhapsody hiding that gun all these

years because she thought her father was the murderer. But it had been Ethan all along.

"Why did you give John an alibi for that night if you wanted him to take the fall?"

"I panicked when the police showed up at his place. And—this may sound strange—but with Mariama gone, I saw no need to make him suffer. He was my friend."

"And yet, you shot him."

"Once he decided to go after Darius, he would have found out the truth sooner or later. He was already suspicious of that alibi."

I glanced at Devlin's still form. "Please call 911. It may not be too late to save him."

"You know I can't do that."

"Then tell me why you killed Gerrity."

"He'd been blackmailing my father for years. He claimed to have evidence that would prove my father killed my mother. It was nonsense, of course, but Father paid him at first in order to salvage his reputation. And perhaps because he knew about me."

"You killed her?"

"You don't know what it was like, watching her suffer all those years. Mariama helped me. She knew exactly how to do it so that no one would suspect. That's when I knew she really loved me."

"So now you're going to shoot me, too." My fingertips touched Devlin's hand and I closed my eyes. He was so cold. "What will be your excuse this time? Mariama isn't here. You can't blame this on her."

"Don't be so sure," he said, and I turned to see his numinous smile. Or was that Mariama's smile? Was he still doing her bidding?

A slight movement from the back door caught my attention. I couldn't see her face, but I smelled her haunting perfume. Isabel Perilloux eased into my line of sight with a fingertip to her lips. From the front door, Clementine's voice rang out. "Amelia! Are you in here? Grandmother had a dream. She thought that I should come check up on you."

Synchronicity, I thought. Those two women had been brought into my life for a reason.

Ethan leaped to his feet, his head cocked toward the sound of Clementine's voice. It was a perfect distraction. I grabbed Devlin's gun from his holster and when Ethan turned back to the kitchen, I fired without hesitation.

I was astounded by my action. I lay there in shock as Isabel dropped to her knees beside Devlin. Within moments, her hands were covered in his blood.

Forty-One

I stayed by Devlin's bedside day and night, clinging to his hand, willing him to come back to me. The temptation to stay with Shani must have been irresistible because he showed no sign of coming around.

On the third night, I had just nodded off when I felt another presence in the room. I opened my eyes to find Darius Goodwine in the doorway.

"I know what you tried to do," I said. "You used Shani to lure me through the veil so that Mariama could inhabit my body."

"You're strong," he said with what I thought was grudging admiration. "Far stronger than Mariama."

I didn't feel all that strong at that moment. I felt… helpless.

"You said I had untapped power. Show me how to use it to bring him back," I begged.

"There are always unintended consequences when you bring back the dead," he warned.

"I just want him back."

I lifted my head and glanced around. I was alone in the room except for Devlin.

A moment later, his eyes fluttered open. "Amelia?"

"Yes, it's me. Welcome back," I whispered, with only a momentary trepidation as I pondered those unintended consequences.

Epilogue

Devlin was released from the hospital two weeks later. He would need months of physical therapy, but he was already able to get around with the aid of a cane. He hadn't been well enough to attend Ethan's funeral. I had gone only to pay my respects to Dr. Shaw. His health was deteriorating rapidly, his mind slipping into a place that couldn't process the reality of what his son had done. I thought that might be for the best, but I would miss his counsel. I had dropped in on him earlier, only to find that Layla had been replaced. I wondered if she'd disappeared with Darius. I hadn't seen or heard from him since that day in the hospital, and I still wasn't certain his visit had been real. I wanted to believe Devlin had come back to me on his own, without any unintended consequences, but sometimes when I lay awake beside him in bed at night, my mind would drift to a dark and disturbing place. What if he had brought something back with him from the other side? What if I had?

Shani had moved on. Robert Fremont had moved on.

Even Mariama had vanished. Devlin was free of his ghosts, and I wanted to believe that we could finally be together. But something tormented. Something haunted. *What you are, I once was. What I am, you will someday become.*

I thought of the sightless woman's prophecy as I watched Devlin kneel at Shani's gravesite.

My name is Amelia Gray, she'd said.

A chill wind whispered through the trees and I shivered. Devlin rose and I went to him at once. He pulled me into his arms and I melted against him. He was my sanctuary now. My only safe haven.

The sun glimmered through the trees as we walked hand in hand through the lichgate.

* * * * *

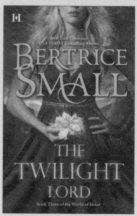

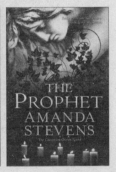

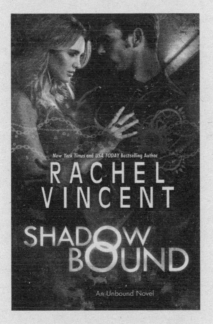

AMANDA STEVENS

31400 THE RESTORER	___	$7.99 U.S.	___	$9.99 CAN.
31277 THE KINGDOM	___	$7.99 U.S.	___	$9.99 CAN.

(limited quantities available)

TOTAL AMOUNT	$ ________
POSTAGE & HANDLING	$ ________
($1.00 for 1 book, 50¢ for each additional)	
APPLICABLE TAXES*	$ ________
TOTAL PAYABLE	$ ________

(check or money order—please do not send cash)

To order, complete this form and send it, along with a check or money order for the total above, payable to MIRA Books, to: **In the U.S.:** 3010 Walden Avenue, P.O. Box 9077, Buffalo, NY 14269-9077; **In Canada:** P.O. Box 636, Fort Erie, Ontario, L2A 5X3.

Name: ______________________________

Address: ______________________ City: ______________

State/Prov.: ____________________ Zip/Postal Code: ____________

Account Number (if applicable): ______________________

075 CSAS

*New York residents remit applicable sales taxes.
*Canadian residents remit applicable GST and provincial taxes.

MAS0512BL